VI KEELAND

Inappropriate

Edited by: Jessica Royer Ocken
Proofreading by: Elaine York, Eda Price
Cover Model: Simone Curto
Photographer: Wander Aguiar
Cover designer: Sommer Stein, Perfect Pear Creative
www.perfectpearcreative.com
Formatting by: Elaine York, Allusion Graphics
www.allusiongraphics.com

No rain
No flowers

CHAPTER 1

Ireland

God, *I feel like crap.*

I lifted my head from the pillow and winced. This is why I rarely drank. A belligerent hangover and a 3:30 a.m. wakeup time don't make for good bedfellows. Reaching over toward the annoying buzzing sound, I patted around my nightstand until I somehow managed to find my phone and silence the alarm.

Ten minutes later, the sound returned. I groaned as I dragged my body out of the comfort of my bed and headed to the kitchen for some much-needed coffee and Motrin. I'd probably need to ice my eyes, too, in order to look halfway presentable on air this morning.

I was mid-pour, steaming coffee filling my mug, when suddenly the reason for last night's inebriation and my resulting hangover hit me. How the hell had I forgotten?

The letter.

The damn letter.

"Ouch! *Shit!*" Hot coffee spilled over the top of the mug and scalded my hand.

"*Shit.*"

"*Ouch.*"

"*Shit!*"

I ran my hand under cold water and shut my eyes. What the hell had I done? I wanted to crawl back into bed and go back to forgetting.

But instead, all the details from yesterday came flooding back like a tsunami. An hour after I'd wheeled my luggage through the front door, returning from a week in paradise, a letter had arrived via messenger.

Fired.

In a form letter.

The day before I was scheduled to return to work from vacation.

I felt nauseous. It was the first time I'd been unemployed since I was fourteen years old. Not to mention, the *only* time my departure wasn't of my own accord. I turned off the water and hung my head, trying to recall the exact wording in that damn letter.

Dear Ms. Saint James,

We regret to inform you that your employment at Lexington Industries has been terminated, effective immediately.

Your employment has been terminated for the following reasons:

- Violation of Conduct Policy 3-4. Committing any acts which constitute sexual assault or indecent exposure.

- Violation of Conduct Policy 3-6. Using the Internet and/or other communication media to engage in sexual conduct or lewd behavior.

-Violation of Conduct Policy 3-7. Engaging in other forms of sexually immoral or objectionable conduct.

Severance pay shall not be paid because your termination was for cause. Within thirty days, we will issue a letter to you outlining the status of your benefits. Insurance coverage will continue for the time required by New York State employment law.

The personnel office will coordinate your final paycheck and work with your supervisor on the collection of your personal items.

We regret this action and wish you the best of luck in your endeavors.

Sincerely,

Joan Marie Bennett
Director of Human Resources

There had been a thumb drive included in the padded envelope, which contained a thirty-second video one of my friends had taken on the beach. I felt a burn traveling up my throat, for reasons other than the likely alcohol poisoning I'd subjected my body to.

My job. It had been my life for the past nine years. And some stupid, grainy video had made everything I'd worked my ass off for vanish like a puff of smoke.

Poof. Goodbye, career.

I groaned.

"God. What the hell am I going to do?"

Standing upright clearly wasn't the answer to that question, so I took my pounding headache back to the bedroom and crawled under the covers. I pulled the comforter up and over my head, hoping the pitch black might swallow me alive.

Eventually I managed to fall back asleep. When I woke up a few hours later, I felt slightly better. Though, that didn't last for very long—not once I realized I'd only remembered *half* the events of last night.

• • •

My roommate and best friend, Mia, poured me a cup of coffee and heated it up in the microwave. She looked pretty hungover herself.

"How'd you sleep?" she asked.

Elbows propped on the kitchen table, I held my head upright in my hands—sort of. I looked at her through one squinted eye.

"How do you think?"

She sighed. "I still can't get over the fact that they fired you. You have a contract. Is it even legal to sack someone for something that happened when they weren't at work?"

I sipped my coffee. "Apparently so. I spoke to Scott about it a few minutes ago." I'd sucked up my pride and called my ex. He was an asshole, and the last person I wanted to talk to, but he was also the only lawyer in my contacts. Unfortunately, he'd confirmed that what my employer did was perfectly legal.

4

"I'm so sorry. I had no idea a day at the beach could turn into something like this. It's all my fault. I was the one who suggested we go to the topless section."

"It's not your fault."

"What the hell was Olivia thinking, posting it on Instagram and tagging all of us?"

"I'm thinking the piña coladas that cute cabana boy was serving us with an extra shot of rum had her not thinking at all. But I don't understand how my job knew about it. She tagged my private account—the Ireland Saint James one—not my public Ireland Richardson account the station runs for me. Or *used* to run, I suppose. So how did they even see it? I double-checked my settings this morning to make sure I hadn't somehow changed them to open—and I hadn't."

"I don't know. Maybe someone from your job follows one of us who has a public account."

I shook my head. "I guess."

"Did the asshole respond to your email, at least?"

I furrowed my brow. "What email?"

"You don't remember?"

"Apparently not."

"The one you sent to the president of your company."

My eyes widened. *Oh shit.* Things just kept getting better.

• • •

Apparently rock bottom has a basement.

Fired.

No severance pay.

One week *after* I paid the second and biggest payment required on the construction contract for my first home.

The likelihood of getting a good recommendation from my current employer? *Zilch* after I went on a drunken rampage and told the guy who works in the ivory tower what I thought of him and his company.

Awesome.

Just awesome.

Great job, Ireland!

Between plunking down most of my life savings for the down payment on the land I bought in Agoura Hills, and being a big shot and covering the entire bachelorette party's alcohol tab for a full week in the Caribbean, I had about a thousand dollars to my name. Not to mention, soon my roommate would be getting married and moving out, taking half the rent she paid each month with her.

But...don't worry, Ireland. You'll get another job.

When hell freezes over.

The news media industry was about as forgiving as my bank account after a day at the mall.

I was screwed.

So screwed.

I'd have to go back to independent contract work, writing magazine articles for pennies per word to make ends meet. That part of my life was supposed to be over. I'd *killed myself*—working sixty hours a week for nearly ten years to get where I was now. I couldn't walk away from that without a fight.

I had to at least attempt to salvage things—enough to get a recommendation that wasn't scathing. So I took a deep breath, pulled up my big-girl panties, and opened my laptop to refresh my memory on the specifics of what I'd written to the president of Lexington Industries, since more than half of it was fuzzy. Maybe it wasn't as bad as I thought. I clicked into my sent box and opened the message.

Dear Mr. Jong-un,

I shut my eyes. *Shit.* Well, there goes that wishful thought. But maybe he won't get my humor; he'll just think I got his name wrong. That's possible, right?

I reluctantly went back to reading while holding my breath.

I'd like to formally apologize for my minor indiscretion.

Okay...not a bad start. This is good. This is good.

If only I'd stopped reading there.

You see, I hadn't realized I worked for a dictator.

Ugh.

God, I'm such an asshole when I drink too much. I blew out a loud stream of shaky breath and ripped the Band-Aid off.

I was under the impression that I had the right to do what I pleased while on my own time. Unlike your silver-spoon ass, I work hard. Therefore, I deserve to blow off some steam once in a while. If that entails getting a little sun on my ta-tas while on a girls-only private vacation, then that's what I'll do. I wasn't breaking any laws. It was a nude beach. I could have gone fully nude, but I just chose to go topless. Because, let's be real—I have great tits. If you've watched the "offending video," which your uptight human resources director saw fit to provide me on a thumb drive along with a bullshit termination letter, you should consider yourself lucky you got a glimpse of them. You might even consider adding it to your spank bank, perv.

I've spent more than nine years working my ass off for you and your stupid company. You can both go to hell.

Bite me,

Ireland Saint James

Okay. I had a steeper uphill battle to smooth things over than I'd hoped. But I couldn't let that deter me. Maybe *el presidente* hadn't even read my first email yet, and I could start my next attempt by asking him to ignore the original one.

If I wanted any shot of finding a job within the industry, I couldn't have a bad recommendation. Since they'd violated my privacy, the least they could do was be neutral. I broke out in a panicky sweat and chewed on my fingernail. I wasn't above begging. So I copied and pasted the president's email address and opened a new message. Time was of the essence here.

But just as I started to type, my laptop pinged, letting me know a new email had arrived. I clicked on it, and my heart nearly stopped as I read the email address: Grant.Lexington@LexingtonIndustries.com

Oh God.

No.

I tried to swallow, but my mouth was suddenly dry. This was not good. I just wasn't sure how bad it was yet.

Dear Ms. Saint James,

Thank you for your email...which this silver spoon read at two in the morning, because I was still at the office working. From the tone of your letter—one littered with grammatical errors from a woman with a journalism degree—I'm assuming you wrote it while drunk. If that's the case, at least you no longer need to get up in the morning. You're welcome.

For your information, I have not viewed the video you referred to. But if my spank bank ever runs a little low, perhaps I'll dig it out of my trash folder—along with the standard letter of recommendation your superior had planned to give you.

Sincerely yours,
Richie Rich

I let out the breath I'd been holding. *Oh fuck.*

CHAPTER 2

Grant

"Mr. Lexington, would you like me to order you some lunch? Your two o'clock just called and is running a half hour late, so you have a little break."

"Why can't people ever be on damn time?" I grumbled and pushed the button to the intercom to speak to my assistant. "Can you please order me Boar's Head turkey and Alpine lacy swiss on whole wheat? And tell them one slice of swiss. The last time we ordered from the deli, the guy who made my sandwich must've been from Wisconsin."

"Yes, Mr. Lexington."

I opened my laptop to catch up on emails since my back-to-back meetings had turned into back-to-wait yet again. Scanning for anything important, my eyes stopped on one particular name in my inbox: *Ireland Saint James.*

The woman was obviously a drunk, or nuts, possibly even both. Though her email had been more amusing than half the mundane shit waiting for me. So I clicked.

Dear Mr. Lexington,

Would you believe my email was hacked and someone else wrote that ridiculous letter?

I'm guessing probably not. Considering how well educated, intelligent, hardworking, and successful you are.

Am I pouring it on too thick?

Sorry. But I have a lot of shoveling to do.

Is there any chance we can start over? You see, contrary to what you probably think, I don't drink that often. Which is why when a very unexpected termination letter showed up at my door, it didn't take much to bury my sorrow. And apparently my sanity.

Anyway, if you're still reading, thank you. Here's the letter I should've written:

Dear Mr. Lexington,

I'm writing to request your assistance in what I believe was a wrongful termination of my employment. As background, I've been a dedicated employee of Lexington Industries for nine and a half years. I started as an intern, received promotions through various news-writing positions, and eventually reached my goal of on-air reporter.

Recently, I went on a much-needed vacation to Aruba with eight women for a bachelorette party. Our hotel had a private section of the beach reserved for nude sunbathing. Though not generally an exhibitionist, I joined my friends for a few hours of topless tanning. A few innocent photos were taken, none of which were posted by me, and my on-air name was not tagged. Yet somehow, I returned home to a letter of termination for violating company policy regarding lewd behavior.

While I understand the reason for having an inappropriate-behavior policy, I adamantly believe my conduct while on a private vacation, on a private beach, was not what it was meant to protect Lexington Industries from. As such, I respectfully request that you review the policy and the termination of my employment.

Respectfully yours,

Ireland Saint James (Ireland Richardson, on air)

Saint James. Why do I know that name? It had sounded familiar when the first email arrived, so I'd looked her up in the company directory. But she was in the news division, which my sister ran and I'd avoided like the plague since I took over as president when my dad died eighteen months ago. Politics, propaganda, and bureaucracy weren't my thing. Though I was president in name, I generally stuck to the financial side of Lexington Industries.

I dug out the first email I'd received from Ms. Saint James and reread it. While the newest one was certainly more appropriate, the first amused me more. She'd signed the letter with the closing, *Bite me*...which had actually made me chuckle. No one talked to me like that. Oddly, I found it a bit refreshing. I had the strangest urge to have a conversation with Ms. Richardson after a few drinks. She'd certainly piqued my curiosity. I pressed the button of the intercom on my phone again.

"Millie, could you call down to the Broadcast Media division—the morning news segment producer? I think it might be Harrison Bickman or Harold Milton... something along those lines."

"Of course. Would you like me to set up a meeting for you?"

"No. Tell him I'd like to see the personnel file for one of his employees—Ireland Saint James. Her stage name is Ireland Richardson."

"I'll get it taken care of."

"Thank you."

My afternoon meeting only lasted fifteen minutes. Not only did the guy show up an hour and a half late, he was also completely unprepared. I had no patience for people who didn't value my time, so I'd called it quits and walked out of the conference room after telling him to lose my number.

"Is everything okay?" Millie looked up at me as I strode past her desk. "Do you need something from your office for your meeting?"

"My meeting is over. Hang up on anyone who calls from Bayside Investments, if they ever call again."

"Uh...yes, Mr. Lexington." Millie got up and followed me into my office, holding a notepad. "Your grandmother called. She said to tell you they don't need a security system and she sent the installer home."

I rounded my desk and shook my head. "Great. Just great."

"I retrieved Ms. Saint James's file for you and printed it out. It's on your desk in a folder. There's also a video of some sort that was on file in Human Resources, which I emailed to you."

"Thank you, Millie." I sat down at my desk. "Would you mind closing the door on your way out?"

• • •

Jesus Christ. Now I remembered her. It was a long time ago, but her story wasn't one you'd forget too easily. Back when Ireland Saint James was hired, my father was still running things. I'd been sitting in his office when Millie had brought him the file on her. He'd used her story as a teaching example—an example of decisions you sometimes have to make to protect the company image.

I leaned back in my chair. Every employee gets a background check—the extensiveness of it depends on the position. The more visibility someone has, the more their name and face can affect the brand of the company, so the deeper we delve. Human Resources and an outside investigation company usually do the vetting. When a person comes back clean, a manager does the hire with a signoff from the division's director. For the most part, senior management isn't involved—unless someone poses a possible threat to our name and a department head still wants to make an offer. Then the file gets sent up the flagpole.

Ireland Saint James. I rubbed at the stubble already forming on my chin. Her first name was a bit unusual, so that was probably what rang a bell. Though I blocked out a lot of shit from ten years ago.

I flipped through the pages of her personnel file—her background summary was barely a page. Yet the file had to be two inches thick.

UCLA undergraduate with a major in communications and minor in English. Berkeley Graduate School of Journalism with a postgraduate fellowship in investigative reporting. Not too shabby. Never arrested, and only one parking ticket. We'd done an update to her background eighteen months ago, when she'd gotten the position she was in now. It seemed she was dating a lawyer. All in all, her investigation was unremarkable—she was an ideal employee and an upstanding citizen. But her father was a different story...

The next fifty pages were mostly about him. He'd been some sort of low-level security guard in an apartment complex here in the city—though it was the time after his departure that was the focus of all of the news articles. Flipping through, I scanned the pages, letting them fan slowly one at a time until I got to one with a photo of a little girl in it. When I lifted it closer, the name in the caption confirmed it was Ireland. She had to be about nine or ten in the picture. For some reason, I stared at it like a bad car accident. She was crying, and a female police officer had a hand wrapped around her shoulder as they walked out of her house.

Good for you.

Good for you, Ireland—getting where you are today after that start.

As fucked up as it was, I smiled at the picture. Things could have very easily gone the other way for her. It made sense that she'd written me a second time now—she was a fighter.

I hit the intercom on my desk phone, and Millie answered.

"Yes, Mr. Lexington."

"Would you get me some recent segments of the morning news with Ms. Saint James? She's Ireland Richardson on air. Have them email up a link from the archives."

"Of course."

• • •

I might've paid more attention to the Broadcast Media division if I'd known it looked like this. Or I could have at least watched the morning news.

Ireland Saint James was a damn knockout—big blue eyes, sandy blond hair, full lips, white teeth that showed often because she smiled a lot. She reminded me of a younger version of that tall actress from the last *Mad Max* movie.

I watched three full segments before clicking back to the email Millie sent me earlier—the one from Ireland's HR file. Three sets of tits greeted me when the video opened. I pulled my head back. Definitely not the news. The women were on a beach, wearing nothing but skimpy bikini bottoms and sipping drinks from coconuts with a straw. I forced my eyes up to examine their faces—none of them was Ireland. But a few seconds before the end of the short video, a woman walked up from the beach. Her hair was slicked back from the water and looked darker wet, but the smile was unmistakably Ireland's.

With the other women, I'd noticed their bodies first, yet it took me until the video ended and froze on Ireland to even look down—and it wasn't because her body wasn't impressive. Her breasts were full and natural. They went with the rest of her luscious curves. But it was the curve of her *smile* that made me feel like I should suit up in armor.

I shifted in my seat and toggled to the X at the corner of the video to close it. Though she'd suggested I add it to my spank bank, I wasn't going to be disrespectful. Now, if she'd sent me the video herself, that might be a different story. But I certainly wasn't going to work up a stiffy in my office replaying the video a dozen times—no matter how tempted the asshole part of me was.

I turned in my chair to look out the window. *Ireland Saint James. You seem like a real handful.* A woman I should steer clear of, that was for damn sure. Yet I felt compelled to learn more. For a few minutes, I debated digging further, maybe listening to more of her side of the story. But why would I be doing that?

Because I was curious about Ireland Saint James, that's why.

Though was it because I wanted to ensure fairness at my company?

Or because she had a mesmerizing smile, a killer rack, and a fucked-up history that made me curious?

After a few minutes of deliberating, I knew the answer. Every warning sensor in my brain told me to delete the emails and run the personnel file through the shredder. That was the smart thing to do...definitely the right business decision to make. Yet...

I hit the space bar to power my laptop back up and opened a new email.

Dear Ms. Richardson,

After further review...

CHAPTER 3

Ireland

Harold Bickman is such an asshole.

Though I loved my job, my boss was the one thing I wouldn't miss. The man was a dirt bag. He hadn't been a fan of mine almost from the very beginning, ever since I'd found out he hired my male counterpart—who had less experience than me and less time with the company—with a salary of twenty grand more than mine. I'd brought it to his attention in a professional manner, and he'd proceeded to explain that there were pros and cons to every employee and every position. He'd said I shouldn't worry, that I'd see benefits Jack Dorphman didn't have someday soon—like when I took advantage of the great *maternity leave* policy the company had.

I'd filed a formal complaint about my salary with Human Resources and gotten equivalent pay. But there was no going back from what Harold Bickman considered treason on my part. We'd found a way to work together without too much friction—mostly by avoidance, though his email today proved once again what a colossal jerk he was. And something in my gut made me think he'd had a hand in the station getting ahold of that topless beach video. Lord knows the man wanted to give my job to Siren Eckert bad enough.

Side note, Siren is her real name, not her stage name. What were her parents thinking? Anyway...

Harold Bickman, a fifty-four-year-old, overweight, balding man who smelled like day-old cheese, wasn't the brightest bulb in the bunch when it came to women. I bet he thought he had a chance with Siren—the twenty-four-year-old former Miss Seattle runner-up—just because she batted her eyelashes at him. I bet he also thought I would follow the directions in his email.

Dear Ms. Richardson,

In light of the unfortunate events and your recent departure from Broadcast Media, I have scheduled you to visit the office at 10 a.m. on Thursday, June 29th to collect your belongings. I trust you will conduct yourself professionally during your visit. As your employee identification and building card have been deactivated, you will need to check in at the security desk.

Regards,

H. Bickman

Seriously? I wanted to crawl through my laptop and strangle the man. It made me cringe to think that he might've viewed the "unfortunate events." He probably jerked off while watching the twenty-two-second glimpse of topless women, right before walking over to Siren and offering her my job.

God, the one good thing about getting fired was that I'd finally get to tell that man what I thought about him on Thursday. Although, I wouldn't put it past the wimp to be MIA when I came to "collect my belongings."

I sighed and hit the trashcan icon to get rid of Harold once and for all. But just as I was about to close my laptop, I saw another new email waiting. This one from Grant Lexington. Curious, I immediately clicked to open.

> *Dear Ms. Richardson,*
>
> *After further review of your file, I've determined the decision to terminate your employment was warranted. However, I'll reach out to your immediate supervisor and suggest he provide you with a neutral letter of recommendation based on your performance.*
> *Sincerely,*
> *Grant Lexington*

Great, just great—leave it up to *Harold* to give me something neutral. I probably should have shut my laptop and cooled off. But the last forty-eight hours had brought me to a boiling point. So I typed back, not bothering with the formality of a greeting or anything.

> *Great. Harold Bickman hates women almost as much as he hates foot tapping. Oh...unless he thinks he*

has a chance to bang you—like he does my replacement.
Thanks for nothing.

• • •

Two days later, on Thursday morning, I was no less bitter when I arrived at the office. I was, however, almost forty-five minutes early since I had no idea how long it took to get to the office during rush-hour traffic. The roads were always empty when I left for work at four-thirty in the morning. Since I wouldn't put it past Bickman not to allow me in early, I decided to go next door to the coffee shop. It would give me a chance to mentally prepare for cleaning out my desk, and dealing with him, too.

I ordered a decaf, since my nerves were shot already, and went to sit at a corner table. Whenever I was feeling stressed, I watched Instagram video clips from the *Ellen* show. They always cracked me up, and that, in turn, helped me relax. I clicked on a funny clip where Billie Eilish scared Melissa McCarthy, and I laughed out loud. Looking up from my phone when it ended, I was caught off guard to find a man standing next to me.

"Do you mind if I share your table?"

I looked him up and down. Tall, gorgeous, expensive suit...probably not a serial killer. Then again, my ex always had perfectly tailored suits, too.

I squinted. "Why?"

The man looked to his left and then his right. When his greenish gray eyes returned to meet mine, I thought I detected the slightest twitch at the left corner of his lip. "Because all of the other seats are taken."

I surveyed the room. *Oh. Shit.* They *were* all taken now. Lifting my purse off the table, I nodded. "Sorry. I didn't realize the place had filled up. I thought... Well, never mind. Please, help yourself."

That lip made the slightest twitch again. Did he have a tic, or was I amusing him?

"I said *Excuse me*, but you didn't seem to hear. You were engrossed in what you were doing."

"Oh. Yeah. Lots of work. Busy, busy." I clicked to close YouTube and opened up my email.

The handsome guy unbuttoned his suit jacket and sat down in the seat across from me. He lifted his coffee cup to his lips. "The one with Will is my personal favorite."

My brows furrowed.

He smirked. "Smith. On *Ellen*. I couldn't help but notice what you were watching. You were smiling. You have a beautiful smile, by the way."

I felt my cheeks heat, but not because of the compliment. I rolled my eyes. "So I lied. I wasn't working. You didn't have to call me out on it."

His little smirk turned into a full-blown grin, yet there was still something very cocky about it.

"Did anyone ever tell you that you have an arrogant smile?" I asked.

"No. But then again, I haven't seemed to use it too much the last few years."

I tilted my head. "That's a shame."

His eyes roamed over my face. "So why did you lie about working?"

"Honestly?"

23

"Sure. Let's try that route."

I sighed. "It was a gut reaction. I just recently lost my job, and I don't know... I guess I felt like a loser sitting here watching *Ellen* clips."

"What do you do for a living?"

"I'm a newscaster for Lexington Industries—or at least I was until a few days ago. I did the early-morning segment."

Mr. Doesn't Smile Often didn't respond the way most people did when I told them I was on TV. They usually raised their brows and had a million questions. But it sounded way more glamorous than it was. Yet the man across the table didn't seem impressed. Or if he was, he didn't show it. Which I found curious.

"And what do you do that you wear a fancy suit and yet can sit in a coffee shop so leisurely at..." I looked at the time on my phone. "...nine forty-five in the morning?"

That little twitch was back. He seemed to like my sarcasm.

"I'm the CEO of a company."

"Impressive."

"Not really. It's a family business. So it's not like I started at the bottom."

"Nepotism." I sipped my coffee. "You're right. I'm a lot less impressed now."

He smiled again. If what he'd said about not doing it often was really true, it was a damn shame...because those full lips and that cocky smile could melt hearts and win poker games.

"So tell me about getting fired," he said. "That is, if you don't have to get back to all that work you were doing on your phone."

I chuckled. "It's a long story. But I did something I thought was harmless, and it turned out to be in violation of the company's policy."

"And you're an otherwise good employee?"

"Yes, I worked my butt off for more than nine years to get where I was."

He studied me and sipped his coffee some more. "Have you tried talking to your boss?"

"My boss has wanted me gone for years—ever since I complained that he hired my male counterpart for more money than I was being paid." Which reminded me, I needed to get to the office to see that asshole boss. "I should get going. Said boss is waiting for me to clean out my desk."

Mr. CEO rubbed his chin. "Would you mind if I offered you a little advice? I've dealt with a lot of employment issues."

"Sure." I shrugged. "Can't hurt."

"Retaliation for reporting an illegal gender pay gap is illegal. I suggest you make an appointment with the Human Resources department and lay out your support for that claim. Sounds to me like there should be an investigation, and your boss might be the one who should be in here watching *Ellen* videos."

Huh. Scott hadn't mentioned that retaliation was illegal when I'd told him what happened. But that didn't surprise me. He was too busy lecturing me for being topless on the beach.

I stood. "Thank you. Maybe I'll do that."

The handsome man rose from his chair. He stared at me, almost looking like he wanted to say more, but had to deliberate over his words. I waited until it got awkward.

"Umm... It was nice meeting you," I said.

He nodded. "Likewise."

I started to walk away, and he stopped me by speaking again. "Would you...want to have lunch later? You can't very well give me the excuse that you're too busy now that I know you're unemployed."

I smiled. "Thanks. But I don't think so."

Mr. CEO nodded and sat back down.

I walked out of the coffee shop, not quite sure why I'd said no. Of course there was *stranger danger* and all. But meeting him for lunch in a public place wouldn't be any more dangerous than going out with a guy I met at a bar. And I'd done that before. If I were being honest, something about the guy intimidated me—not unlike how I'd felt when Scott and I first got together. He was just too good-looking and too successful and, well, I guess I felt gun shy about the type.

But that was just stupid. The man was seriously sexy, and my morning was going to be shitty enough. Why not go out to lunch and take a chance?

I halted in place on the street, causing the person behind me to bang into my back. "Sorry," I said.

The guy made a face and walked around me. I rushed back to the coffee shop and opened the door. The CEO was standing and picked up his cup like he was about to leave.

"Hey, Mr. CEO, you're not a serial killer, right?"

His brows jumped. "No. Not a serial killer."

"Okay. Then I changed my mind. I'll have lunch with you."

"Well, now I'm glad I didn't go on that rampage after all."

I chuckled and dug into my purse for my phone. "Put your number in. I'll text you my contact info."

He typed into my cell, and I immediately sent him my contact information. When his phone buzzed in his hand, he looked down. "Ireland. Beautiful name. Fitting."

I looked down at my own phone, but he hadn't entered a name. "CEO? You're not going to tell me your name."

"Figured I'd keep you curious until lunch."

"Hmmm... Okay. But I'm guessing you have some sort of uppity CEO name that gets passed down, along with a trust fund."

He chuckled. "I'm glad I stopped in for coffee today."

I smiled. "Me too. I'll text you later about lunch."

He nodded. "I'm looking forward to it, Ireland."

I left the coffee shop and headed for the office in a much better mood than I'd started with. Maybe today wouldn't be so bad after all...

• • •

"Seriously? You couldn't even have her wait until I'd cleaned out my desk?"

Our office space was a large, open square with cubicles in the middle and private, fishbowl-type glass offices lining the perimeter. Security had escorted me to Bickman's office like I was a prisoner, and now I could see Siren on the other side of the large space, moving boxes from her cubicle into my office.

Bickman yanked on his belt buckle and pulled his pants from beneath his belly to up and over it. "Don't cause a scene, or I'll pack up your crap for you."

I scowled and began to tap my foot as I spoke. "I hope you at least gave her pay parity with a male of the same education and experience. Oh wait...that might be hard since a man with her qualifications works in the *mail room* still."

He pushed a few buttons on his phone and looked across at my office as he spoke on speakerphone. "Ireland is here to clean out her office. You might want to give her some space and finish setting up your new office when she's done."

"Yes, Mr. Bickman."

I rolled my eyes. *Yes, Mr. Bickman.*

The asshole waved his hand, dismissing me to go do what I needed to do. "Don't take too long."

Disgusted, I turned to walk out of his office and then stopped and backed up. I hadn't decided if I was going to go to HR about him firing me for retaliation. I really didn't have any proof—I couldn't show that Bickman was the one who'd surfaced the video that was my reason for being fired. And I knew threatening wouldn't bother him at all. Still, I needed to make him feel like shit, so I could at least feel better.

I stepped back into his office and quietly closed the door behind me, turning to say one last thing.

"You've been looking for a reason to fire me for years. But it's hard to justify when I've been a model employee, and our ratings have gone up consistently since I joined the show. Finally you found a reason. I don't know how you did it, but I know you were behind Human Resources getting ahold of that video. Tell me, did you keep a copy for yourself? I hope you did, because that'll be the only piece of ass you'll ever see from this office. You certainly won't be seeing any skin from the unqualified, barely-out-of-high-school girl you gave my job to. You *think* that will make her like you, but she's busy banging that new intern from advertising. Oh, and remember Marge Wilson—the divorced, middle-aged temp you got drunk at the office Christmas party a few years back? The one you think no one knows you went home with?" I smiled and held up my pinky, waving it in the air. "Well, we *all* know. Her nickname for you was *Inchworm*."

I opened the door, took a deep breath, and headed over to clean out nine years of my life.

Literally three minutes later, Security was at my office door, and Bickman stood right behind them.

I put the last of my things from the top drawer into a box and glowered at him. "I'm not done yet."

"You've had long enough. We have work to do around here."

I mumbled under my breath and opened the second drawer to continue packing. "God, you're such an asshole, Inchworm."

Apparently, I wasn't very good at mumbling. Bickman's face turned red, and he pointed toward the exit. "Out! Get out."

I yanked the second drawer off the track and unceremoniously dumped the contents into my box. Then I did the same thing for two others and tossed the empty drawers onto the guest chairs on the other side of my desk. I grabbed the framed pictures that sat on my desk and my degree off the wall and jammed it all into the box.

The two uniformed security guards he'd summoned looked completely uncomfortable.

I smiled at one sadly. "I'll leave so you don't have to deal with this jerk."

The guards followed me to the elevator bank and got into the car with me. Bickman at least had enough common sense to take a different elevator. Though when we stepped out on the lobby level, he exited the car next to us.

I shook my head and kept walking. "I think the two security guards are enough. You don't need to escort me, Bickman."

He kept his distance but followed behind, nonetheless. When I got to the main lobby area, there were a lot of people standing around. So I decided to go out with a bang. I stopped and turned around to face Bickman. Setting my heavy box on the floor in front of me, I pointed my finger at him and began to shout at the top of my lungs. "This man uses his position to try to take advantage of women. He just fired me and gave my job to some young girl because he thinks she might spread her legs to say thank you. I guess he isn't familiar with the #MeToo movement."

Bickman rushed forward and grabbed my elbow. I yanked it out of his hand.

"Don't touch me."

He took a few steps back when he realized people were watching and turned to scurry back to the elevator bank.

I needed to get the hell out of here before Security called the actual cops. So I took a deep, cleansing breath, lifted my box back up, and held my chin high as I marched toward the glass doors. Only...a man was walking directly in my path, heading right toward me with rapid, long strides. My steps faltered as I took in his face. *His very pissed-off face.*

"Keep your damn hands to yourself," he barked over my shoulder at Bickman.

Mr. CEO.

Great. Just great. The first guy I'd met in months that I was actually a little interested in, and he had to walk into my building just as I was making a scene and acting like a crazy person. The timing couldn't have been worse. Then again, it went with the rest of my shitty day.

The stress of the last few days must have gotten to me, and I cracked. I started laughing like a nutjob. At first it was a burst of laughter, but it turned into a snort, followed by a belly laugh that made me sound like I'd lost my mind. I tried to cover my mouth and stop, but my words came out between hysterics. "Of course I had to run into you here. I swear, I'm not really like this. It's just been a *really* bad few days."

CEO continued to stare over my shoulder. The look on his face was positively lethal—jaw tight, muscles flexing in his cheek, and his nostrils flaring like a bull's. I turned to follow his line of sight and saw Bickman walking back toward us instead of away.

I sighed, knowing the scene wasn't over yet, and shut my eyes. "I'll understand why you don't call me for lunch."

The man's eyes flickered to me, then Bickman, and then back to me once again. "Actually, I'd still love to take you to lunch. But I'm guessing you're about to change your mind."

CHAPTER 4

Grant

"**M**r. Lexington, it's so good to see you."

Ireland's head swung back and forth. If I'd had any doubt about whether she'd known who I was in the coffee shop earlier, the confusion on her face now confirmed she'd had no clue.

"Did he just call you..."

Bickman appeared at Ireland's side, and I glared at him. "Give us a moment. I need to speak to Ms. Saint James."

Ireland's eyes lit up. "You son of a bitch. You knew who I was the entire time?"

Bickman was still standing behind her like I hadn't just told him to beat it. "Did you not understand what I said?" I growled at him.

"Sorry, Mr. Lexington. Of course. I'll go back up to my office. I'm on the eleventh floor if you need me."

Yeah. You've done enough already. I told the security guards to go back to their posts and went to take the box from Ireland's hands. "Let me hold that."

She pulled it away from my reach. "*You're* Grant Lexington?"

"I am."

"And you knew who I was at the coffee shop?"

I swallowed. "Yes."

"God, I gave my number to a liar. That's *worse* than a serial killer."

"I never lied to you."

"Yes, but you neglected to mention the fact that you're my boss's boss's boss." The box she held started to slip, and she almost fumbled it. "Oh God. Our emails! We've exchanged emails, and you didn't think it was relevant to mention who you were when you knew who I was?"

"I honestly didn't know who you were when I first walked over to take the empty seat. But I would've mentioned it at lunch..."

She shook her head. "Lunch? *Screw you*. Better yet. Screw your whole damn company."

Ireland walked around me and stalked toward the door.

"Ireland!" I called after her.

She kept walking. I probably needed my head examined, but watching her out Bickman and tell me off made my dick twitch. It was even better than the current view of her sexy ass as she tore out of my building.

I smiled and shook my head. Maybe we were both a little nuts. "So I'll call you about our lunch date later then?" I yelled after her.

She raised a hand without looking back and gave me the finger.

I chuckled.

My gut told me it wouldn't be the last time I saw Ireland, but for the moment, I had other pressing things to attend to.

• • •

"Mr. Lexington, it's nice to see you. I'm sorry you had to witness the unfortunate events in the lobby. We had a disgruntled terminated employee who wanted to make a scene."

A young woman popped her head into Bickman's office. She didn't immediately notice me since I was standing to the side of the doorway. "Can I go back into my office..." She spotted me and trailed off. "Oh, I'm sorry to interrupt. I didn't realize you weren't alone."

"It's fine," I said with a nod.

Bickman made the introductions. "Siren, this is Grant Lexington. He's the President and CEO of the company that owns our little station."

"Oh. Wow," she said.

I extended my hand. "Nice to meet you."

Bickman puffed out his chest. "Siren's just been promoted to on-air reporter."

So this is the unqualified woman Ireland was going off about?

Bickman told the woman she could continue moving into her new office, and I watched his eyes drop to her ass when she turned around. Once she was out of earshot, I confirmed my suspicion.

"Is she Ms. Saint James's replacement?"

The asshole looked proud. "Yes. She's a graduate of Yale and..."

I cut him off. "How did you get ahold of Ms. Saint James's vacation video?"

"Excuse me?"

"Do I need to speak more slowly? How. Did. You. Get. Ms. Saint James's. Vacation. Video?"

"I...uhh...saw it on social media."

I arched a brow. "On her public social media?"

"No, her private Instagram account."

"So you're friends on social media then? Since you can see things posted to her private accounts?"

"Yes. Well, not technically me. But I have access to an account she's friends with."

"Elaborate." I was starting to lose my patience.

"I have some social media set up in an old employee's name. A basic profile."

"So you're telling me you're using someone else's name to stalk all your employees' private social media?"

Bickman tugged at the knot of his tie. "No. Just the troublesome ones."

"The troublesome ones?"

"Yes."

He didn't need to tell me any more. Ireland hadn't been exaggerating. This guy was really a piece of work. I walked to his desk, picked up the receiver to his phone, and pushed a few buttons. When Security answered, I said, "This is Grant Lexington. Can you please come up to the eleventh floor? I have a terminated employee you need to escort off the premises."

When I hung up, Bickman still didn't seem to get it.

I put my hands on my hips. "You're fired. You have until Security gets up here to clean out your desk, which I'm pretty sure is more than the amount of time you afforded Ms. Saint James."

The dumbass blinked a few times. "What?"

I leaned in and spoke slowly. "What part of *you're fired* didn't you understand?"

Bickman said something—though I don't know what the hell it was, because I walked out of his office and went to the woman I assumed was his assistant based on where she sat.

"Are you Bickman's assistant?"

The older woman looked nervous. "Yes."

I looked down at the nameplate on her desk and extended my hand. I guess I really should've stopped by this building more often. Half the people didn't even know who I was. "Hi, Carol. I'm Grant Lexington, the CEO of Lexington Industries, which owns this station. I work in our other offices across the street. Mr. Bickman is no longer with the company. Don't worry about your job, though. It's safe."

"Okay..."

"Who covers for Bickman when he's on vacation?"

"Umm... Well, Ireland used to."

Great. "Well, who is the most senior person besides Ireland?"

"I guess that would be Mike Charles."

"And where does he sit?"

Carol pointed to an office.

"Thank you."

I spoke with Mike Charles and put him in charge, and then I watched as Security escorted a flustered

Bickman out of the building. When I was done, I went back across the street.

Millie stood as I entered and followed me into my office, reading me a list of calls I'd missed and some other shit that went in one ear and out the other. I took off my jacket and rolled up my shirtsleeves.

"Can you please send an email to my sister to let her know I fired Harold Bickman in Broadcast Media? Mike Charles is going to hold the reins while things get sorted out over there."

"Umm...sure. Though the last time you *hired* someone for Kate's division, she wasn't happy. She'll probably be in your office within ten minutes once I call."

I sat down and blew out a deep breath. "Good point. I'll tell her myself. Ask Kate if she can come across to my office to talk."

Millie eyed me over her notepad. "She'd probably like it if you went to her for a change..."

Millie was right. My sister definitely begrudged that she always had to come to me. "Good point. Tell her I'll be coming over to talk to her in ten minutes."

"Is there anything else?"

"Can you also send a messenger with an apology letter to Ireland Saint James? Tell her I've reviewed the circumstances surrounding her termination and to be back at work by Monday."

Millie scribbled in her notebook. "Okay. I'll get right on that."

"Thank you."

As she got to the door, I thought of something else. "Can you please add a dozen roses to go with the letter to Ms. Saint James?"

Millie's brows drew together, but she rarely questioned my judgment, and she'd already commented on how my sister was going to react. So she scribbled more in her notebook and simply said, "Will do."

. . .

The next afternoon, Millie walked into my office carrying a box of flowers. She looked nervous. My name was scribbled across the top of the box in red marker. "These came for you via messenger just now."

I opened the long, white box and unwrapped the tissue paper. Inside were a dozen roses, but all the heads had been cut off the stems. A folded piece of stationery lay at the top. I picked it up and opened it.

Keep the flowers. I'll need a fat raise if you want me back.
—Ireland

I laughed out loud. Millie looked at me like I was nuts.

"Can you please call Ms. Saint James? Tell her I don't negotiate via messenger. Set up a lunch meeting for today at La Piazza at one o'clock."

. . .

I looked at my watch. If it were anyone else, I'd have walked out the door by now. Yet fifteen minutes after my scheduled lunch, I was still sitting at the table alone, drinking a glass of water, when Ireland Saint James walked in. She looked around the restaurant, and the hostess pointed to where I was seated.

As she made her way toward me, she smiled. It caught me off guard when my heart started to pump faster. Unlike yesterday and in the clips I'd watched, today her hair was pulled back into a slick ponytail. It showcased her high cheekbones and full lips, focusing attention on just her face. Some women needed window dressing in the form of hair and makeup, but Ireland was even more beautiful without that shit. She had on a royal blue silk shirt and a pair of black slacks. The outfit was pretty conservative, yet she still managed to snag the eye of every man and woman as she made her way through the dining room.

I stood and tried not to let her see how much her appearance affected me. "You're late."

"I'm sorry. I was early, but when I walked out to my car, my tire was flat. I had to grab an Uber."

I extended my hand. "Please sit."

Ireland took her seat, and the waiter came right over. "May I get you something to drink?"

I looked to Ireland. She smirked and unfolded her napkin. "I don't usually drink during the day, but since I'm unemployed, not driving, and he's paying, I'll have a glass of merlot, please."

I tried to contain my smile. "I'll just have a sparkling water." I glanced at Ireland. "Since I *am* gainfully employed."

The waiter disappeared, and Ireland folded her hands in front of her on the table. Ordinarily, people deferred to me to lead the conversation, but this woman wasn't ordinary.

"So," she said. "I spoke to my attorney, and he says I have a case against your company for harassment, breach of contract, and emotional distress."

I sat back into my chair. "Your attorney? And who might that be?"

"His name is Scott Marcum."

I knew the name from her background investigation a few years back. He'd been her boyfriend at the time. I wondered if they were still together.

"I see. Well, I came to offer you your job back, with an apology and perhaps a small raise. But if you'd rather go through our attorneys, that's fine, too." I started to get up from my chair—calling her bluff.

She fell for it. "Actually, I'd rather not deal with attorneys. I was just letting you know what mine said."

I folded my arms across my chest. "Letting me know so you can use it as leverage against me?"

She folded her arms across her chest, mimicking my stance. "Are you going to sit down so we can have a conversation or stomp out like a child?"

The woman had giant balls; I had to give her that. If she only knew how her attitude made me want to take a peek between her legs and check for some. We stared at each other for a full sixty seconds, and then I caved and sat down.

"Alright, Ms. Saint James. Let's put our cards on the table. What is it that you want?"

"I heard you fired Bickman. Is it true?"

"Yes."

"Why?"

"Because I don't like the methods he used to monitor his employees."

"Good. Me either. Plus, he's a dick."

My lip twitched. "Yes, there's that, too."

"Did you follow me to the coffee shop?"

"No. And for the record, I don't follow women or my employees around. I happened to walk in to grab a cup of coffee. My phone had rung in the car, and the connection was bad and dropped the call. I needed to compose a text to the caller so she wouldn't worry."

"Why didn't you tell me who you were when you realized who I was?"

"I already answered that question for you the other day. It was a coincidence that I sat down at your table. And then when I realized...I was intrigued about what you might say."

The waiter brought her wine and my water, and Ireland alternated between watching him and looking at me.

"We'll need a few minutes," I said. "We haven't looked at the menus yet."

Ireland's eyes were on me again when the waiter disappeared. She seemed to be mulling something over.

"Any other questions?"

She nodded. "Who was on the phone?"

"Pardon?"

"You said you were on the phone while you were driving, and the call got dropped, and you didn't want the person to worry."

I sipped my water. "My grandmother, not that it's any of your business. Are we done with the interrogation now? Because I was considering putting the drunken emails you sent me behind us. But if you'd like to rehash every last interaction we've had, we can discuss those, too."

She squinted at me and drank some of her wine. "I want a twenty-percent raise, and consideration given to Madeline Newton for Bickman's position."

Interesting. I scratched my chin. "One thing at a time. I'll give you ten percent."

"Fifteen."

"Twelve and a half."

She smiled. "Seventeen."

I chuckled. "That's not the way this works. Once you go down in a negotiation, you don't get to go back up if you're not liking the way things are going."

She frowned. "Who said?"

I shook my head. "I'll tell you what. I'll give you your fifteen, but for that, you'll also have to sign a release form, giving up your right to any potential lawsuit for anything Bickman might have done during his tenure."

She thought about it. "Okay. That's fair. If I'm being honest, I wasn't going to sue you anyway. I think our society is litigious enough. Plus, I don't like dealing with lawyers."

"What about Scott Marcum?"

"*Especially* Scott Marcum."

Good to know. "So we have a deal then?"

"As long as you'll give consideration to Madeline Newton for Bickman's position. She's the best person for the job, and has been passed over twice."

"If she applies, I'll make sure she's given due consideration."

"Thank you." She put out her hand. "Then I guess we have a deal."

I shouldn't have noticed how tiny and soft her hands were, how much her skin felt like silk, but I did.

I cleared my throat after we shook. "I'll let Mike Charles know you'll be taking the reins back immediately. I have to admit, I'm surprised you won't try for Bickman's position yourself."

She shook her head. "I'm not ready for it. But Madeline will do a great job. Unlike Bickman, she's smart and fair, and people respect what she says. Well, actually, to be fair, Bickman was smart, too. Just not when it came to women."

This woman just kept surprising me.

"You thought Bickman was smart?"

She nodded. "He was. It was everything else that was horrible."

"How did you two manage to co-exist for so long if he was that bad?"

"He was rude and demeaning, and I got my joy from the little things I did that drove him nuts. I pretended it balanced things."

My brows narrowed. "What little things?"

She smirked. "Well, he had certain pet peeves. For example, he couldn't stand when someone tapped their foot. It would make him turn the color of a tomato while he held in exploding about it."

"Okay..."

"So I would tap my foot and watch the vein in his neck pulse when he pissed me off."

My brows rose.

"He also once mentioned that he hated when people wore too much perfume or cologne. So I kept a bottle in my desk drawer for those times when I saw him ogling a woman's ass. I'd douse myself before going into his office and pretending I needed help with a story."

"Creative," I said.

"I thought so."

Ireland Saint James had a wicked side, that was for sure. I probably shouldn't have, but I found it rather sexy.

The waiter came back over to take our order, but we still hadn't checked out the menu. "Have you decided yet?"

Ireland held her menu up to the waiter. "Actually, I'm not going to be staying for lunch. So it's just Mr. Lexington."

"Alright." The waiter nodded and then turned to me. "For you, sir?"

"I need a few more minutes."

After the waiter walked away, I raised a brow. "Not hungry?"

"I'm always hungry. But I need to change the flat to my spare so I can drive the car to the tire shop. My roommate has to work at three, and she's going to give me a lift back home so I don't have to wait there. Last time they took hours, and now that I'm employed again...I have a ton of work to catch up on."

I nodded. "Do you have AAA?" I wasn't sure why the hell I'd asked. Was I going to go over and roll up the sleeves of my custom-made shirt and change it for her if she didn't?

"No. But I know how to change it. I've done it before." She laughed. "I once went on a date with a guy who got a flat while driving me home. He'd never changed a tire, so I changed it for him."

I smiled. "I bet he didn't get a second date."

She finished off her wine. "Definitely not."

My mind conjured up a quick flash of Ireland changing a tire. Only she wasn't changing some guy's tire while dressed for a date. She had on a pair of Daisy Dukes, a shirt tied in a knot exposing a fuck of a lot of tanned skin, her hair was in pigtails, and she had a smudge of grease on her cheek. The grease was fucking hot.

I shook my head and cleared my throat. "I'll let people know to expect you back at work."

Ireland stood, and I followed suit. She extended her hand. "Thank you for getting involved. Obviously, you didn't have to. Especially after the horrible emails I sent."

I nodded and shook. "I think everything worked out the way it should have."

She gathered her purse and started to walk away, then turned back. "Oh...and I gave you my number for lunch. Obviously this means I can't go out with you."

"Of course." I smiled. "Turns out you're not my type anyway."

Ireland narrowed her eyes. "And what exactly is your type?"

"The non-pain-in-the-ass type. Have a good day, Ms. Richardson."

CHAPTER 5

Ireland

"You look insane, you know." Mia looked up at the hat on my head. It was totally lopsided and had two weird points that stuck up. It gave off sort of a homeless-jester vibe. Not to mention it was going to be seventy-five degrees today. But I wore it on my drive to work every day anyway.

"You're just jealous because Aunt Opal doesn't crochet for you."

"I love Opal. But, yeah...not jealous your aunt who is almost blind left me off her Christmas crochet gift list."

I opened the passenger door and grabbed my bag. "Thank you for getting up and driving me at this ungodly hour. I didn't want to call an Uber and risk getting to work late on my first day back. I owe you one."

"You owe me a thousand. I'll just add it to your tab."

I smiled. "Thanks."

"What time should I pick you up?"

"You don't have to. I'll get a ride or grab an Uber to the tire shop to pick up my car. I'll just see you at home later." The tire shop had called to tell me I also desperately needed brakes and an alignment. So my flat tire had turned into two days without a car.

"Are you sure? I have coverage at the spa today. In fact, I have no idea what to do with myself since Christian talked me into not doing treatments and only managing the place now. I can pick you up. We can even grab some lunch. Better yet, I'll bring you back to the salon, and we'll get a couple's massage. My treat!"

Mia owned a successful medi-spa—the kind that did facials, Botox injections, massages, and laser treatments. Her fiancé was trying to teach her to be a manager instead of a worker bee, so she could prepare to open a second location.

"I'd love to. But I'm going to have to work late to catch up. Maybe we can grab some dinner when I get home?"

She wrinkled her nose. "I can't. I promised Christian I'd make him his favorite dinner—tortellini ala Mia."

"What's that?"

"Tortellini in a cream sauce. He loves the sauce, so I let him paint it on me when he's done."

"TMI, friend." I laughed. "TMI. But I thought he wasn't coming home until tomorrow?"

"He changed his flight." She smiled like a bride three weeks away from her wedding day. "He said he missed me too much to stay another night after his last meeting. So he's taking the last flight home. I'll probably just crash over there tonight."

I opened my mouth and pointed inside it with my finger, making a gagging noise. But the truth was, I envied her relationship with her fiancé. I wouldn't believe most men were coming home early just to see their girlfriend of three years, but Christian was as head over heels for Mia now as when they first got together.

I got out of the car and held the door.

Mia wagged her finger at me. "Now be a good girl while you're all alone tonight, and don't email any CEOs to tell them what you think of them."

I was never going to live that down. "I have a job again, don't I?"

She shook her head. "No idea how that managed to work out."

Yeah. Me either.

• • •

"Great show today, Ireland."

"Thanks, Mike."

My first day back on the air in two weeks felt good, and my adrenaline was already pumping to get started on tomorrow's show. I had a renewed sense of pride in my work.

Siren poked her head into my office. She looked nervous. "Hey. So I wanted to clear the air. I hope you know I had nothing to do with Bickman giving me your job. I was shocked when he came to tell me he was promoting me."

I could have pretended I believed her bullshit and gone back to the two of us playing ignorant, but she was young and needed someone to set her straight.

"Come in, Siren. Close the door behind you."

She did, but stood right in front of the door.

I motioned to the chairs on the other side of my desk. "Please, take a seat."

The poor thing looked pale. She'd played up to Bickman, and I'm sure she'd been thrilled when he handed her my job on a silver platter. But the bottom line was he'd abused his position, and really, she hadn't done anything wrong...except maybe break girl code.

I sighed. "Most people think a beautiful woman doesn't have to work as hard to get what she wants. And that might be true when she's at a bar trying to get a drink, or when she's in Home Depot trying to find someone to help her down the plumbing aisle. But it's not true in the workplace. A beautiful woman often has to work twice as hard to be seen for who she is here. Because, unfortunately, there are still men out there who can't see past beauty. I think you're going to be a great reporter someday. But you're not there yet. I wasn't at your age either. And when you play into men like Bickman, and take a position you haven't earned, you devalue yourself and all women. We need to stick together, not use beauty as a weapon against each other."

Siren looked down at her lap for a long time. When she looked up, she had tears in her eyes and nodded. "You're right. It didn't feel right when he gave me the job. It felt like I hadn't earned it...because I didn't."

"I'm not going to pretend I'm totally innocent. You know the mailroom won't ship anything they receive after three o'clock until the following day. I've thrown my share of smiles and batted my damn eyelashes at George to get things out at four thirty. But be careful around men in positions of power who give you something you didn't earn—they're going to expect you to earn it after the fact, in a way you won't like."

"Thanks, Ireland."

"Anytime."

An hour later, my desk phone rang, and the name on the caller ID surprised me. Speaking of men in power...*Grant Lexington* flashed on the display. I shut my laptop and leaned back in my chair as I picked up the phone. "To what do I owe this pleasure?"

"I was just calling to see how things were going— that you settled back in okay." His deep voice was even raspier on the phone than in person. Despite the lecture I'd given Siren earlier, here I was thinking *Hmmm...I'd like to hear that voice late at night when my hands are under the covers.*

I tamped down that thought and instead went with being difficult. "Did you call any other employees that don't work directly for you today?"

"Only the ones that sent me drunk emails, and I stupidly gave them back their jobs anyway."

I smiled. "Touché."

"How are things going?"

"Fine. No one seems too disappointed that Bickman is gone, and the show went off without a hitch this morning."

"It was a good show."

"You watched?"

"I did."

"Do you always watch the six o'clock news?"

"Not normally, no."

"So you watched it today because..."

The line went silent; he wasn't going to fill in the blank for me. *Hmm... Interesting.* He could have easily said he watched it to make sure things went smoothly. Or he watched it because he's the damn boss, and he felt like it. But his lack of a reason made me think he'd watched it just to watch me—and not for professional reasons.

Or maybe I was reading too much into things and that's what I *wanted* to think.

"Anyway..." he said. "I was also calling to invite you to be part of a new committee I'm chairing."

"Oh? What kind of committee?"

He cleared his throat. "It's...uh...for improving the workplace for women."

"*You're* chairing a women's workplace initiative?"

"Yes. Why does that surprise you?"

"Ummm... Because you're not a woman."

"That's a pretty sexist statement. Are you saying a man can't be involved with something to foster a better work environment for women?"

"No, but—"

"If you're too busy..."

"No, no, no. Not at all. I'd love to be part of it. What can I do? When does the committee meet?"

"My assistant will get back to you with the details."

"Oh. Okay. That sounds great. Thank you for thinking of me."

"Yes. Alright. Well, then...goodbye, Ireland."

He hung up sort of abruptly. But it was just as well, because I liked talking to him *way* too much.

CHAPTER 6

Grant

"Millie!" I shouted without getting up from my desk.

My assistant rushed into the office. "Yes, Mr. Lexington?"

"I need to start a new committee."

Her brows knitted. I avoided committees like the plague, and here I was telling her I wanted to *start* one. "Okay...what kind of committee, and who will be involved?"

I shook my head and grumbled the answer. "The focus of the group is to improve the workplace for women."

Millie's eyebrows jumped.

Yeah. I know. I'm fucking shocked, too.

"Okay..." she said hesitantly, like she was waiting for the punch line. "Do you have committee members already picked out?"

I waved my hand. "Get a bunch of women. I don't care who they are. And maybe my sister Kate. She loves to have meetings."

"You don't care who the women on the committee are?"

"No." I picked up a pile of papers and shuffled them, trying to pull off casual. "Maybe invite Ireland Saint James to be part of it."

"Ireland? The woman who sent you the decapitated flowers?"

Well, when she said it like that, it sounded a little nuts to create a committee out of thin air and invite someone who cut the heads off of the expensive flowers I sent her and walked out on our lunch date before we'd even ordered.

I sighed. "Yeah, her."

"When would you like me..."

"Soon."

"Do you have an agenda in mind for this committee's first meeting?"

"Women's shit. I don't know. You must know better than me. Pull something together."

Millie looked like she was seconds away from walking over and feeling my forehead to see if I had a fever.

Maybe that's what it was. Maybe I was sick instead of losing my mind? It damn well better be one or the other. I dragged a hand through my hair. A committee on women's initiatives? I wanted to be part of that almost as much as I wanted someone to grip my nuts in their fist and twist. Yet here I was, apparently spearheading the group.

What the fuck?

Ireland Saint James. That's what the fuck. In my entire life, I'd never had to go out of my way to talk to a woman, yet this woman had me calling her to check how her day was going and then inventing a fucking committee when she asked the reason for my call. Stress, too much work—it wasn't entirely out of the realm of possibility that I could be experiencing a breakdown.

While I debated a quick trip to a therapist, my assistant was still standing in my office, looking at me like I had two heads. I picked up a file and looked at her pointedly.

"Do you need anything else from me to get it started?"

"Umm... No, I don't think so."

"Good. Then that'll be all."

Millie stopped in my doorway and turned back. "The mail came. Would you like today's letter—"

"Throw it out," I barked.

"I'll get right on it. And don't forget about the photo shoot tonight."

The confused look on my face told her I had no fucking idea what she was talking about, so she filled in the blanks.

"You have an interview and photo shoot for *Today's Entrepreneur* magazine. It was scheduled a few months ago, and it's on your calendar."

Shit. Photo shoots and interviews were right up there with committees on women in the workplace on my list of crap I had zero interest in being part of. "What time?"

"Four thirty. At Leilani."

I looked at my watch. *Great.* I had an hour to finish up six hours of work.

● ● ●

A half dozen people were already sitting on the dock in front of Leilani when I parked at the marina. It was four thirty, right on the nose. They must've been early.

A familiar-looking redheaded woman smiled as I approached.

"Mr. Lexington. Amanda Cadet." She extended her hand to me. "It's so nice to see you again."

Again. Well, that explained why she looked familiar. Though I had no idea where we'd met. Probably some industry function. "You, too. Please, call me Grant."

"Alright. And please call me Amanda."

I looked around at a shitload of equipment. "Are you moving in?"

She laughed. "We brought a lot of camera and video equipment, because we weren't sure of the setting. To be safe, we even packed some props and a few canvas backgrounds. Though we can obviously put that all back in the truck." She turned to eye my boat. "This sailboat is stunning, and the scenery is better than any movie set."

"Thank you. It was my grandfather's. First sailboat he ever built in 1965."

"Well, you could have told me it was brand new."

I nodded my head toward the *Leilani May.* "Why don't I show you around, and you can decide where your crew wants to set up."

I gave Amanda a quick tour. The sixty-foot ketch was eye candy, even to non-boaters. Navy hull, satin finish teak wood, cream upholstery, stainless steel galley, an owner's stateroom more luxurious than most apartments, and three guest cabins made it look more like a Vineyard Vines ad than a sixty-year-old sailboat.

"So...what do you think? Where should we do this?"

"Honestly, anywhere would make for a great shoot. The boat is beautiful." She lifted a painted nail to her bottom lip, calling my attention to it. "And the subject is flawless. This cover is going to pull big numbers."

Amanda Cadet was attractive, and she knew it. She also knew how to use it to get what she wanted. Though whatever she thought she was getting from me—a story with some major revelation or my mouth between her legs—she wouldn't be. Because business and pleasure don't mix. I almost laughed at that thought after the way I'd been acting around Ms. Aruba Tits.

I held out my hand to indicate she should exit the cabin first. "Why don't we go out on the rear deck and set up on the left side with the marina in the background?"

"That sounds perfect."

I posed for pictures for the better part of an hour, hating every moment of it, but keeping my contempt to myself. When they had enough shots to plaster the walls of my office, Amanda told everyone to pack it up.

"Do you want me to video the interview?" her cameraman asked.

The piece she was putting together was for print, but it wasn't uncommon to record a session so the reporter could go back later and listen for things they'd missed in their notes.

Amanda's eyes swept over me. "No, that's okay. I think I'm good taking care of this one all by myself."

After the crew left, we sat alone on the back deck.

"So how often do you get down here to go boating? My brother is an orthopedic surgeon with a fifty-foot Carver down in San Diego Bay. I think he used it twice last year."

The truthful response to that question was *every damn day*. But I preferred to keep my private life private. The fact that I lived on the *Leilani May* was none of her business, and definitely not something I intended to share with her readers.

I nodded like I could relate to her brother. "Not often enough."

"I love that you still have your grandfather's first boat. I think the things a man holds on to say a lot about him."

If she only knew the half of it. "This boat built my family's company."

"How so?"

"This was his first model, and he used it to take the initial orders for Lexington Craft Yachts. Thirty years later, Lexington Craft went public, and my family used the proceeds to expand into different entertainment-related businesses. My dad had started a sports magazine, and my grandfather bought a few more publications. Eventually that led to buying a news station and chain of movie theaters. So without this boat, you wouldn't be interested in interviewing me today."

She flaunted a flirtatious smile. "Something tells me I'd be interested in interviewing you whether you were the CEO of one of the top 100 growing companies in America or your job was to clean this boat."

"I'm not that interesting."

"Humble, too, huh? I like it." She winked. "Tell me about your family's foundation. Your mother started it, correct?"

"That's right. It's called Pia's Place. My mother was put into the foster care system because of abuse when she was five. She moved around a lot, so it was difficult for her to keep the same therapist for too long. She had a different counselor every year at Child Protective Services, because those people are underpaid and overworked, so they tend to have a revolving door. She always felt different than the other kids in school, most of whom didn't know what foster care was. So it was difficult to connect with someone who understood what she was going through. Pia's Place is sort of like a big brother program for foster kids, except all of the big brothers and sisters are former foster children themselves, so they can really connect with the kids they're assigned to. The foundation trains the volunteers and covers the cost of all of their outings, meals, and entertainment when they spend time with their Little Sister or Brother. It also pays down a chunk of any student loans the volunteers have or helps them pay for a college education."

"That's amazing."

It was amazing, and that's because my mother was a very special person. But all this shit was readily available online. So if this was news to Amanda, she hadn't done her homework.

I smiled. "My mother never forgot where she came from."

"And you and your two sisters were adopted from foster care, right?"

I nodded. More shit anyone with access to Google could find in two minutes. "That's right. My parents became foster parents when I was five. I was first, and then my sister Kate, then Jillian. We were all originally foster placements. My mother continued to take in children until she became sick."

"I'm sorry about your loss."

"Thank you."

"And do you have a Little Brother? I mean, in the program. I know you don't have an actual one."

"I do. He's eleven, going on twenty. My sisters are paired up, too."

She smiled. "What's his name?"

Finally, one probing question. Though I wasn't about to give her Leo's name. The relationships between a Big and a Little were private—especially mine and Leo's tangled one. "I prefer not to divulge anything about kids who are part of the program."

"Oh. Sure. Yeah. I understand. They're minors. I wasn't thinking."

Over the next half hour we talked about more things that would find their way into the puff piece she'd write—who runs what at Lexington Industries, how well the company is doing, and the direction I'd like to take things in the next few years. Then she attempted to get some personal questions in.

"Are you single?"

I nodded. "I am."

"No special someone to take sailing on the weekend on this beautiful boat?"

"Not at the moment."

She tilted her head. "That's a shame."

My phone started to buzz. I looked down. "It's the office. Please excuse me for a moment."

"Of course."

I swiped to answer, knowing full well who would be on the line, and took a few steps away from Amanda.

"Hi, Mr. Lexington. It's Millie, and I'm about to head out for the day. It's just about six o'clock. You wanted me to call and let you know when it was six."

"Yes, that's great. Thank you."

I held the phone up to my ear for a minute after my assistant hung up, and then turned back to my interviewer. "Sorry. I have an overseas call I'm going to need to take in a few minutes. Do you think we can finish up?"

"Oh. Of course. No problem." She stood. "I think I have everything I need for now anyway."

It's gonna be one hell of a dull article. "Great. Thank you."

Amanda packed up her notepad and dug a business card out of her purse. Writing something on the back, she extended it to me with a tilt of her head. "I wrote my home number on the card." She smiled. "I love to sail."

I smiled back like I was flattered. "I'll keep that in mind the next time I'm going out." *Which will not likely be anytime soon...considering the boat hasn't moved from the dock in close to a decade.*

Offering a hand, I helped Amanda over to the dock.

She lifted the strap of her bag onto her shoulder and looked down at the name painted in gold across the back of the navy hull. *"Leilani May,"* she said. "Who's the boat named after?"

I winked. "Sorry. Interview is over."

CHAPTER 7

Grant - 15 years ago

I couldn't stop staring.

The snow was coming down pretty heavy, and the new girl stood out front with her mouth open, tongue sticking out, and no shoes on as she spun around with her eyes shut. She laughed as she caught snowflakes in her mouth.

Lily.

Lily. I needed to get some of those flowers to see what they smelled like. Not that I was dumb enough to think Lily would actually smell like a lily, but I somehow knew the smell was going to be the best smell ever.

I had a gnawing ache in my chest as I watched from the window. The logical reason for it was the grilled cheese and tomato soup Mom had made for lunch earlier. But I knew that wasn't it. Even at fourteen, I knew what love felt like. Well, I hadn't until an hour ago when the doorbell rang. Yet now I was absolutely certain of it.

Lily.

Lily.

Grant's Lily.

It even sounds right, doesn't it?

Grant and Lily.

Lily and Grant.

If we have kids, maybe they'll be named after flowers, too—Violet, Poppy, Ivy. Wait. Ivy isn't a flower. It's a damn weed. I think?

Whatever.

It's not important.

I leaned closer to the window in my father's office, and my warm breath fogged the view. Raising a hand, I wiped it clear with the cuff of my sweatshirt. The movement caught Lily's attention down below. She stopped spinning, cupped her hands around her eyes to shield them from the snow, and squinted up at me. I probably should've ducked so she didn't see me, but I was frozen—completely and totally mesmerized by this girl.

She yelled something I couldn't hear with the window shut. So I unlocked it and slid it open.

I had to clear my throat to get words out. "Did you say something?"

"Yeah. I said, are you some sort of a creeper or something?"

Shit. Now she thinks I'm weird. First I'd practically run out of the room when my mother introduced her to us, and now she'd caught me watching her like some sort of stalker. I needed to play it cool.

"No," I yelled. "Just watching to see if any of your toes are going to turn black and fall off from frostbite. Didn't you see *The Day After Tomorrow*?"

She shook her head. "I've never been to a movie."

My eyes widened. "You've never been to a movie?"

"Nope. My mom doesn't believe in television or movies. She thinks TV makes us believe stupid things."

"But if you'd watched *The Day After Tomorrow*, you might have shoes on."

She smiled, and My. Heart. Literally. Skipped. A. Beat. It felt like it had done a quick somersault the moment she flashed her pearly whites. I rubbed at the spot on my chest, though it didn't hurt at all.

Looking down again at Lily, I yelled, "Hey, do that again."

"Do what?"

"Smile."

And there it was—an unmistakable skipped beat inside my chest.

Lily turned to look all around her. "Did you hear that?"

"Hear what?"

"Bells jingling?"

Maybe we were both imagining things.

"No. No bells."

She shrugged. "Maybe it's Santa Claus. I heard you rich people believe until you're, like, thirty because you keep getting gifts every year."

Suddenly the outside motion detector light flashed on, and I heard my mother's voice. "Lily? What are you doing out there? Come inside before you catch a cold."

"Yes, Mrs. Lexington. I was just checking out the snowflakes. I've never seen snow before in person."

"Oh, my. Okay. Well, come inside, and let's get you properly dressed. Kate has a snowsuit and boots that should fit you...and a hat."

Lily looked up at me and smiled one more time.

My heart squeezed inside my chest. *Again.*

Damn...who knew love could be so painful?

• • •

The next morning I couldn't find her anywhere. Mom usually made the new kids take the bus to school with me on their first day, and then I'd walk them to the office where she'd already be registering them and talking to the guidance counselor.

I poured cereal into a bowl and grabbed the milk out of the refrigerator, but when I went to put the container back, I heard a loud bang coming from the door that led to the garage. I scooped up a mouthful of Golden Grahams and went to see what was going on, carrying my cereal bowl.

Opening the door, I halted mid-chew.

"What are you doing?"

Lily's brows drew tighter. She seemed legitimately confused by my question.

"Painting. What does it look like I'm doing?"

"It looks more like you painted yourself."

Lily stood in front of an easel, her arms and legs covered in a dozen different colors of paint. She had on a long T-shirt that covered her ass, but barely. My eyes snagged on her legs, which had less paint than the top half of her, but were so long and smooth. I'd never seen a girl with such long legs before. I had the strongest urge to pick her up and see if she could cross her feet at the ankles behind my back.

I didn't realize how long I'd been staring until she spoke again.

"You're dripping."

My eyes jumped up to meet hers. "Huh?"

She smiled and nodded her chin toward my cereal bowl. I'd been holding it crooked and milk was dripping onto my shoes.

"Shit." I righted the bowl.

Lily laughed. God, this girl was beautiful. Long, black hair, naturally tanned skin in the dead of winter, and the biggest brown eyes I'd ever seen. And she was tall—only a few inches shorter than me. Ever since the summer of eighth grade, when I grew four inches in just a few months, most of the girls didn't come up to my shoulders. But Lily did. And it felt right that she was tall—like she was meant to stand out over all the other girls.

I shook my head and snapped myself out of it. "Does my mother know you're in here painting? The bus comes in, like, fifteen minutes."

Her button nose wrinkled. "Bus?"

"Yeah, you know...school. It's seven o'clock."

"In the morning?"

Now I was as confused as her. "Yes, the morning. You thought it was still nighttime?"

"Yeah. I guess I painted all night. I must've lost track of time." She shrugged. "That happens sometimes."

I walked over and looked at the canvas. "You painted that?"

"Yeah. It's not that good."

My brows rose. The painting, which was some sort of abstract of a bunch of intertwined flowers, looked like it belonged in a museum, if you asked me. "Umm... If that's not good, I hope you don't see the crap I make in art class."

She smiled. And again, my chest tightened.

"My mom took me to Hawaii once. The flowers there were so beautiful. It's the only thing I like to paint." She shrugged. "I'm sort of obsessed with doing it. I name them all. This one is called Leilani—it means heavenly flower and child of God in Hawaiian. It's a popular name there. My grandmother was Willow. My mom is Rose, and I'm Lily. So we're all named after flowers and plants. Maybe when I have my own little girl someday, I'll name her Leilani."

Wow. *That's screwed up.* I'd had the same thought about naming kids after flowers. Except my thought hadn't been about Lily's kids, it had been about *our* kids.

"Leilani," I said. "It's a beautiful name."

Lily closed her eyes and took in a deep breath. "Lay-lah-nee. It is, isn't it?"

"You're beautiful, too." I wasn't sure where that even came from. Well, obviously, I knew where it came from—it was the truth. But I hadn't expected it to come out of my mouth.

Lily set the brush down on her easel and wiped her hands on her T-shirt. She walked over and stood directly in front of me—right in my personal space. Every hair on my body rose, and my palms immediately started to sweat. *What the hell is wrong with me?* I'd made out with girls before, and yet this girl made me nervous to even be around her.

Pushing up on her toes, Lily kissed my cheek gently. "I think this might be the first foster home I like living in."

Yeah, I think I'm going to like you living here, too.

CHAPTER 8

Ireland

"**O**h good. It didn't start yet." A woman in a gray suit took the seat next to me at the conference table. She seemed flustered. "I heard he's a stickler for being on time."

"Grant?" I asked.

Her brows drew together. "Mr. Lexington, yes."

Oh, right. Mr. Lexington. I guess he was Grant when he was a guy I was going to go out with, but now he's back to Mr. Lexington. "His secretary came in a few minutes ago," I said. "He's running a few minutes late."

The woman smiled. "Great. My daughters called, and I had to referee an argument over a hairbrush." She extended her hand. "I'm Ellen Passman, by the way. I'm the accounting manager over in Finance."

I shook. "Ireland Saint James or Richardson. I'm in the News division of Broadcast Media. Richardson is my on-air name."

"Oh, I know who you are. I love your show."

I smiled. "Thank you."

"I'm really excited about this new committee. But I wish we had a little more notice. It's the end of the month and crunch time for my department."

I'd been curious about how this committee came about ever since Grant had called. I couldn't shake the crazy thought that he'd made up the entire thing while on the phone with me. Of course that was ludicrous— not to mention egotistical and self-absorbed—yet the idea kept nagging at me.

"When did you get invited?" I asked.

"Just this morning. You?"

"A few days ago. Did you receive an agenda for the meeting or anything?"

"Nope. Nothing."

The air in the room changed, and I knew who'd walked in before I turned my head. Grant Lexington stood just inside the door with the VP of the News division, Kate Benton, my boss's boss, who was also his sister. He scanned the room, and his eyes stopped upon finding me—as if he'd found what he was looking for, which was crazy.

His gaze was so intense that it made me want to fidget in my seat.

"Sorry I'm late," he said. "Thank you all for coming." He turned to his sister. "I'm sure you all know Kate. She's the Vice President of Broadcast Media."

People thanked him for inviting them, but I stayed quiet, observing.

There were a few open seats: the head of the table, one down at the far end of my side, one directly across from me, and one to my left. Without discussion, his sister moved to the open seat a few spots over—I got the feeling this man took the power seat in every room he walked into.

But then he surprised me. He pulled the chair from the head of the table and held it out. "Kate."

His sister seemed just as surprised, but she turned back and took the seat anyway. Grant unbuttoned his jacket and pulled out the chair next to me. He leaned close as he settled in and whispered quietly, "Good to see you, Ireland."

I nodded. No one at the table seemed to notice anything strange—certainly not that he'd taken the seat next to me and moved it a little closer than it had been before, and luckily not that my mind was reeling from the way he smelled: clean, but with a masculine, woodsy edge.

For the next half hour, I tried to ignore the man sitting next to me and tried not to fidget. But I had to look at Kate while she spoke, which meant Grant's profile was directly in my line of sight. It also meant I noticed how tanned his skin looked, and that he had a slight white line on the sides of his head from sunglasses. I wouldn't have taken him for the outdoorsy type. But it looked like he spent a lot of time in the sun. His skin was bronzed, his hair slicked back, and it could use a trim at the edges where it reached his collar. He had the start of a five o'clock shadow, even though it was only ten in the morning. I wondered if he shaved at night or if he just had so much testosterone that a beard started sprouting just a couple of hours after he put down the razor.

My gut said it was the latter.

Possibly feeling eyes on him, Grant turned and looked at me. His eyes immediately dropped to my lips, and I lost the battle I'd waged not to fidget. I forced my attention back to Kate, but I didn't miss the slight lip twitch from the man next to me before he refocused on his sister.

"Why don't we go around the room and open the floor for possible agenda items for our next meeting?" Kate said. "I'd love to hear what you all think are some of our most pressing women's issues here at Lexington Industries."

"That's a great idea," Grant said.

Some of the women were more enthusiastic than others. One woman spoke about the need for a breastfeeding room. Another spoke about mixing family responsibilities with work and how flexible hours in the workplace would be a great asset to working moms and dads. An older woman advocated for equal pay for women, which had been the issue I'd planned to speak about since I had personal experience with it. Two women passed on speaking, saying they needed to give it some thought, and then it was my turn. I'd been about to second the other woman's comments on equal pay when I felt Grant's eyes on me. At the last second, I decided to screw with him.

"I think sexual harassment needs to be addressed. Things like a boss or a boss's boss's boss asking a woman out to lunch."

Grant kept his face stern, yet I caught the slight tick of the muscle in his jaw.

"Absolutely," Kate said. "Things like that should never happen."

Grant cleared his throat. "I do a lot of business over meals. It's partially out of necessity because there are only so many hours in the day. Are you saying we should put an end to the practice of people sharing lunch altogether?"

I addressed him directly. "Not at all. But it's a slippery slope, and it's often difficult for a woman to know if a man is inviting her to lunch to discuss business or if there's more to it."

Grant held my eyes for a few heartbeats and then gave a curt nod. "Very well. Add that to the agenda for our next meeting." He stood abruptly. "I think this has been a good start. I'll have my assistant type up notes and schedule the next meeting."

Kate looked just as confused as most of the people at the table. But I got the feeling she was used to her brother's abruptness. She smoothed things over. "Yes, we appreciate you all taking time to kick things off with us, and we look forward to addressing the many unique needs of women in the workplace. I think this committee is going to do very good things for Lexington Industries. Thank you for making the time, everyone."

I stayed in my seat as people got up, eavesdropping on a conversation between Grant and Kate.

"You decide to create this committee, come up with a flimsy agenda three hours ago, and stick me at the head of the table to punt." Kate shook her head. "I finally get things going, and you grow bored. Do me a favor, don't take an interest in any committees anymore." She shuffled the papers in front of her and turned on her heel to walk out.

I rose and headed for the door. But I felt Grant walk up behind me. He discreetly took my elbow and steered me to the right as we exited the conference room.

"Can we speak for a moment?" he whispered.

"Sure. Would you like to hear more about my thoughts on sexual harassment?" I offered a smug smile.

His jaw flexed, and I continued to walk by his side down the hall to his office. Arriving, he extended a hand for me to walk in first. "This is me being a gentleman. I hope it's not a form of harassment."

Grant spoke to his assistant from the doorway while I took a look around his office. It was large, the proverbial corner office with floor-to-ceiling windows covering two walls, a masculine-looking, carved, dark wood desk in the center, and a separate seating area to one side. A framed photo on a credenza caught my attention—Grant and his two sisters with an older woman, who I assumed might be his mother. Though I didn't ask when he walked in and joined me.

He motioned to the seating area. "Please, have a seat."

He took the seat across from me, unbuttoned a cufflink, and started to roll up one of his shirtsleeves. "So...your boss's boss's boss asking you to lunch is sexual harassment?"

My eyes had been glued to his muscular forearms. I blinked a few times and looked up. I'd been teasing him when I said that in the conference room, but the look in his eyes wasn't playful. "I was just screwing around with you."

"So you didn't find it harassing when I asked you to lunch to discuss your reinstatement?"

I'd actually been referring to when he'd asked me to lunch before I knew who he was. But Grant looked genuinely concerned that he'd upset me. I felt like I should let him off the hook.

I shook my head. "I never felt harassed. Sexual harassment is an unwelcome sexual advance. You never propositioned me once I knew who you were, and, if I'm being honest, any advance you made in the coffee shop wasn't unwelcome."

His shoulders visibly relaxed. "I apologize if I put you in a precarious position in the coffee shop."

I was honest. "It's okay. Like I said, it wasn't unwelcome."

Grant seemed to avoid looking at me. He nodded and finished rolling up the other sleeve before standing. "Thank you for your candor."

I stood. "Of course."

A moment of awkwardness settled in between us. I was acutely aware of how much my body liked being this close to him. The air had a crackle to it whenever he was near, and I didn't think I was the only one who felt it—probably not the best thing to be thinking about right after the meeting we'd just had.

"Okay...well...I'll see you at the next meeting, I guess."

Grant nodded. He looked like he wanted me to leave his office almost as much as I wanted to leave... which was not at all. Nevertheless, I took a few steps toward the door. Then I changed my mind. If I could be candid, so could he.

"Can I ask you something?" I said.

"What is it?"

"Did you make up the women's committee while you were on the phone with me? Or was it something you had in the works?"

Grant raised one brow. "You're very full of yourself, aren't you? The president of a multinational company makes up an entire initiative just to have the chance to spend a little time with you?"

I felt my cheeks heat. I knew how egotistical it sounded... I laughed nervously. "I guess that is a little insane."

Grant stepped closer to me. "It would also be highly inappropriate, wouldn't it now?"

I could've sworn there was a glimmer of amusement in his eyes. Damn, my imagination was really having a field day. I needed to get the hell out of here. "Yes. Yes, I suppose it would be." I shook my head. "I should get back to work."

I suddenly had the urge to flee and headed for the door.

As I reached the doorway, Grant called after me. "Ireland?"

I turned back. Dear God, the man was handsome. He was the kind of gorgeous your eyes snagged on while walking and made you trip over your own two feet— basically the dangerous kind women should keep away from, particularly with the cocky smile he wore on his face.

"I'm glad we've cleared up that any advance wasn't unwelcome. I'll see you around...soon."

My brain felt like it was misfiring as I walked out of his office. What the hell had just happened? I'd admitted that I welcomed any advance by him, and he'd admitted what...?

I played the conversation over in my mind as I headed for the elevator. While I had been forthcoming, Grant hadn't actually admitted anything. In fact, when I asked him if he'd created the meeting just for my benefit, he'd turned the question around on me. He never did give me a straight answer, did he?

CHAPTER 9

Grant

"A committee on women's initiatives? Seriously?"
I sighed as my sister Kate helped herself into my office. "We already did this dance after the meeting ended, remember?"

"I'm not done discussing it."

"Of course you're not," I mumbled under my breath.

"Why the committee? There's a reason."

I shuffled papers on my desk. "It's an initiative I've been thinking about for a long time. I thought I'd mentioned it to you."

Kate squinted. "How long?"

"How long what?"

"How long have you been thinking about this initiative?"

"A long time." I stacked the papers I'd gathered into a pile in the middle of my desk and straightened them. My sister stayed quiet. She was waiting for me to look at her. I took a deep breath and raised my eyes to meet hers.

She studied my face before speaking again. "Why don't I believe you?"

I rolled my eyes. "Because you're a man-hating narcissist."

"True. But that's not it."

I knew all of my sister's tones. There was the pissed-off one when she thought I was an asshole and was starting to lose patience, and there was the warm and caring one she used when she discussed subjects like our parents. Most commonly I was on the receiving end of the snarky tone, which I generally deserved. But the tone right now? This was her bloodhound tone, the one where she sank her teeth into every word I said to look for underlying meaning. She knew I was full of shit about my interest in a women's initiative, and it was killing her not to know the real reason I'd done what I did.

I opened my desk drawer and pulled out a file. Plopping it down on the desk, I said, "I have a meeting in five minutes, so why don't you go play detective in your own office. If you come up with any more clues, have your assistant send a memo to my assistant."

My sister scowled at me. "You're an ass, you know that?"

My lips curved to a genuine smile. "Love you, too, sis."

Kate rolled her eyes. "Don't forget about the One World Broadcasting fundraiser Friday night. Are you bringing Arlia?"

"Arlia and I aren't seeing each other anymore." I made a mental note to let Arlia know about that.

"Oh. Who are you bringing?"

"I don't always need to bring a date to functions."

"Yet you always do..." She walked toward my doorway. "Oh, I almost forgot. The woman you recommended to replace Bickman—Madeline Newton—came back clean on her updated background check. I interviewed her after my director finished. We both agree she'd be a good fit. I'll be making her an offer at the end of this week. But we can invite her to the fundraiser if you'd like. Bickman always went, and we have the empty seat at our tables."

"Sure, that's fine."

Kate turned to leave.

"Wait," I called after her. "Who usually gets invited to these things if there's no department head?"

She shrugged. "No one. Or sometimes the acting department head."

"On second thought, let's hold off on making Madeline an offer for a week or two." I pulled a lie out of my ass. It was so believable that when I said the words, I wondered if maybe they were true. "I heard she applied over at Eastern Broadcasting. I'd like to see if she takes that job if we don't give her the position right away—see how loyal she is and what she's willing to risk to stick around with us."

My sister looked surprised, but she bought the story.

"Oh. Okay," she said. "That's a good idea. I'll hold off on her offer and won't invite her to the fundraiser, which would give her a hint she was getting the job. I'll see if the interim department head can attend instead."

Nice, Kate. Your idea to invite Ireland. I waved my hand like I wasn't thrilled at the prospect of the interim department head coming to the fundraiser decked out in a sexy-as-shit dress. "Fine. Whatever you want."

Kate went to turn around a second time, and I stopped her yet again. "Also, since the topic of sexual harassment came up in our new committee meeting, I'd like to read our policy—brush up on how we handle things. And also whatever policy we have on workplace relationships."

Maybe I'd pushed my bullshit too far. My sister's brows jumped. "Really? You want to read *policy?*"

"Yes."

"Well, there's a first time for everything, I suppose. We have a sexual harassment policy, of course. But we don't actually have a corporate policy prohibiting office relationships and dating. Eighty percent of people have either observed or been involved in an office relationship. Who are we to tell people that work ninety hours a week that they can't date a coworker?"

I scratched at the scruff on my chin. "So what Ms. Saint James referenced in our meeting—a boss asking an employee on a date—that's permissible?"

"Well, that's where it gets tricky. It's not illegal or against policy for a manager to ask out his employee, per se. But sexual harassment is illegal under Title VII of the federal Civil Rights Act, as well as California law and our own corporate policy, which prohibits creating a hostile workplace based on a person's sex. A manager and an employee get friendly, maybe one misreads the other's signals, and then all of a sudden a rebuffed request for a date creates a difficult workplace environment."

I nodded. "Good to know. Thank you."

After Kate disappeared, I sat down in my chair and stared out the window. I'd never dipped my pen in company ink. In fact, I didn't get involved with anyone in the goddamned industry. I liked my private business kept private. Yet here I was inquiring about policy and procedure, ready to rewrite it if I needed to, just to keep my fantasy about getting in Ireland Saint James's pants alive.

Fuck. I dragged a hand through my hair.

That thought alone could probably get me in hot water. Though, like my sister said, federal and state laws only pertained to *unwelcome* advances. And Ireland had been clear that my previous advance—before she knew who I was—hadn't been unwelcome. Now all I needed to do was to have my employee welcome further advances—like telling her I can't stop thinking about her wicked mouth wrapped around my cock.

• • •

Two days later, I'd managed to get my head back in the game and get some actual work done—work that didn't involve Ireland Saint James. I'd just finished a conference call with our London attorneys when Millie knocked and opened my office door.

"I'm sorry to interrupt. But you have a visitor."

I looked at my watch. "I didn't think the meeting with Jim Hanson was for another hour."

"It's not. Arlia is here."

I tossed my pen on the desk and leaned back in my chair with a sigh. I should have texted her back earlier.

Better yet, I should have taken her to dinner and broken things off. The last thing I wanted was a scene in my office.

Millie saw my face. "I told her you were in a meeting, so I can let her know you're going to be a while, if you want."

I seriously considered it. But I liked loose ends even less than confrontation, so I might as well get it over with.

I shook my head. "It's fine. Just give me a minute to clean up my desk."

Millie nodded, and a few minutes later, she showed Arlia in. Arlia was dressed in a body-hugging black mini dress that showed off a mile of tanned legs. I stayed behind my desk to avoid an intimate greeting.

"I was starting to think you were avoiding me."

I smiled. "Just busy." I motioned to the chair on the other side of my desk. "What brings you by?"

Arlia Francois was a beautiful woman. A professional model, she knew exactly how to play up her best features. With long legs and two different-colored eyes—one bright blue and the other deep brown—she captured everyone's attention. Though when she took a seat and very slowly and purposely crossed her toned legs, neither my dick nor I got too excited.

"I have to leave for Paris this weekend, and I'll be gone for two weeks. I thought maybe we could get together before then. I'm free Thursday night."

Thursday night was the fundraiser. "I have a work event Thursday evening."

She pouted. "I have to work Friday, but maybe a late supper?"

I wasn't the type of man who ignored women and blew off their invitations as a way of ending things. I preferred direct, and in the long run, most women did, too. Though sometimes they didn't appreciate being dumped in the short run.

I leaned forward. "You're a wonderful woman, Arlia. But we're in different places, and I think it's best we stop seeing each other."

Her flirty, pouty mouth twisted to angry. "What?"

"I was upfront when we started seeing each other a few months ago. I'm not interested in a relationship right now. Things were casual at first, but I don't think we're looking for the same thing anymore."

She raised her voice. "So you just wanted to fuck me, then?"

I thought explaining that I didn't want a relationship *before* we went out the first time had clarified that whatever we might have was physical and for companionship. But apparently in the future I needed to spell it out even more.

"Please keep your voice down. I was clear about my intentions from the beginning."

Tears flooded her eyes. *Shit.* I should have taken Millie up on the offer to pretend I was still on my call and done this in a public place where I had an escape route.

"But I thought we'd grown to more..."

And therein lay the problem. Some women *say* they're good with casual—but they aren't. They think they can change what I want and then get pissed off at me for only wanting exactly what I'd said I wanted at the beginning.

"I'm sorry if you misunderstood."

Apparently, that was the wrong thing to say.

Her entire face contorted. "I didn't misunderstand. You led me on."

I hadn't led her on one bit. But I knew when it was best to eat crow. "I'm sorry if I did that."

Her face softened, and she sniffled. "Fine. We can keep it the way things were when we started. No strings attached."

I could've ended this more easily if I agreed to that and then avoided her in the future. But leaving no strings attached still kept a string between us. And I didn't want to be tethered to her anymore.

"I think it's best we just end things here completely."

Her eyes grew wide. She wasn't used to rejection. "But..."

"I'm sorry, Arlia."

She recovered by shifting from upset and shocked back to pissed off. Abruptly, she rose to her feet.

I joined her in standing.

Arlia surprised me by smoothing out her dress. It looked like she was going to leave without too much of a scene after all. Thinking we were good, I made the mistake of walking around the desk to escort her out.

But apparently, her composure was only the eye of the storm. Once I got near, her fury reignited.

"*You're a user.*"

"I'm sorry you feel that way."

She raised her voice again. "Your apartment is as dull as you are. The only thing interesting about you is your dick."

Okay, I'm done. I put my hand behind her back, careful not to touch, but to *guide* her to walk toward my office door.

She practically spat at me. "Don't touch me."

I pulled my hand back and raised them both in the air. "I was just going to show you out."

She reared back and slapped me across the face. The impact was so unexpected and hard, my cheek turned from the momentum of the connection.

"I'll show myself out."

I stayed put until the door opened and slammed shut. It had been a long time since I was slapped. *A long-ass time.* Only now, I was smarter and would be keeping far away after that shit happened.

CHAPTER 10

Grant – 14 years ago

"I don't want to go back."

I rubbed Lily's shoulders. "I don't want you to go either."

Her eyes filled with tears. "It's just going to happen again. My mom is fine for a while, and then she stops taking her meds and disappears. Eventually someone realizes I'm living alone and calls the cops, who then call Social Services."

Lily had been with us for more than nine months. She'd told me how when her mom would disappear, she had to steal food from the grocery store and sell shit from their apartment just to eat. She'd stopped going to soup kitchens because they asked so many questions about where her parents were.

"Listen, I want you to take this." I held out an envelope with five hundred bucks stashed inside. "Just in case she disappears again."

The tears she'd held back began to stream down her face. "I don't need it. You're going to come see me all the time, right? If she disappears, I'll just tell you, and you can bring me something then."

"What happens if she makes you move again, Lily?" They'd moved dozens of times over the last fifteen years. Me showing up at her apartment one day and finding it empty wasn't out of the realm of possibility.

"I won't go. How would you even find me?"

"If you move, you'll write to me. Do you know the address here?"

Lily nodded and rattled off the house address.

I smiled. "Good. If you ever have to move, you'll tell me in a letter. And I'll come see you every week on Sunday—even if you move all the way to New York. I promise." That probably seemed crazy, but I knew I'd find a way to do it. Lily and I were meant to be together. "Take the envelope. It's not much. But you might need it for stamps. Or stuff for school."

She hesitated, but took it. Once she figured out how much I'd shoved inside, she wouldn't be happy. But she'd be back at her mother's, and neither of us was going to be very happy anyway.

My mom knocked on Lily's bedroom door. "Lily, sweetheart? Are you ready? The social worker is here."

The look of terror on her face killed me. It freaking *killed* me. I knew from personal experience that going back home once you'd been removed rarely worked out. Yet the damn judges always wanted to put you back—as if mothers and fathers were entitled to have children, and they had to prove to the guy in the black robe why they were incompetent. Birth parents usually had to screw up a half-dozen times before they'd stop sending you back. The system sucked.

I motioned toward the door with my head and whispered, "Tell her you're getting dressed, and you'll be down in a few minutes."

Lily did, but her voice broke. Mom said she'd meet her downstairs.

It was only a matter of time before my mother noticed I wasn't around. Lily and I had kept our relationship a secret. We were afraid my parents would think it was a bad idea to keep two fifteen year olds who were in love in the same house. I mean, *it was*...but they didn't need to know that. They also didn't need to know that I snuck into her bed every night after everyone was asleep. *That* would most certainly freak Mom out.

"I don't want to lose you," Lily sobbed quietly.

I cupped her face and wiped away her tears with my thumbs. "Don't cry. You're never going to lose me, Lily. Not ever. I love you."

"I love you, too."

We held each other for a long time. Eventually, though, we had to let go.

"I'll write to you every day we can't be together."

I smiled. "Okay."

"You don't have to write back. I know you don't like writing stuff. Just promise me one thing."

"What's that?"

"You'll write to me if you fall in love with someone else, and tell me all about her so I'll know you're happy and I should stop writing. Otherwise, I'll never give up on us."

I grinned and kissed her nose. "You got a deal. Works out pretty good for me. Because I'll never have to write one damn letter."

• • •

I'd never met anyone who had hallucinations before. My mom had been an addict, and she would sleep for hours on end, sometimes days when she was on a binge. But even when she was at her worst, she never heard voices in her head.

This was the second Sunday I'd visited Lily since she moved out, but the first time her mother had been home. Rose had a job waitressing on weekends, so she'd been at work last week, but apparently this week she was incapable of going. I understood why now. Rose was lying on the couch smoking a cigarette so small that I couldn't imagine it wasn't burning her fingers. Her mouth kept moving as she spoke quietly to herself, but I couldn't figure out what she was saying.

Lily tugged my hand when she caught me staring and told me to come to her room. "But..." I leaned and whispered, "What about the cigarette?"

Lily sighed and walked over. She slipped the cigarette from between her mother's two fingers and dropped it into a half-full glass of water on the coffee table, which already had a dozen other tiny remnants of filters. Her mom didn't even seem to notice.

I took a seat on Lily's bed, and she hopped onto my lap.

"I guess she stopped taking her medicine?"

"She ran out a week ago and didn't refill it. I hadn't been checking, so I didn't notice right away. But I called the pharmacy, and I can pick up the new one later."

"How long will she stay like that?"

Lily sighed. "I don't know. But she was doing so good."

Things had been normal for me for more than ten years now, but I still remembered the constant disappointment of my mom sleeping all the time—not to mention all the scary guys who hung around our apartment. It was easy to forget my life had once been like Lily's.

"Maybe we should call someone. Like CPS?"

Lily's eyes widened. "No!"

"I thought you wanted to stay with us. If they see her like that, they'll remove you again, and you'll probably come back to our house."

Lily frowned. "I *do* want that. But now that I'm back with her, I can't leave her like this. She needs me. They drug her up too much in the hospital."

"I know. But she doesn't look so good."

"The medicine will make her better. I swear."

I didn't like it, but I understood wanting to take care of your mother, even when she should've been taking care of you. I sighed. "Fine."

Lily wrapped her arms around my neck. "Did you get my letters?"

"I did. You really don't want me to write back? I couldn't do it every day like you. I wouldn't know what to say. But maybe I could write once or twice a week."

"Nope. If I ever see a letter from you in my mailbox, my heart's going to be broken, because it will be your goodbye."

I wasn't going to argue, considering I hated writing anything, especially letters. Plus, I had better things to do. I brushed Lily's hair from her shoulder and leaned in for a kiss. "I missed you this week."

"I miss sleeping with you at night. I haven't been sleeping well without you. I got used to the sound of your heartbeat lulling me to sleep."

"Well, you might not hear it at night anymore. But it still belongs to you."

Lily and I hung out in her room until I had to go. My mom was picking me up, and I wanted to wait downstairs so she didn't come up and see the condition of Lily's mom. Reluctantly, we untangled our bodies, straightened our clothes, and headed back to the living room. Lily had slipped out a few times over the last few hours to check on her mom, but I hadn't seen her since I came in hours ago.

Rose wasn't spacing out on the couch anymore. Now she walked back and forth from one side of the living room to the other, pacing. When you spent a good chunk of your childhood around junkies and addicts, you learned to read how stable a person is from just a quick look into their eyes. And Lily's mother looked the opposite of stable right now. Noticing me looking at her, she stopped pacing and stared at me. Her face twisted with anger, and she walked toward me with purpose. I stepped in front of Lily.

Rose's eyes looked crazed. "I know you told them."

My brows furrowed. "Who?"

"The doctors. It's your fault."

"I'm sorry, Mrs. Harrison. I'm not sure what you're talking about."

Before I could register what the hell was happening, she wound up and slapped me straight across the face. "Liar!"

Lily jumped between us and pushed her mom back. "Mom! What the hell? What are you doing?"

"He tells the doctors." She wagged her finger at me. "He tells them everything."

"Mom." Lily put her arm around her mother and guided her to the couch. "You're confused. You stopped taking your medicine, and it made you sick again." They sat down. "I'm going to go get it from the pharmacy."

Her mom started to cry. All of the anger in her face was gone, replaced by sheer sadness. It was the craziest transformation I'd ever seen. It took Lily a few minutes to calm her down, but eventually she got her back into the position she'd been in when I walked in: lying on the couch, smoking a cigarette in an almost catatonic state, and whispering to herself. Lily walked me to the door and waited until we were in the hall to speak.

She reached up and stroked my cheek. "I'm so sorry. Are you okay? She...sometimes gets hallucinations, and they always seem to center on the doctors."

Jesus. "Yeah, I'm fine. But I don't think you should stay here."

"No. I can't leave her like this. She needs me."

I shook my head. "I don't know, Lily. That was fucked up. How do you know she won't hurt you?"

"She won't. I promise. Please don't say anything to anyone."

I hated to leave her, but a part of me did understand the need to help a screwed-up parent, right or wrong. I used to cook mine dinner at five years old.

"Okay. But get her back on the meds tonight. And if she isn't a little better by next week, we need to get you out of here."

CHAPTER 11

Ireland

I wondered if he'd be here.

I was mid-conversation with some former colleagues I hadn't seen in a few years when I got my answer. The sight of him made me lose my train of thought.

On the other side of the room, Grant Lexington stood wearing a classic black tuxedo. He was talking to an older gentleman, which gave me the opportunity to really take him in—tall, broad shoulders, yet not overly bulky, a narrow waist with one hand resting casually in his pants pocket. Even from a distance, his confidence registered. There was something about the way certain men held themselves that showed they were in charge, and that really worked for me. It could take a man who was a seven and make him an eleven in my book. On the other hand, a handsome ten with a meek personality could be reduced to a five.

Mr. Confident held a drink in his left hand and raised it to his mouth, but he stopped before drinking.

He seemed to sense something and looked around the room. When his eyes caught mine, a slow, wicked smile spread across his face. He excused himself from the conversation and strode toward me.

My body tingled as I watched him approach with long strides, and I turned from the group I'd been standing with.

"What a pleasant surprise," he said.

I tried to appear casual as I sipped my champagne. "I'm filling in for Bickman."

He nodded. "Of course."

Grant eyed the group next to me. "Are you here with a date?"

"No. You?"

He smiled and shook his head. "Would a compliment be unwelcome? I wouldn't want to sexually harass you."

"Compliments are always welcome, Mr. Lexington."

His eyes sparkled. Taking hold of my elbow, he led me a few feet away from the group I'd been standing with. "That's a dangerous thing to say to a man like me."

"What was the compliment anyway?"

Grant's eyes swept over me. "You look beautiful tonight."

I blushed. "Thank you."

Grant stopped a waiter as he passed. He gulped back the rest of the amber liquid in his glass and slipped the flute of champagne from my hand, setting them both down on the waiter's tray.

"I was drinking that."

He motioned for the waiter to move along and returned his attention to me. "I'll get you more when we're done."

"Done with what?"

He held out his hand. "Dance with me."

I shook my head. "I'm not sure that's such a good idea."

He smirked. "I'm fucking positive it's not."

Grant took my hand and led me to the dance floor. I debated arguing, but when he pulled me close and I felt the firmness of his chest and took in his delicious masculine scent, I forgot what I was even about to argue over. He led with the same kind of confidence he exuded—a quiet dominance mixed with natural grace.

"So why no date tonight, Ireland?" He looked down at me as we glided around the dance floor.

"No suitable candidates, I guess."

"Surely in the entire city of Los Angeles there's at least one eligible bachelor."

"I must keep missing him."

Grant smiled.

We had good banter, that's for sure. Even that first nutty email exchange.

"Why no date for you tonight?" I asked.

"I guess I keep missing her, too."

We both laughed.

"So how are things going without Bickman?"

"Honestly, it's going fine. He's not really missed."

Grant nodded. "Good to hear. Though I expected nothing less."

A minute later, the song ended, and the emcee asked everyone to please find their seats in the main dining room. As soon as we stepped back from each other, a man approached Grant and asked to have a word with him.

He looked like he didn't want to leave my side. "Where are you seated?" he asked.

"Table nine. You?"

"Table one. I'll catch up with you later," he said. "Thank you for the dance."

I smirked. "It wasn't like you gave me any choice. Enjoy your evening, Mr. Lexington."

For the rest of the night, Grant and I didn't cross paths. But that didn't mean my eyes lost track of him at any point. He was busy; everyone in the room wanted a piece of him. Which was probably for the best, since the piece I seemed to want of him wouldn't be the wisest business decision. Still, our gazes caught a few times, and we exchanged what I thought were flirty, private smiles.

When the coffee came out, I knew it was time for me to make my exit. Three thirty would roll around soon enough. I scanned the room for Grant, figuring I'd wave goodbye, but he was engrossed in a conversation with a group of men who all looked old enough to be his dad. I weighed the right business etiquette—did I go over and interrupt him to say goodnight, or simply leave? Undecided, I picked up my purse and said my goodbyes at my own table. When I was done, I looked back at where Grant had been talking, but he was no longer there.

I figured fate had decided how to handle things for me.

Though when I turned from my table, I crashed directly into a hard body.

I backed up. "Sorry. Oh...it's you."

"You sound disappointed. Would you have preferred to walk into someone else?"

I laughed. "No. I was going to come over and say goodnight, but then you disappeared."

"I guess I beat you to it. I'll walk with you. I was just heading out myself."

He hadn't looked like he was getting ready to leave a few minutes ago. Nevertheless, Grant put his hand on the small of my back and escorted me out of the ballroom.

Outside, I took out my phone.

"Did you drive?" he asked.

"No. I Ubered so I could have a glass of wine."

"I have a car. I'll drop you."

"That's not necessary."

"I insist."

A minute later, a stretch limo pulled around. Apparently, him having a car meant a chauffeured one. The uniformed driver got out and went to open the back door, but Grant waved him off and opened it for me instead.

"Thank you."

I slid across the backseat to make room for Grant. The rear of the limo was spacious enough to hold ten people. Yet when he climbed in and joined me, it suddenly felt very small. I was hyperaware of his thigh brushing against mine.

As we started to move, I looked forward, but sensed Grant's eyes on me.

"What?" I asked.

"Nothing."

"You were staring at me."

He looked back and forth between my eyes. "What's your address?"

For some crazy reason, I debated giving it to him.

Grant must have seen the conflict written on my face and chuckled. "The driver needs it to take you home, Ireland. I wasn't inviting myself over."

"Oh, right. Of course."

Feeling like an idiot, I spouted off my address. Grant leaned forward and relayed it to the driver. When he settled back into his seat, his leg now firmly pressed against mine.

"Tell me something about you, Ireland Saint James."

"What do you want to know?"

"Anything."

"Okay..." I thought about it. "I've had four promotions within Lexington Industries over the last nine years."

"Tell me something I don't know."

I arched a brow. "You've looked me up."

"How else would I have decided to give you your job back?"

I shifted in my seat to face him. "I'll tell you what. I'll tell you something about me you don't know, if you promise to answer a question for me honestly."

He nodded. "I can do that."

It's not easy to come up with a little-known fun fact about yourself when you're under pressure, but I did my best. "I can do a backflip from standing still."

Grant smiled. "Interesting."

"Thank you. My turn. Did you decide to hire me back because of what I looked like?"

"Truth?"

"That would be nice, yes."

I watched the wheels in his head turn. "If I say yes, that could be sexist and inappropriate based on our work relationship."

I leaned over to him and lowered my voice. "It'll be our little secret."

He chuckled and shook his head. "I decided to hire you back because you have balls and don't put up with shit from people like Bickman. I respect that."

"Oh. Okay." As screwed up as it was, my shoulders slumped a bit.

Grant leaned in to me and whispered, "The fact that you're gorgeous is just a bonus."

If I were a peacock, my feathers would have fanned. I smiled. "Thank you. My turn. Tell me something about you that I don't know."

I liked that he seemed to actually give it some thought, when he could've rattled off some business accomplishment. Instead he said, "I'm one of three children. We were all adopted from different families after being foster children."

"Oh, wow. That's really personal. I feel like I owe you more than a backflip now."

Grant's eyes dropped to my lips before returning to meet my gaze. "I'll take whatever you want to give me."

There were a million things I could've shared—that I have a scar on my torso from a bicycle accident when I was seven, that I sleep with the light on because I don't like to be alone in the dark... Hell, I could have shared my bra size. Yet I had to go and share the most screwed-up thing about me.

"My father is in prison for killing my mother."

Grant's smile immediately fell. But while it affected him and changed the mood, there was no sign of surprise.

I blew out a stream of air and closed my eyes. "You already knew that, too, didn't you?"

He nodded. "I pulled your file. We do extensive background checks on employees...."

I forced a consolatory smile. "Of course."

Grant bumped his shoulder with mine. "But it still counts. I appreciate you sharing that with me."

Thanks to my big mouth, the fun mood had been transformed to gloomy. Though a thought popped into my head that might change that. "So, if you pulled my file, does that mean you watched the *offending video*?"

Grant cleared his throat and looked forward. "I had to see what I was dealing with."

I watched him for a second. He looked slightly uncomfortable with the direction I'd taken the conversation, which only made me want to take it further down that path.

Leaning in slightly, my voice registered lower. "Did you watch it more than once?"

Grant struggled a moment. He looked relieved when his cell phone rang.

Pulling it from his pocket, he read the name flashing on the screen. "Excuse me. I have to take this."

He swiped. "What's going on?"

I heard a woman's voice on the other end, but couldn't make out what she was saying.

"How long ago did he leave?"

The woman spoke louder. She sounded upset.

"Alright. I'm nearby. Don't leave the house. I'll find him."

He swiped to end the call and leaned forward to speak to the driver. "Get off at the next exit. Make a right on Cross Bay and a left on Singleton."

"Yes, sir."

Grant blew out a jagged breath. He frowned. "I'm sorry. We need to make a detour."

"Is everything okay?"

He shook his head. "My grandfather has dementia. He's still in the early stages, but sometimes he takes off. My grandmother can't handle him anymore by herself, but they also won't let anyone help until things blow up. It's the third time he's gone missing in the last two months."

"I'm sorry. That must be tough to deal with."

"It wouldn't be happening if they'd let the alarm installer do the job I hired him to do when he showed up at their house the other day. But they won't even let me have someone put in a monitor so my grandmother could be alerted to a door opening while she's sleeping."

The driver got off at the exit and made the turns Grant had instructed him to make. Then Grant directed him into the side streets of a pretty exclusive area. The homes were all set back on sprawling front lawns, and one house was bigger than the next. He told the driver to slow down and put on his brights.

"This is their house. He usually takes the same path. Go to the end of the road and take a left and a quick right. Follow the winding path down to the water."

"You sound like you have a pretty good idea where he's heading," I said.

Grant looked out the windows, searching as he spoke. "He always goes to the same place."

A few minutes later, I spotted someone walking along the side of the road.

"There!" I pointed. "I see someone up ahead."

Grant let out a deep breath. "That's him." He instructed the driver to pull up behind him slowly, and he jumped out of the car before it had even rolled to a complete stop.

I watched the interaction between the two men through the front window of the limo. Grant's grandfather was dressed in a brown bathrobe and slippers. His hair was disheveled, and he turned around, seeming confused when the headlights caught his attention. But his entire face lit up as he shielded his eyes and got a look at the man stalking his way. He definitely recognized his grandson. He opened his arms wide and waited as a tuxedoed and clearly frustrated Grant approached.

I couldn't help but smile when Grant gave in and let the old man swamp him in a hug. The two of them spoke for a minute, and then Grant led him back to the limousine.

Grant helped his grandfather climb in first.

The man smiled at me warmly as he took a seat. "Well, aren't you pretty."

Grant got in and pulled the door shut. He shook his head. "Don't let the charm fool you. He's a dirty old man."

Grant's grandfather laughed and winked at me. "He exaggerates. I'm not that old."

"You gotta stop disappearing, Pops. It's almost midnight."

"I needed to see Leilani."

"This late?"

"A man needs to see his girl when he needs to see his girl."

Grant sighed. "I'll tell you what. I'll take you to Leilani, but you have to agree to let me put an alarm on the house tomorrow. You worry Grams when you disappear."

Grant's grandfather folded his arms over his chest. He reminded me of a little boy who was told he couldn't have dessert until he ate all of his vegetables. "Fine."

Grant ran his hand through his hair and turned to me. "Do you mind if we make another stop? It's just down the road."

"Of course not. Whatever you need to do."

"Thank you." He leaned forward to speak to the driver. "Head down to Castaway Marina, please."

CHAPTER 12

Ireland

L eilani wasn't a woman. She was a boat.

A gorgeous sailboat.

Grant helped his grandfather board and then held out his hand to me.

"Thank you," I said as I stepped onto the back deck.

His grandfather disappeared into the cabin immediately.

"He's going to put on Frank Sinatra. Sometimes he forgets his wife. Sometimes he wanders off and gets lost. But he never forgets about this boat or Frank."

I looked around the wide back seating area. "I can see why. This boat is incredible."

"Thank you. Pops built it almost sixty years ago. He gave it to me as a gift on my twenty-first birthday."

"Oh, that's really special."

"He built it as a sample, to use it to sell boats and take orders when he started his boat-manufacturing business. He borrowed the money from a loan shark who would have broken his legs if he didn't get his money back. But he sold more than he could possibly build the first time he unveiled it at a boat show." Grant laughed. "The loan shark's grandson actually has the newest model, and Pops plays cards with the shark, who lives in assisted living now."

I looked at the logo on the side of the boat. "I didn't realize your family owned Lexington Craft. I don't know too much about boats, but those are really beautiful. I see them in movies every once in a while."

Grant shook his head. "My family doesn't own it anymore. Well, we have a chunk of stock from when it was sold, but it's been a public company for a long time. Pops stayed on to run it after the sale, but he retired ten years ago after he made sure the new management was as passionate about boat building as he is. He and my grandmother used to have a big boat over at the marina down the road, but they put it in storage a few years back, after he was diagnosed. This one is special to him, and he likes to come visit her."

I smiled. "That's understandable."

Frank Sinatra started to play through the speakers, and a minute later Pops came out from the cabin. He had a box of cigars in one hand and a lit one in the other. His robe hung open, revealing a white T-shirt and white boxers.

"Pops, why don't you tie your robe?"

Pops handed Grant the box and pointed his cigar at me. "You look like that actress..." He snapped his fingers a few times, trying to recall. "What's her name—you know the one?" *Snap. Snap.* "The one with the big..."

I thought I knew where he was going with this. But then he snapped a few more times and shouted, "The one with the big *balls*!"

Grant and his grandfather went hysterical with laughter. I had no idea what the hell they were cracking up about, but watching them made me smile anyway. I also noticed how different Grant looked when he was relaxed and had a genuine smile. He seemed so much younger, so much less intimidating.

Grant was still chuckling when he explained what was so funny. "A couple of years ago, I took Pops to the store to get new shoes. He'd just started to struggle with his memory, and he wanted shoes with support soles, but he couldn't remember the words *support soles*. For some odd reason, he thought the word he was searching for was *balls*—so he yelled that he wanted *balls* at the top of his lungs."

He wiped tears from his eyes. "The salesperson had a good laugh, and from then on, Pops started to fill in words he can't remember with *balls*. It's interesting because he can always remember *balls*, but not the word he's searching for. Anyway, it cracks us up every damn time."

I'd thought being near cocky, confident, handsome Grant was dangerous, but seeing how sweet he was with his grandfather and how much he cherished their good times, made my heart swell in my chest.

Pops snapped his fingers a few more times. He seemed to get stuck on certain things. "Who the heck does she look like? She's tall...I don't remember her name."

"She looks like a younger Charlize Theron, Pops." Grant studied my face and winked. "Except she's not as tall, and Ireland is prettier."

"Yeah, that's it." Pops nodded and smiled. "Great balls on that one."

I'd been told I resembled that actress a few times over the years, but it had never made me blush before.

The three of us sat at the back of the boat for a while. Pops kept us amused with stories about when he'd first started building boats and all the trial and error that went into it. It was pretty amazing how far his memory stretched back, yet he would sometimes forget who family members were or where he was. At one point, he stood and announced he was going to go listen to his baby purr.

"He likes to listen to the engine," Grant explained. He blew a ring of smoke from the cigar he'd lit a few minutes ago and held it up. "I think he comes for these more than anything these days. My grandmother won't let him smoke anymore—not since he lit one and walked away and the rug caught on fire."

"That's just as well. They're not good for you. And I never understood the appeal anyway. You don't even inhale. I always thought they were a kind of phallic symbol men like to flaunt."

Grant examined his cigar and grinned. "Glad I got the extra-thick Cohiba now."

"Seriously, what's the appeal with cigars?"

"It's more about the moment it forces you to take. Sitting out here without this cigar in my hand, I'd probably take out my phone and scroll after a few minutes—or get up and do something around the boat. But a good cigar causes me to sit back and take a minute, reflect on my day or the beauty around me." His eyes roamed my face, and his gaze heated. "There's a lot to appreciate at the moment."

Rather than squirm under his scrutiny, I opted to retake control. He had the cigar in the hand opposite me, so I leaned over him and plucked it from his fingers.

"Show me how to do this." I raised the smoldering cancer stick to my lips.

Grant arched a brow. "You're going to smoke my cigar?"

"Does that bother you?"

A dirty grin tugged at the corner of his lips. "Of course not. You're welcome to wrap your lips around my Cohiba."

I rolled my eyes, but a shiver moved through me, even though there was no breeze.

"Hold it up to your lips."

"Okay."

"Pretend you're sucking through a straw. But don't inhale. Just take the smoke into your mouth and then blow it out. Don't pull the air in deep from your diaphragm."

I did what he instructed—at least I thought I did. But after I inhaled, I inadvertently swallowed some of the smoke and started to cough.

Grant chuckled. "I told you not to inhale."

I sputtered. "Apparently that's easier said than done." I held out the cigar, and he took it back.

We sat together in quiet after that for a while. Grant kept his eye on Pops, who had his head buried in the engine on the other side of the boat while he tinkered. I looked around at the other boats and the marina.

"You must get some beautiful sunsets here."

"I do."

"Probably romantic. Do you bring your conquests here to get them in the mood?"

Grant brought his cigar to his mouth and wrapped his lips around the end. I was slightly turned on by the sight, especially knowing my lips had been there earlier. He puffed four or five times, then blew out a thick cloud of white smoke. "If by *conquests* you mean *dates*, then the answer is no. I don't bring them here to *get them in the mood*."

"Why not?"

He shrugged. "I just don't."

A loud slam brought our attention back to Pops. Grant jumped up, but it had only been his grandfather letting the engine hatch door drop.

Pops brushed his hands together. "Still as sexy as the day she purred to life for the first time. The carburetor could probably use an adjustment though. You'll get better fuel efficiency with a little tweaking."

"I'll take care of it. Thanks, Pops."

"You two kids ready to go? I need my beauty sleep."

"Ready whenever you are." Grant stood and attempted to help his grandfather up the gangplank and over to the dock, though Pops wasn't having it. He swatted Grant's hand away and climbed off the boat on his own.

Grant and I exchanged smiles, and I let him help me off the boat. The three of us walked together back to the waiting car.

It was a short ride back to Grant's grandparents' house, and Pops climbed out of the car as soon as we stopped. Grant hopped out to follow him.

When he got to the front door of the house, Pops turned back and yelled, "Goodbye, Charlize!"

I poked my head out the car door. "Later, Balls!"

Pops spoke to Grant, although I could still hear him. "Boy, she's a looker, ain't she?"

Grant smiled. "That she is, Pops. That she is."

The two men disappeared inside, and a few minutes later, a woman I assumed was Grant's grandmother opened the door again. She hugged Grant, and he waited until the door was closed, then double-checked to make sure it was locked before coming back to the car.

He climbed inside and shut the door. "Sorry about that."

"Oh no. Don't be. Your grandfather is a pistol. That was fun, and your boat is beautiful."

"Thank you."

"Do you get to use it often?"

Grant hesitated before answering. "Every day. I live on it."

"Really? That's very cool." I raised an eyebrow. "But you said you don't bring dates on the boat."

"I don't. I also have an apartment downtown in Marina Del Rey. Some people use a house as their primary residence and a boat for fun. I do the opposite."

Hmm... Interesting.

We talked the rest of the short drive to my place. Our conversation was casual, but it was impossible to feel completely relaxed near Grant. He just took up too much space—both literally on the seat next to me and metaphorically inside my head. The driver slowed as we turned down my street.

I pointed to the tall apartment building, suddenly glad I lived in a nice neighborhood. "This is me."

The limousine pulled to the curb, and the casual and relaxed mood abruptly came to a halt. It felt like the end of a date with an awkward goodbye, rather than saying goodnight to the CEO of the company I worked for.

I put my hand on the door latch and spoke really quickly. "Thank you for the ride home."

Grant leaned forward to his driver. "Give me a few minutes, Ben. I'm going to walk Ms. Saint James to the door."

"That's not necessary," I said.

Grant reached and put his hand over mine, which was still holding the door handle, and pushed open the car door. He climbed out first and extended his hand. "It's necessary."

With his hand on my lower back, Grant guided me ahead of him up the narrow walkway. I felt the heat from his palm scorching my skin and wondered if it was my body or his that was on fire. Maybe it was the connection between us.

My apartment was on the third floor, and he insisted on riding the elevator up with me, too. At my door, Grant shoved his hands into his trouser pockets.

"Thanks again for the ride," I said.

"Of course."

"Okay...well...you have a good night." I did some sort of a curt, clumsy wave and fumbled to open the lock.

Stepping inside, I looked back and smiled awkwardly one last time before shutting the door. Then I proceeded to lean my head against it and bang a few times. "God, you're such a doofus around that man."

Sighing, I walked toward the kitchen. But the bell stopped me after a few steps. Grant must've forgotten something. I walked back and checked the peephole before opening the door.

I smiled playfully. "Miss me already?"

Grant shook his head and frowned. He looked like he wasn't very happy to be standing where he was. Blowing out an audible breath, he said, "Go out with me Friday night."

"*Uh...* You sort of look like you're asking me something dreadful."

He raked a hand through his hair. "Sorry. I know it's probably not the smartest idea, but I'd really like to take you out."

I nibbled on my bottom lip. "Is it not the smartest idea because I work for you, or not the smartest because we met by me sending you a drunk email to tell you off?"

Grant smiled. "Both."

I liked his honesty. And his jawline. And that tiny little dimple on the left side of his cheek that I'd just noticed for the first time. In fact, I couldn't think straight when gazing at his handsome face.

So I looked down to gather my thoughts, but all that did was remind me of the other things I liked about him: his broad shoulders, narrow waistline... Damn, *big feet, too.*

Yet even with all that beautiful packaging, I still wasn't sold. Though my reasoning wasn't the same as his. Grant was wary because I worked for him. I was wary because something told me this man could eat me alive.

After inwardly debating the pros and cons, I looked up. "How about drinks? We see how it goes?"

"If that's what you prefer."

I exhaled. "I think so."

"Then drinks, it is. I'll pick you up at seven."

"Could we have them on Leilani?" I asked. "Maybe watch the sunset?"

The muscle in Grant's jaw flexed. "My apartment overlooks the harbor and faces west. The terrace gets a beautiful sunset. Or there's a nice bar down at the pier."

"I'd prefer your boat, rather than your porn palace."

Grant's lip twitched. "Porn palace?"

"You said you use your boat to live and your apartment for fun."

His eyes roamed my face. "If I say yes, is it a date?"

I wanted to say *yes* in the worst way. I was incredibly attracted to him physically, but I also found his direct, no-bullshit attitude a turn on. Not to mention, he'd let down his guard around his grandfather and shown there was more to him than the gruff exterior. Yet... something about him terrified me.

I looked him in the eyes. "Do you just want to sleep with me, or do you want to actually take me out?"

Grant smiled. "Yes."

I laughed and shook my head. "I appreciate the honesty. But can I think about it?"

His cocky smile fell. "Of course."

"Thank you. Have a good night, Grant."

I shut the door feeling deflated, but inside I knew I'd done the right thing. Nothing about Grant Lexington was simple. Especially the fact that he was my boss.

CHAPTER 13

Grant

"Mr. Lexington?" My assistant buzzed into my office. "You have Ireland Saint James on line one. Would you like me to tell her you're about to go into a meeting?"

I stood with a file in my hand, ready to head to a ten o'clock meeting, but I sat back down. "No, I'll take it. Tell Mark Anderson I'll be a few minutes late and to start without me."

I tossed the file onto my desk, picked up the receiver, and leaned back in my chair. "Ms. Saint James. It's been three days. You must've had a lot to *think* about."

"Sorry. I've been busy. But I wanted to get back to you on your dinner invitation, or rather our discussion about having drinks."

"Okay..."

"You seem like a really nice guy—"

I sat up in my chair and cut her off. "Let's finish this conversation over lunch."

"Uh...well, can't we just—"

I interrupted a second time. "No. I have a meeting now. Be in my office at one o'clock. I'll have lunch waiting."

"But—"

"We'll talk then."

She sighed. "Fine."

On my way to my meeting, I stopped at Millie's desk. "Can you please order lunch for me and Ms. Saint James for one o'clock?"

"Of course. What would you like?"

"Whatever."

"Do you want salads, sandwiches? Is she vegan?"

"How the hell would I know? Just order a few things."

Millie's forehead wrinkled. "Okay."

"And if I'm late, tell her to start eating without me."

"The mail just came. Would you like me to put today's letter on your desk?"

"Shred it," I bit out.

When my meeting finally broke at five after one, I was impatient. Some people took ten minutes to dance around and spit out one damn fact. For the last hour, I'd found it hard to focus, too busy wondering if my next appointment was going to stand me up.

The tension in my shoulders dissipated as I walked into my office and found Ireland snooping. I shut the door behind me. "Looking for something?"

She turned with a framed photo in her hand. "Is this you and your grandfather?"

I walked over. The photo had been on the credenza since I'd moved into this office eighteen months ago, but

I hadn't really looked at it since. Pops and I were fishing off the side of Leilani. I must've been about seven or eight. "He caught a thrasher shark that day. I caught a sunburn."

Ireland smiled and set the frame back down.

Lunch was set up at the small seating area, rather than at my desk. I held out my hand. "Please, have a seat. I'm a few minutes late, and the food is probably getting cold."

Ireland sat on the couch, and I took the seat across from her.

"Are more people joining us?" she asked. "There are six different lunches here."

"I didn't know what you liked."

Her face softened. "Thank you. I'm not picky. But I'll take this cheeseburger, if you don't mind. I'm starving."

"Whatever you like."

I grabbed a turkey sandwich and wasted no time getting to the point. I preferred to discuss business first, so I could actually enjoy my food after. "So, you were about to give me the *you're a nice guy, but...* brush-off speech. It's one I don't hear too often."

"Because no one says no to you?"

"No, because I'm not that nice of a guy."

Ireland picked up a French fry and pointed it at me. "Well, that in itself is a reason I shouldn't be having dinner or drinks with you, isn't it?"

I leaned over and bit the fry from her fingers. "Probably. But I'd like a chance to change your mind anyway. I get the feeling you're wary of me because you sense I'm not being forthright with you. But I'm in a difficult position here. I can't say whatever is on my mind because you work for me, and I don't want you to feel pressured."

"I don't feel pressured by you as a boss. Even though you *did* bark at me to come up here for lunch. I somehow know my job isn't at stake, and it's just you being you. If I'm being honest, your barking felt real, and I'd rather see that man than the hesitant one who is trying to be appropriate."

"So you prefer me inappropriate and barking?"

She laughed. "I prefer you to just be you and not filter what you're thinking."

My eyes locked with hers. I've found that often a woman thinks she wants unfiltered honesty, but it turns out not to be the case once she hears it. "You sure about that?"

"Positive."

I reached over and took her hand. "Good. Then let's be honest. I haven't been able to stop thinking about you in days. Hell, since you told me off in that email. You asked me the other night if I just wanted to sleep with you. I absolutely want to be inside you. I'd lock that door and take you on my desk right now, if you were game."

She swallowed.

"But if you'd like to have drinks and watch the sunset on my boat, I'm up for that, too. I haven't had anything but a sexual relationship with a woman in seven years, and to be candid, I'm not entirely sure what I'm capable of offering anymore. But if you'd like to start with drinks, we can most definitely see where it goes."

Ireland started to shake her head. I couldn't get a read on the surprised look on her face—whether it was a good surprise or one that confirmed she should run the other way.

"Was that supposed to be you pleading your case for me to go out with you? Because you basically told me you suck at relationships and might just only want to have sex with me. And oh *by the way*, if I'm up for banging on your desk, that's an available option, too."

"That depends. Did it work?"

She laughed. "Oh my God. I think I've lost my mind. Because I think it might have."

"Good. Then shut up and eat your lunch because your food is getting cold."

Ireland was still laughing and shaking her head as she bit into her cheeseburger. I'm glad I wasn't the only one that had started to lose his mind. Especially since watching her sink her teeth into her lunch made me salivate at the thought of sinking my teeth into her skin.

With the important stuff out of the way, we managed to have a relaxed meal. We talked about work, our routines, and she asked if my grandfather had attempted any escapes again—which I liked. She was thoughtful, and her interest seemed genuine.

Too soon, Ireland's phone buzzed. She had a reminder set on her phone, and it made me think of how I had Millie call to get me out of stuff. I eyed her cell.

"Is that a made-up appointment to help get you out of here?"

She brushed a hair from her face. "No. I wish it were. I have to run out to meet my contractor. I'm building a house in Agoura Hills. Construction is supposed to finish in a few weeks, but my builder said there might be some sort of a delay, and he wants to discuss plans."

"That doesn't sound good."

"No, it definitely doesn't. Especially since my roommate is moving out in two weeks when she gets married, and our lease is up in just a couple of months."

"I have a good real estate agent who can help you locate something temporary if you need it."

"Thank you." She squinted at me. "So is that something you do on a regular basis?"

"What?"

"Make up appointments to get out of a meeting faster."

I smirked. "Occasionally."

Just then, my desk phone buzzed, and Millie came over the intercom. "Mr. Lexington? Leo arrived a few minutes early. He just ran to the bathroom."

Ireland raised a brow.

"That was a total coincidence. Leo is an actual person. I'm sure he'll be busting in here when he gets back if I'm not out. So you'll get to meet him. He has a button on his ass that makes him pop up after more than ten seconds of waiting if he doesn't have a video game in his hand."

"Is Leo an adult or child?"

"Child. Who thinks he's an adult. He's my... We spend time together every Wednesday afternoon. It's part of a program my mother started twenty years ago for foster kids. It's sort of like a Big Brothers, Big Sisters program, except all the kids in it are in foster care and all of the Bigs are former foster children. Bigs make a commitment to mentor a Little from five to twenty-five. Foster kids get bounced around a lot, and having the same Big for years gives them consistency."

She shook her head. "That's awesome. But there are really two sides to you, aren't there? You should have told me that story the other night. I probably would have said yes to dinner."

I chuckled. "*Now* you tell me."

Ireland smiled. "But I'm also glad you didn't make up an appointment to ditch me."

"Likewise."

"I should get going anyway. We both have things to do." Ireland stood. "Thank you for lunch. Next time you don't need to go overboard and order so much. I'm not picky. I eat anything."

"Glad to know you're planning a next time. I'll pick you up Friday at seven?"

"I'll come to you."

"I'm capable of picking you up. Besides, I already know where you live."

She smiled. "And I'm capable of driving myself."

I shook my head. "You're always a pain in the ass, aren't you? I'll see you Friday at 7 at the marina."

Ireland picked up my empty food container and hers from the table and shoved them into a bag. She held the garbage out to me. "Oh. And I should tell you I don't kiss on the first date."

I took the handle of the bag, along with her hand, and used it to yank her closer to me. "That's good. Because *this* was our first date. See you Friday, Ireland."

• • •

"I don't want the alarm connected to the police station. I don't like guns in the house."

The installer looked at me, and I motioned for him to keep working as I guided Grams into the kitchen to talk. "Grams, if the alarm goes off and you don't hear it, they'll know to go looking for Pops. I registered him with the police department, so they'll understand that it's more than likely a missing person and not a break-in they need to show up for with guns blazing."

She sat down. "I'm capable of taking care of him."

The worse Pops got, the harder things grew for her, too. She felt disabled herself for needing any help with her husband of fifty years.

I sat across from her and covered her hand with mine. An older, independent couple didn't view taking help much differently than a foster kid might—they didn't want to rely on anyone but themselves. Logical arguments don't work, because what they're fighting is emotional and not practical. So just like with Leo, I knew the best thing to do wasn't reason with my grandmother. She needed her emotions validated.

"I get that you don't *need* any help, Grams. You could handle him all on your own. But I *want* to help. If Mom were still here, she'd be moved in and sleeping on your bedroom floor to make sure Pops didn't wander off and get hurt. Letting me help Pops is for Mom and me. Not because you can't do it yourself."

Grams's eyes watered. I'd broken out the big guns mentioning Mom, but it was the truth, and we needed to get past her unwillingness. Unfortunately, things weren't going to be improving.

She squeezed my hand and nodded. "Fine. But if I'm taking your help, there're some other things I could use a hand with."

"Name it."

Leo busted into the kitchen, and Pops followed behind. "Look at this thing Pops made. It's an electric chair!"

Great. More shit I'd have to explain to Leo's social worker at some point. In his retirement, my grandfather had taken up building replica miniature houses. All of his years as a wooden boat builder had come in handy, and he'd spent the first two years of being home building an exact miniature replica of his and Grams's house, down to the bathroom fixtures and chipped bluestone in the yard. Leo and I visited Grams and Pops a lot, and he'd tried to get Leo interested in his little hobby. But being a typical eleven year old, Leo thought making a dollhouse was boring. That is, until Pops started to work on a *creepy* dollhouse. The entire thing was a freak show of weird shit. But Pops and Leo had built every little bit of that freak show, and Leo had gotten pretty good with woodworking.

I took the miniature electric chair from Leo's hands and checked it out. The details were pretty amazing, down to the tiny black leather wrist straps on the arms of the chair and what looked like a few drops of blood stained on the seat.

"It's great. But do me a favor and don't bring it home to your foster mom. She already suspects I might be a devil worshiper after you brought home that creepy miniature doll so you could work on mangling it."

"Fine." He rolled his eyes. "Whatever."

Grams got up. "What can I make you to eat, Leo? How about a peanut butter and banana sandwich for a snack?"

He grinned. "With no crust?"

Grams walked to the bread drawer and opened it. "People who eat crust can't be trusted."

Leo took a seat on a stool at the granite kitchen bar and propped his feet up on the one next to him.

I knocked them off. "Feet off the furniture."

Pops said he was going to go take a nap, so I told him I'd tag along to check on the ceiling fan Grams had said wasn't working.

When I came back to the kitchen a few minutes later, Grams and Leo were laughing. "What's so funny?"

"You. In a Santa suit." Leo chuckled.

I swiped a piece of his peanut butter and banana sandwich from his plate and shoved it into my mouth. "What are you talking about?"

Grams answered. "Earlier, when we were talking about how you like to help, you said you'd do anything I needed, right?"

I narrowed my eyes. "Yeah. But why does the way you're asking me now feel like a trick question?"

Leo laughed. "Because she's gonna sucker you into playing Santa this weekend, instead of Pops."

I pointed a finger at Leo. "Watch your language."

"What did I say? Sucker? That's not even a bad word. I've heard you say way worse."

"I'm an adult."

"So?"

"So, you're not."

Grams got up and took Leo's empty plate. "He has a point, Grant. If you want him to act a certain way, you need to mind your own rules."

Leo boasted a smug smile. The little shit knew I wouldn't argue with Grams. "Yeah, Grant. I only say bad words because I hear them from you."

I made a face that screamed bullshit. "My ass."

Leo pointed to me and looked at Grams. "See, there he goes again!"

Grams sighed and turned on the sink to rinse Leo's plate. "Settle down now, boys."

The brat was just about to eat the last bite of his sandwich when I swiped it from his hand and popped it into my mouth.

"Hey..." Leo whined.

I grinned. "You heard the lady. Settle down now, kid."

Grams came back to the table. "Grant, I really do need you to play Santa this weekend at the Pia's Place Christmas in July party. You know Pops usually does it. But I don't think he's up to it this year. Sometimes he forgets what he's doing, and I don't want him to scare any of the little kids."

"Can't you find someone else?"

Grams frowned. "It's a family tradition now. I think it should be passed down to you."

Leo grinned from ear to ear. "Yeah, Grant. It's a family tradition."

The little shit was in rare form today. But I couldn't say no to my grandmother. Even though I suspected I'd been set up from the get-go today. She'd lured me into the conversation about doing things for her, just so I couldn't refuse.

"Fine." I pouted. "But if any little kids pee on me, I'm telling you now, next year the tradition will be passed to Kate's husband."

Grams walked over and cupped my cheeks. "Thank you, sweetheart. It means a lot to me."

Later in the evening, on the ride to Leo's house, he mentioned he was going up to San Bernardino next weekend so he wouldn't be at the Christmas in July festival this year.

I glanced over at him and back to the road. "San Bernardino? What are you doing there?" I knew of only one reason he might be making that trip, and I hoped I was wrong.

"My mom's back in town. She's picking me up and taking me to visit my sister."

Shit. "Rose is taking you to see Lily?"

Leo frowned. "That's what my social worker said."

CHAPTER 14

Grant – 11 years ago

"**D**on't let her drive. She was up all night again, you know?" Mom whispered as we sat in the kitchen drinking coffee together.

"Yeah, I know. She was in the garage painting. She'll probably pass out in the car on the drive up. I won't let her behind the wheel."

Lily had been living with us again for a few months now—her fourth time back in four years. The foster care system had created a vicious cycle. Every time Lily would start to get settled in with us, they'd put her back with her mom—even though she never wanted to go at first. Then once she was living with her mom again, she would feel responsible for taking care of her and not want to put her back into a mental health facility. Things would eventually get really bad, and Lily would be removed and upset. She'd come back to our house, and it would take a few months for her to settle in again. Seven or eight months later, the entire circle jerk happened again.

Broken system. Though, as of today, Lily was officially not part of the fucked-up world of foster care anymore. Because today was her eighteenth birthday. Unfortunately, the only thing she wanted for her birthday was to drive upstate and visit her mom. Which was one of the reasons she'd been up all night painting again. She got anxious when there was anything to do with Rose, and painting soothed her when her mind couldn't rest.

"Dad and I were talking," Mom said. "We think maybe Lily should see a counselor. Someone privately, outside of the social services system. She's had five different counselors since she first came here, and I think she would benefit from some consistency. She's been through a lot—the constant moves back and forth, being taken away from her mother, us moving from Big Bear Lake closer to LA because of all my appointments, my being sick…"

Of course it was a lot, and she was right. Lily took Mom's ovarian cancer diagnosis just as badly as I did. I had no doubt Lily *should* talk to someone on a regular basis. But she'd been looking forward to her eighteenth birthday mainly because the state couldn't force her to go see a shrink once a month anymore. To her, seeing a therapist of any kind meant she was crazy like her mother.

"I don't know, Mom. She's not going to want to go."

"If anyone can talk her into it, you can. You two are closer than brother and sister."

I frowned. I felt bad that we were still lying to my mom, and to everyone. But if my parents had known we were a couple when we were fifteen, they might not have taken Lily back. The state definitely wouldn't have allowed it. Then as we got older, we didn't say anything because it was easier to have our privacy. If Mom knew we were together, we'd never be allowed behind a closed door again—especially not with my little sisters around.

"I'll see what I can do."

Lily swept into the kitchen and sing-songed, *"Good morning."*

She was full of energy, even though she'd been up all night painting. It seemed like she had two moods lately: up or down. There was no real in-between anymore. But I could understand it; she'd been through a lot.

"Happy birthday." Mom stood and brought Lily in for a hug. She cupped her cheeks, along with some hair. "Eighteen. Today brings you a lot of freedom. You've spent time with us over the years because you had to, but I hope you'll stay for many more now because you want to. You're part of this family, Lily."

"Thank you, Pia."

Mom sniffled and shook her head. "I don't want to ruin your birthday and get all emotional. So let me just give you your gifts." She turned around, took two wrapped boxes off the kitchen counter, and handed them to Lily. "Happy birthday, sweetheart."

Lily thanked her and opened the first one. Her eyes lit up as she found a big set of expensive oil paints she always visited in the store. "Thank you so much. I've wanted these for so long. But they're so expensive. You shouldn't have."

"Grant told me how much you admired them."

She opened the second box—stationery with *Lily* imprinted on it and lilies wrapped around her name.

She ran her finger across the top. "This is beautiful."

"I figured you could use it to write to Grant when he goes away to college."

Lily's eyes jumped to me, but then she smiled at Mom. "Thank you. It's perfect. I really love it."

Four years ago, when Lily moved back in with her mom the first time, she'd told me she would write to me every day we couldn't be together. I'd thought she was exaggerating, but the last time I counted, I had over five hundred letters. Some days she sent me three or four pages about her day, other days she'd just write a few sentences, and sometimes I'd get a poem or a picture she'd drawn. But she never missed a day. So the stationery was a great idea, though she wouldn't be using it when I went away to college. I'd decided to stay home. Yet another thing neither Lily nor I had mentioned to my mom yet.

I looked at my watch. "You ready to get going?"

"I am."

"You two be careful," Mom said. She turned to Lily. "Enjoy your visit with your mom."

If today was anything like most days with Rose, there was about a fifty-fifty shot of that happening.

• • •

A psychiatric center might be a hospital, but it's a hell of a lot different than the place you go when someone has a baby or something, or at least this one was. The white walls were bare, with no cheerful art or framed pictures to soften the hardness of the environment. Since the floor we were visiting at Crescent Psychiatric Hospital was an adult-only wing, everyone was dressed casually, mostly in street clothes. But a few people were milling around in pajamas, even though it was the middle of the day.

Rose, Lily's mother, wasn't in the activity center or any of the common areas. We found her in her room, lying in bed in the fetal position with her eyes open. Her big belly was really showing now. Three months ago when she was admitted, we'd found out Rose was four months pregnant. She'd been in the midst of a manic episode then, rambling on about all the plans she and the baby's father had. Though as far as I knew, the mystery man who had gotten her pregnant had never shown his face even once to check on her since her admission. And something told me he never would.

Rose's eyes acknowledged us as we walked in, but she didn't move.

"Mom, how are you?"

Lily went to sit down on the bed. She brushed her mom's hair back the same way I'd seen my mom do to my sisters a hundred times.

Rose mumbled something incoherent.

Lily leaned down and kissed her mother's cheek. "Your hair is nice and soft. Did you wash it today?"

More incoherent babbling, yet Lily went on like they were having an actual conversation.

"Look, Grant's with me." She pointed to where I stood near the door, and her mom's eyes followed along for a few seconds, but then Rose went right back to staring into space.

I wasn't sure what kind of drugs they were giving her, but she was only slightly more alert than catatonic. Or maybe they weren't giving her any. She was pregnant, after all.

Lily got up, went around to the other side of her bed, and climbed in behind her mom to snuggle her. "I missed you."

I blinked a few times as the scene before me brought back a flash of a memory. About six months ago, Lily had been sad when her mom hadn't called or shown up for their scheduled weekly visit again. After waiting all day on Sunday, Lily had climbed into bed and spent a few days there...lying in the fetal position. I'd thought she was just sulking and sad, and I had done my best to cheer her up—including spending hours snuggled in bed behind her, a lot like she was doing to her mother now.

That thought made me antsy. "I'm going to go for a walk—give you two some time alone."

Lily nodded.

I grabbed my jacket and opened the door, but I glanced back over my shoulder one more time before leaving. A fucked-up feeling settled into my chest as I thought how much the two of them looked like Lily and me had a while back.

Except Lily just had a lot to deal with. She wasn't sick like her mom.

CHAPTER 15

Ireland

I was *so* damn nervous.

Grant's boat was only a twenty-minute drive from my apartment, but I wanted to pick up something to bring with me, so I'd left an hour early. The liquor store pit stop only ate up a few minutes, so I arrived at the marina almost a half-hour before I was supposed to. I gave my name to the attendant at the booth, and he pointed out one of Grant's assigned spots. I could see down the long dock that led to where his boat was parked. There was a flurry of activity, people coming and going to their boats, and chairs set up where people sat on the dock and chatted with their neighbors.

It seemed like a friendly community, and it made me wonder why Grant didn't bring dates down here. His boat was impressive, and the setting was definitely made for romance. I made a mental note to dig deeper into the no-dates-on-the-boat zone, and I pulled down the mirror to check my makeup. When I flicked it back up, I saw Grant outside on the back of his boat. He was dressed casually, in a pair of shorts with an untucked short-sleeve button up and sunglasses. When he hopped over the back transom, I saw he had no shoes on.

An older man walked over to talk to him, and it gave me the chance to observe him outside of a work setting. God, he was sexy. I'd always had a thing for a man in a well-fitted suit. The way they wore them gave off an air of power, but looking down the dock, I realized the suit had nothing to do with the air Grant Lexington gave off. He stood casually talking to the gentleman, yet there was something about the way he held himself—his feet planted wide, broad shoulders back, arms folded across his chest. The man oozed confidence even with bare feet. With some guys, a good suit made the man. Not Grant. He made the suit.

I watched for a few minutes more while he finished his conversation with the man. Then he tightened some ropes and carried out a set of portable stairs and set them on the dock. The next time he went into the cabin, I took a deep breath and got out of the car.

His boat was docked next to last, probably thirty boats down at the far end of the marina. I'd made it about ten when he emerged from the cabin again. He caught sight of me right away and stood watching me make my way toward him. I became self-conscious about each step. And whatever nerves had settled in the car came back with a roar. Though I wouldn't let him see me stress. So I straightened my spine and added a little bounce to my walk that I knew would make the bottom of my sundress shimmy from side to side.

"Hey." I stood on the dock next to the boat, and Grant offered a hand so I could board using the stairs he'd set out. "Well, these certainly make it easier. Especially in these wedges."

Grant didn't let go of my hand once I was safely onboard. "Had to dust off those stairs. Never use 'em."

"I could have climbed on like we did the other night. You didn't have to dig them out. Sorry if I'm a little early. I wasn't sure how long it would take to get here, and I wanted to stop and pick this up." I handed him the bottle of wine.

"Thank you. I was wondering how long you were going to sit in the car and watch me."

My eyes widened. *Shit.* He'd seen me. "I wasn't checking you out, if that's what you think. I was just really early and didn't want to impose."

He pushed his sunglasses down on his nose so I could see his eyes. "That's too bad. You're welcome to check me out whenever you want. It would only be fair since I won't be able to stop looking at you in that dress."

I'd changed three times and settled on a spaghetti strap white and navy sundress with a V-neck. It showed off more cleavage than I normally put on display, but my roommate had talked me into wearing it. Now I was glad I'd listened.

"Come on. I'll give you the tour and open the wine."

I followed Grant into the cabin. We'd stayed outside the other night with his grandfather, so it was the first time I was seeing the inside and where he lived. The room we entered was a big living room. It had a wraparound couch, two matching chairs, a long credenza, and a big-screen television. The living room I shared with Mia was probably the same size.

"It's easy to forget you're on a boat in here, isn't it?"

He pointed to the wall-to-wall windows. "There are two different shades that come down. One blocks out some of the sun and keeps it cool, but you can still see outside through them, and the other totally blacks out the outside. You can't tell if it's day or night when those are down, much less where you are."

I followed Grant into the kitchen and was surprised to find it was almost as big as the living room. "I don't know why, but I expected a small galley kitchen, not something like this."

"It was smaller originally. There used to be a bedroom up here, but I took out the wall and opened it up. I like to cook."

I raised a brow. "You cook?"

"Why does that surprise you?"

"I don't know. I guess it just seems so domestic. I took you more for the type that went to restaurants and grabbed takeout."

"My mom was Italian and cooked a big meal every night. The kitchen was the center of the house growing up. We had foster kids coming and going, and she used cooking to get us all together at least once a day."

I smiled. "That's really nice."

"I did pick up food tonight on my way home, but not because I can't cook. I was running late, and you didn't want a date, so I figured that meant I shouldn't sneak in a full meal."

Grant showed me the rest of the boat: a small bedroom downstairs that he'd turned into an office, a guest bedroom, two bathrooms, and then he opened the door to a giant master bedroom.

"This is huge."

"That's the kind of thing I like to hear in here." He winked.

I took a few steps in and looked around. The room had dark wood and a king-size bed with plush navy linens. One of the walls was covered in black and white photos of boats sailing on the water with matte black frames. I walked over and looked at some of them.

"These are beautiful. Did you take them?"

"No. They're all the different models my grandfather built over the years. The photos are all of the prototypes taking their first sail."

I pointed to the one in the center. "Is this this boat?"

Grant stood close behind me, close enough that I felt the heat emanating from his body. "It is. That was taken in 1965."

"Crazy. I can't get over how old this boat is. If you told me it was a year old, I'd believe it."

"That's what people loved about his models. They have a timeless quality about them."

I looked closer at the photo. "There's no name on the back yet."

"The showroom samples and prototypes were never named. It's bad luck to change a boat's name. So it was up to the first owner to name her."

I turned around, and suddenly the big room seemed much smaller. Grant didn't back up. "Her? Is a boat always a her?"

He nodded. "Pops would say sailors of the past were almost always men and often dedicated their ships to goddesses who would protect their vessel in rough seas." Grant brushed a hair from my shoulder. "But I think they're women because they're high maintenance."

"High maintenance, huh? Well, you live on a boat, so you must not mind high maintenance, then?"

His eyes dropped to my lips, and he smirked. "Apparently high maintenance is my type. Easy is boring."

I thought he was going to lean in and kiss me, and in the moment, I would have let him, but instead his eyes caught my gaze. "Come on. I promised you a drink and a sunset."

We went out to the front of the boat, and Grant set up a tray of all different finger foods he'd bought at the Italian market. It was enough food for three meals.

"Do you always buy enough for ten people? I'm sensing a pattern here between lunch the other day and all of this."

"The pattern is wanting to make sure you're taken care of, not being wasteful."

I smiled. "Are you always this accommodating to your dates?"

"Considering you're the first woman sitting on my boat for a sunset, I'd have to say no."

I tilted my head. "What's your story? You said the other day you haven't had a relationship in seven years. Is it because you work a lot?"

Grant seemed to consider his words. "Partly. I do work a lot. Contrary to your initial opinion of me— where you assumed I was a spoiled silver spoon who didn't work—I put in a ten- to twelve-hour day at the office most weekdays and a half day on Saturday."

"I'm never going to live that email down, am I?"

He shook his head. "Not likely."

I sighed. "Okay, Mr. Workaholic. So let's back up. I asked if you hadn't had a relationship in seven years because you're busy, and your answer was *partly*. What's the other part? For some reason, I feel like you're leaving out an important piece of the story."

Grant's eyes settled on mine for a few heartbeats, but then he looked away to pick up his wine. "I was married. Been divorced for seven years."

"You must've been married young. Or are you older than you look?"

He nodded.

A few minutes ago, he'd seemed relaxed, but his composure totally changed now. His jaw tightened, he avoided eye contact, and his movements were rigid, as if all the muscles in his body had contracted at once.

"I'm twenty-nine. Got married at twenty-one."

Even though he looked completely uncomfortable discussing the subject, I pushed a bit more. "So you were only married for a year, then?"

He gulped back his wine. "Almost, yes. A few months less."

"Were you high school sweethearts or something?"

"Sort of. Lily was one of my parents' foster kids for a while. Actually, she came and went a lot over the years."

Though he was answering my questions, he wasn't really offering too much information. I sipped my wine. "Can I ask what happened? Did you grow apart or something?"

Grant was quiet for a moment and then looked me in the eyes. "No, she ruined my life."

Okay then. He spoke so sternly that it caught me off guard. I had no idea how to respond. Though Grant took care of that for me.

"Why don't we talk about you? I'm trying to work my way up from drinks to a full-blown date. Dragging out shit about my ex-wife isn't the way to make that happen."

"What would you like to know?"

"I don't know. The game we played in the car on the way home from the fundraiser worked well. Tell me something I don't know about you."

The mood had definitely dampened, and Grant was right. We didn't need to drag all of our skeletons out of the closet the first evening we spent time together. So I said something I thought might tilt the mood back to playful.

"I love accents. Growing up, every time I heard a new one, I'd study it until I nailed it down. Actually, I still do it from time to time."

Grant looked amused. "Let's hear Australian."

I sat up and cleared my throat. "Okay. Let me think." I tapped my finger to my lip. "This is *turn on the air conditioner. It's hot in here. Chuck awn da egg ignisna. Iz hawt innere.*"

Grant laughed. "That's actually pretty good. How about British?"

"Okay. Here is *I don't often use my cell phone.*" I cleared my throat again. "*I don't OF-unh use me MOH-bye-ul.*

He chuckled. "Nice."

"Your turn. Tell me something about you I don't know."

He looked at my lips. "I want to devour your mouth."

I swallowed. "I sort of knew that already."

Grant kept staring at my lips, and I squirmed. Yet he still didn't lean in and go for a damn kiss. The way he looked at me, I was about two seconds away from taking it upon myself to make the first move. But then he looked over my shoulder.

"When did that happen?"

I blinked a few times. "What?"

He lifted his chin to point behind me. "That."

I turned. The sky was the most amazing shade of orange mixed with deep purple hues. "Oh my God. That's incredible."

I stood to take in the full view, and Grant stood behind me. We were both silent as we watched the sky light up with color around the setting sun. He snaked a hand around my waist and rested his head on top of mine.

"I know you said you don't bring dates here, but do you do this often? Appreciate the view, I mean."

"I do, actually. I make a point of taking a few minutes every day to watch either the sunset or the sunrise. I run on the beach in the morning and catch it, or if my day starts early, I make sure I'm back here before sunset."

I leaned my head back against Grant's chest. "I like that."

He squeezed me closer. "Good. I like this."

Time just got away from us after that. We talked for hours, and before I knew it, it was almost midnight.

I yawned.

"You're tired."

"Yeah. I get up at three thirty."

"Want me to drive you home? I can pick you up to get your car in the morning."

I smiled. "No, I'm okay to drive still. But I should get going."

Grant nodded. "I'll walk you to your car."

He helped me off the boat, and the gold-painted name on the back caught in the dock lights. *Leilani May*.

"Who is the boat named after?"

Grant looked away. "No one."

For a businessman, he wasn't a very good liar. But the evening had been so nice that I didn't ruin it by pressing the subject.

We walked down the dock hand in hand, and when we got to my car, Grant took my other one, too. He laced his fingers with mine. "So did I pass your test? Do I get an actual date?"

I smirked. "Maybe."

"Good, then I don't need to be on my best behavior anymore."

Grant let go of my hands and cupped my cheeks. He guided me to take a few steps, and before I realized what was happening, my back was up against my car and he'd planted his lips over mine. I gasped, and he didn't waste the opportunity to dip his tongue inside. His kiss was assertive, yet gentle at the same time. He tilted my head and groaned when the kiss deepened. His desperate sound turned me on almost as much as the feeling of his hard body pressed against mine. My purse fell to the gravel, and my hands wrapped around his back. When I dug my nails into him, he grabbed my ass and lifted me off my feet. We groped each other, my legs locked around his waist as he grinded against me. I could feel how hard he was even through our clothes.

When the kiss finally broke, I struggled to catch my breath. "Wow." I'd been kissed before, kissed really well even, but no one had ever kissed the shit out of me. My mind was in a fog from it.

He smiled and used his thumb to wipe my bottom lip. "God, I wanted to do that so badly all night."

I gave him a goofy grin. "I'm glad you waited until we were in the parking lot. Otherwise I might not have left."

Grant pretended to bang his head against my car. "Fuck. Did you have to tell me that?"

I giggled. "Thank you for sharing your sunset with me. I had a really nice time."

"Sunrise is even better. You're welcome to stay tonight and find out in the morning."

I smiled. "Maybe another time."

It took all of my willpower to pull away from Grant. I'd been teasing, but I was so turned on, I *was* lucky he'd waited until now to kiss me like that. I brushed my lips with his one more time and opened the car door. He stood watching as I buckled up and turned the ignition.

As I put the car into reverse to back out, I rolled down my window. "Goodnight, Grant."

"Dinner soon?"

I smiled. "Maybe. If you'd told me who the boat was named after, my answer would have definitely been yes."

CHAPTER 16

Grant - 8 years ago

The shower door opened and steam billowed out. I smiled, finding a naked Lily ready to join me.

"Hey. You feeling better?"

Lily stepped inside the stall and shut the door behind her. She put both her palms on my chest. "Yeah. It must've been the flu or something."

The flu. That's what she always called it. Lily seemed to get the flu more and more over the last year. Yet the days she spent curled up in bed never came with a cough or fever. Lily was depressed. Of course, she had every right to be. She'd dropped out of college because she hated the non-art classes, her mom had disappeared into the wind a year ago, taking her three-year-old brother, Leo, with her, and both of us had taken my mom's death a few months ago pretty hard.

But Lily's constant, bedridden bouts of depression seemed like more than just regular depression. She would shut down for days every time her *flu* hit. She didn't eat, didn't talk, didn't function as a person. And even though she spent almost twenty-four-seven in bed, she rarely slept. She just stared, unfocused, lost in her own head.

It scared me. I didn't say it, but more and more lately, her highs and lows reminded me of her mom's— so much so that I'd been pushing her to see a therapist. That discussion always turned her depression into anger. Because to her, needing help meant she was like her mom.

Lily leaned in and pressed her body against mine. She shut her eyes and looked up at the streaming water as it rained down. A huge smile spread across her face, and I couldn't have stopped the one that broke out on mine if I'd tried. That's the thing with Lily—her smile was contagious. When she didn't have the flu, she was so full of life and happiness, more so than the average person. The happy times always made me forget about the sad ones...until it happened all over again a few months later.

She pushed up on her tippy toes and pressed her lips to mine. The water from overhead streamed down over our joined lips. It tickled, and both of us started to laugh.

"I've been thinking about something," she said.

I pushed the wet hair from her face and smiled. "I'm hoping you're thinking about bending over and hanging on to that wall behind you."

Lily giggled. "I'm serious."

I took her hand and slid it between us, down to my erection. "So am I. Can you tell?"

She laughed more. "I've been thinking about how much I love you."

"Well, I like the sound of that. Go on."

"And how much I love living down here with you."

My grandfather had given me a boat a few months ago on my twenty-first birthday—the very first boat he ever built. When Mom died, Lily and I decided to move into it and live down at the marina. It wasn't exactly a traditional home, but my girl wasn't exactly traditional either, and it made her happy. Plus, we spent every weekend sailing and exploring new places together. Since I'd started working for my family's company after graduating college a few months ago, we could pretty much afford to live wherever we wanted. But this boat felt right for us. And it made Lily happy, most of the time.

"I love living down here with you, too."

"So what I was thinking was..." Lily looked down and went quiet.

I slipped two fingers under her chin and tilted her head up so our eyes met. "What's on your mind, Lily? Talk to me."

"I was thinking... Well..." She dropped to her knees.

Not the direction I thought she was going, but that sure as shit worked for me.

But then she looked up and took my hand and lifted from two knees to only one. My heart beat out of control,

"I love you, Grant." She smiled. "Will you...marry me?"

I pulled her up from the floor. "Get up here. I should be the one down there, not you. I've actually been thinking about us a lot lately. And I would love to marry you."

Lily smiled.

"But..." I said.

Her smile wilted.

I'd been thinking a lot about having this conversation, though I would have planned it a little better—so we weren't having it naked in this small shower. But this was life with Lily, unpredictable and always an adventure. I'd learned to roll with the punches because of her.

I cupped her cheeks. "I want to marry you more than anything. But you've been getting...the flu...a lot lately. And I really want you to talk to someone, go see a doctor."

The look on Lily's face broke my heart. Any discussion of her needing help sliced straight through her. She abruptly turned, swung open the shower door, and ran out of the bathroom.

"Lily! Wait!" I twisted the water off and jumped out of the shower. On my second step, I hit a patch of water she'd left behind and my foot slipped out from under me. I landed on my ass. "Goddammit. Lily, wait!"

But it was too late. While I climbed up from the floor, Lily just kept running. She was already up the stairs and outside the cabin before I could even grab a towel and follow her. I emerged on the back deck, still wrapping the towel around my waist just as she jumped off the boat, buck-ass naked.

"Lily!"

She ignored me and took off down the dock. When I caught her, I wrapped my arms around her from behind. "Stop. Stop running. We need to talk."

Just then, an older couple came out from the cabin of their boat. Their eyes grew wide. I put my hand up and spoke to them. "Sorry. We're leaving. We were just...playing a little game, and it got out of control. Everything's fine."

Realizing what it might look like, that I was holding on to a naked woman who was trying to run away, I spoke to Lily. "Right, babe? Tell the nice couple everything is good."

Lily had run out upset and angry, but her mood shifted at the calamity we found ourselves in. She started to laugh. "Naked tag," she yelled to the gawking couple. "I guess I'm it now."

We started to crack up. I took the towel from around my waist and wrapped it around Lily's front to cover her up. I kept myself pressed tightly to her back so as to not fully expose myself as we turned back to our boat. I waved as we walked in tandem. "Sorry about that. You have a good day."

Once we were back on the boat, we laughed inside the cabin for a solid five minutes. This was my Lily. My wild, beautiful, adventurous girl who one minute made me panic and the next had tears of laughter running down my face. I plopped down on the couch and pulled her onto my lap, stripping her of the towel in the process. I took her face in my hands.

"I love you, my wild girl. I want to marry you. But I do think you need to see someone."

Lily frowned. "I'm not crazy like my mother."

"I know that. But do it for me anyway."

Lily thought about it, then nodded. "Fine. I'll go see whoever you want. Get me an appointment today."

I smiled. "I didn't mean it had to be this minute. But I'll look for someone. Okay?"

"Then we can get married?"

I looked deep into her eyes. "I promise. But give me a little time to do this right."

• • •

Today was the seven-year anniversary of the day we'd first met. I'd bought a beautiful ring, made reservations at a fancy restaurant, and talked the owner of Lily's favorite art gallery into opening for us privately tonight so I could propose. Everything was going perfect. It had been three weeks since Lily's proposal, and a few days ago she'd gone to her first appointment with a therapist. Surprisingly, she'd come home and said she liked the doctor a lot. Yet even though everything was perfect, my palms were sweating like a bitch as the gallery owner slipped out so we could be alone.

"I can't believe you did all this."

"Anything for my girl."

We walked around hand in hand, taking our time in front of each painting like Lily loved to do. The day I'd come into the gallery to talk to the owner, I'd walked around and looked at all of the artwork. One in particular caught my eye and solidified that I'd made the right choice to propose. Two canvases away was a piece titled *Promises*. It was an abstract of a woman standing at the altar. Only the back of her wedding dress showed, but the focus of the piece was all the flower petals on a white runner along the church aisle. While everything else was black and white, the flower petals were colorful and vibrant. The minute I'd seen it that day, it reminded me of Lily—she *was* those petals on the floor to me. I knew it was the perfect spot to propose.

I took a deep breath as we walked over in front of the painting. Lily's face lit up when she saw it. And just like always, I smiled seeing her smile. While she admired the art, I bent down on one knee.

She screeched and covered her mouth when she noticed. "Yes!"

I chuckled. "I didn't ask anything yet, babe."

She knelt so we were both on one knee. "Grant."

"Yeah?"

"I have a surprise for you, too."

"What's that?"

"I'm pregnant."

CHAPTER 17

Grant

I'd taken to recording the morning news and watching it at my desk.

I had a pile of work stacked up, a shitload of emails waiting for responses, and yet here I was, sitting at my desk on a Saturday watching yesterday morning's show for the second time. Ireland looked good in turquoise. It brought out the color in her eyes. Though I didn't get a good look at the full dress because she was always behind that desk. Maybe I should suggest the anchors get up at some point in the show, change things up a bit.

Jesus Christ. Was this really what I was doing? Analyzing a woman's wardrobe choices to decide what outfit complements her eyes more? And debating calling down to the director of broadcasting to demand that the anchor stand so I can get a better look at her body? I needed my head fucking examined.

Blowing out a stream of hot air, I forced myself to X out of the video recording. I had work to do. Shitloads of it. Before Ireland Saint James, I couldn't have even told you the name of the station we owned, much less what anyone wore. To say the woman had me distracted would be an understatement.

I picked up a file and started to go through a prospective investment that had been sitting on my desk since last week. But two pages into it, my phone buzzed, and though I'd normally ignore it while working, I dug it out of my pocket.

Ireland: Thank you for the flowers. I had a good time last night, too. Especially the end part up against my car.

She'd included a little winky face at the end of her text. Normally, people who used emojis in their texts pissed me off. Yet I found myself smiling at the little yellow face. I texted back.

Grant: Dinner tonight?

Ireland: Can't. I have plans.

Since I had plans on Sunday, I texted back suggesting next weekend, but she was busy then, too. An hour later, the text exchange was still bugging me.

She has plans.

Did she have a date? I'd had drinks with her once, so her having dinner with someone else wasn't exactly off limits. Yet the idea of her going out with another man made me crazy.

I forced myself back to work and tried to ignore thoughts of her out with some other guy tonight. But I reread the same page three times and still had no idea what the words said. So I tossed the file aside and picked my phone back up.

Grant: Are your plans tonight a date?

The little dots started to jump around and then stopped and started a few times.

Ireland: Would that upset you?

Answering a question with a question was right up there next to how much I disliked emojis. This woman was screwing with me. I didn't play games. I didn't have damn time for games. Which reminded me...I needed to get back to work.

I tossed my phone to the side and dug back into the investment prospectus I had been trying to digest.

But twenty minutes later, I had my goddamned phone in my hand again. I was completely distracted by just one simple text. I wasn't sure if I was angrier at myself for needing to know her plans or her for not answering my question.

Grant: Just answer the question.

Her response was immediate.

Ireland: Boy, someone's cranky.

I took a deep breath, which did little to help me relax.

Grant: That would be because I'm still waiting for an answer to my question...

Ireland: Is the muscle in your jaw flexing right now?

I read her text and looked up at the ceiling. This woman was going to be the death of me. And I was starting to get a headache from how hard I'd been clenching my teeth. So she wasn't wrong about the muscle in my jaw.

Grant: Ireland...answer the damn question.

My phone started to buzz for a call, rather than a text. Ireland's name flashed on the screen. I swiped to answer.

"Why must you be so difficult?" I said in greeting.

Ireland laughed, and the sound instantly softened the muscle in my jaw. "You're fun to screw with."

I leaned back in my chair. "I'm much more fun to *screw*. How about we move on to that phase of the relationship instead of you making me fucking nuts?"

I could tell she was still smiling when she spoke. "I do have a date tonight, but you don't have anything to be worried about because he's married."

"Come again?"

She giggled. "I have the rehearsal dinner for my best friend Mia's wedding, which is next weekend. My partner in the wedding is her brother, who is married to a man. So technically, I guess he's my date tonight."

Great. Now I'm jealous of a gay, married man...

"How about Sunday?" she said.

I decided to see if turnabout was fair play. "Can't. I have a date."

Of course, that date was with my grandmother to play Santa Claus at the annual Pia's Place party...

She was quiet for a long moment and then said in a curt tone. "Well, if you have a date, you don't need a second one with me."

I smiled. "You see how that feels, Ireland? It's not very pleasant, is it? Especially not while I'm trying to get work done. My date tomorrow is with my grandmother."

"Oh."

"Next weekend, then?" I said. I really didn't want to wait that long.

Ireland sighed. "Next weekend is the wedding. Mia and I are going to spend the last night in our apartment together Friday night and then Saturday is the wedding and Sunday is a brunch with the wedding party. I don't usually go out on weeknights because I get up so early for work. But maybe we can have an early dinner or something one night?"

"I'm leaving Monday for a business trip to the east coast. I'll be gone until Thursday evening."

"Oh." At least she sounded as disappointed as I felt. "Well, maybe the weekend after, then. Or maybe... would it be too weird if I asked you to come with me to the rehearsal dinner tonight? Spouses are coming that aren't in the wedding. So it's not just the wedding party."

I'd been thinking of our date as being a nice quiet evening with just the two of us, not a night with all of her friends at some wedding rehearsal. But waiting two weeks to see her was not an option. So I'd have to take what I could get.

"What time should I pick you up?"

"Really? You'll come?"

"Apparently that's the only way I'm going to get to see you, so yes. But, full disclosure, I'm only coming because I can't wait to push you up against the car again and suck your face."

She laughed. "That's fair. How about six thirty? The rehearsal is at seven and dinner is right after. They're getting married at the restaurant, so the rehearsal part won't take very long."

"I'll be there at six fifteen. Because I won't be waiting until *after* dinner for my kiss."

• • •

That evening, my heart started to pump at an almost alarming speed the minute she opened the door. Ireland's hair was pulled back from her face and pinned up. She had on another blue outfit; this one a powder blue, body-hugging dress with a wide, scooped neck that exposed her collarbone. It showed a hint of cleavage, which was sexy as hell, but something about that collarbone made me salivate. I'd teased her on the phone about picking her up early because I intended to get round two of the kiss, but I hadn't planned on mauling her the minute she opened the door.

Though you know the old saying about the best laid plans...

Ireland smiled and said hello, stepping aside for me to enter, though I only made it halfway through. Backing her up against the open apartment door, I wrapped my hands around her cheeks and planted my lips over hers. She hadn't been expecting it, but it didn't take long for her to join in. She dug her hands into my hair and yanked, and I sucked on her sweet tongue. Reaching down, I cupped the back of her thigh and lifted so I could move closer. Before I knew it, her legs were wrapped around my waist, and I was grinding a growing erection between her legs. If I'd liked her a little less, I would have dropped to my knees and buried my face between her legs for a taste right there against the door. But Ireland deserved more respect than that. So, begrudgingly, I pulled back from the kiss.

She blinked a few times, and it made me smile that she seemed as lost in the moment as I had been. "Jeez. That was as good as the first time."

I lifted my thumb to her mouth and wiped some of her smeared lipstick from beneath her bottom lip. "I haven't been able to focus on anything but this mouth since you pulled out of the parking lot last night."

She smiled. "I love how honest you are."

I brushed my lips against hers again and spoke with them touching. "If you like my honesty, there're plenty of things I'd be happy to tell you about—things I'd like to do to you."

She giggled and gave me a playful shove. "Why don't you come in so I can shut the door? I've already been fired for indecent exposure once. I wouldn't want it to happen a second time."

"Trust me. If you'd like to prance around naked right now, you most certainly won't be fired."

The inside of her apartment was filled with boxes. She pointed to an empty spot on the couch and said, "Take a seat wherever you can find one. I just need to grab my purse and freshen up my lipstick now that you're wearing half of it."

I wiped my lips with my thumb. "Take your time."

While Ireland disappeared down the hall, I looked around the apartment a bit. There were a few framed photos on the bookshelf, two of her and another woman—who I assumed might be her roommate—one of Ireland, who looked to be about seven or eight with what I guessed was her mother, and another one of her taken recently with an older woman.

Ireland came up behind me while I had that one in my hand. "That's my Aunt Opal. My mom's sister. She raised me after my mother died. She's like a mother to me. Three months ago she moved down to Florida. It's odd not having her close by anymore."

"You two remained close?"

She nodded. "She has macular degeneration, so she's slowly losing her eyesight. She went to live with her daughter in Sanibel Island. Carly is twelve years older than me. She'd already moved out when her mom took me in when I was ten. But we're close. We text every few days. I'm going down to visit next month."

"I was five when I moved in with my mother."

"Do you mind if I ask what happened that you wound up in foster care?"

It wasn't something I spoke about often, but Ireland had been so open about her family history. "My mother was fifteen when I was born. My father isn't named on my birth certificate and was never in the picture. She had a tough home life of her own, and we bounced around from place to place. Eventually, she got into drugs, and we were living in shelters. One night she snuck out and never came back. Haven't seen her since."

Ireland's hand covered her heart. "Oh, God. I'm so sorry."

I put down the framed photo. "Don't be. I was lucky. The first family I was placed with was my parents. I was never bounced around like a lot of kids. I had a good childhood. Pia was the best mom in the world. My dad worked a lot, but he was great, too. They're my parents."

Ireland smiled sadly. "Yeah. I sort of feel the same way. Even though I have nice memories of my mom, I feel like Opal was my parent. Come with me. I want to show you something."

I followed her into her bedroom, and she pointed to a sign over her bed.

No rain. No flowers.

"A lot of my mom's death and everything that happened around that time is a blur. But I remember the priest coming to talk to me after her funeral and saying these words when I was crying. Somehow they've stuck with me over the years. Seems appropriate for your history, too."

I looked into her eyes. *Fuck me.* This woman was something else. I was standing ten feet away from her bed, and all I wanted to do was wrap her in my arms. The fact that I didn't want to bend her over the bed and fuck her sort of freaked me out a little.

I blinked a few times and looked away. "It's a beautiful saying."

Ireland grabbed a sweater from her closet and a purse from her dresser. "You ready to meet my friends?"

"I'd prefer to have you all to myself, but I'm ready to head out, if that's what you're asking."

She smiled and took my hands. "You want to know a secret?"

"What's that?"

"I'm a little afraid to be all alone with you. That's honestly one of the reasons I insisted on drinks rather than a full date."

"Why?"

"I don't know. I guess I sort of don't trust myself with you. You make me...nervous. Not in a bad way, if that makes any sense."

I took one of our joined hands and brought it to my lips to kiss her knuckles. "It makes a lot of sense. You know why?"

"Why?"

"Because you scare the shit out of me, too."

CHAPTER 18

Ireland

"**T**here you are."

Grant had disappeared at some point during the rehearsal. The pastor had stayed after the practice was over, and he'd talked for so long that I couldn't get away to look for my date until now.

"Sorry. I got a work call and had to take it, so I stepped out."

Grant looked away as he spoke. I hadn't known him long enough to really read him, yet it wasn't the first time I'd gotten the distinct feeling he was full of shit. Again, I let it pass.

"Oh. Okay. I lost track of you during the rehearsal. Dinner is about to be served."

Grant nodded.

"Is everything okay?"

"Of course. Just got a little distracted for a moment."

His eyes still didn't meet mine. Maybe I was reading too much into things. Even if he hadn't stepped out to take a call, and just needed some fresh air, it didn't really matter.

I smiled. "I'm guessing a wedding rehearsal where you meet all of my friends at once isn't exactly what you had in mind when you asked me for a second date."

Grant wrapped an arm around my waist. "It wasn't. But I'll take what I can get."

I lifted my arms up and around his neck. "I never would have thought it, but you're a good sport. I'll have to make it up to you later."

Grant's eyes darkened. "I like the sound of that." He leaned in and brushed his lips with mine.

Our private moment was interrupted by the sound of my best friend's voice. "Get a room."

I smiled and introduced Grant to the soon-to-be bride.

"Grant, this is my best friend, Bridezilla. Formerly known as Mia."

Grant and I separated, and he extended his hand. But Mia wasn't having any of that. She went in for a hug. "It's nice to finally meet you, bossman."

He chuckled. "You, too."

She hooked her arm with his and started to walk toward the door. "Come on. I'll introduce you to everyone and tell you all their secrets so you don't feel like an outsider."

Grant laughed, assuming she was kidding, but I knew better.

Inside, Mia introduced Grant to two dozen people, and when dinner started, she sat down with us instead of Christian, her husband-to-be, who was seated at the other end of the long table.

She ate a piece of her salmon and pointed her fork in the direction of our friend Tatiana. "She had her boobs done."

Grant looked over. His eyes dropped briefly to her enormous boobs, and then he turned back with a chuckle. "Not sure that's a secret to too many people."

He was absolutely right. Tatiana's implants were each almost as big as my head, and her chin practically rested on them, they sat so high.

"True." Mia nodded down to the end of the table to the woman sitting across from Christian. "Callie, my soon-to-be sister-in-law—the blonde on my side—sleeps with a teddy bear." She lifted her chin to the table across from us where her dad and his wife were sitting with Christian's parents. "My stepmother, Elaine, has a stack of love letters from an old boyfriend she keeps hidden in the attic."

Grant raised his brows. "You seem to have something on everyone."

Mia continued around the room, telling funny secrets about almost everyone. When she seemed to be done, Grant looked at me, while speaking to her.

"You forgot someone."

Mia bit her lip, like she was considering her options, and leaned over to Grant. "She has porn inside the old Disney DVDs in the living room cabinet. She thinks I don't know about it."

"Mia!" My eyes went wide, and I felt my face start to blush. I *hadn't* realized she knew about that. But the three of us laughed. Of course, the pastor picked that moment to walk over. He put his hand on Mia's shoulder and smiled.

"I'm sorry to interrupt. You three look like you're having a good time. I just wanted to say goodnight to the bride-to-be."

Mia told the pastor she'd walk him out, and after he started to walk away, she leaned back to us and whispered, "I'll be back with his secret in ten minutes."

Grant chuckled. "I like your friend."

"She's crazy, but I'm definitely going to miss her. I've actually never lived alone. I went from my parents' house, to my aunt's, to a roommate at college, and then to sharing an apartment with Mia."

"Will you get another roommate?"

"I had an ad on Craigslist. I've narrowed it down to two men."

"Men?"

"Yes. Jacque is a French underwear model living in the States for a year, and Marco is a fireman."

The look on Grant's face was so serious, I couldn't keep it going any longer. I started to crack up. "I'm teasing. You should see your face, though."

He narrowed his eyes. "Very cute."

"I'm actually really excited to live on my own. I told you I'm building a house. It's not much, but I love the area. It's a new development. The whole community is built around a big, beautiful lake—though my plot isn't lakefront because those parcels were almost four times the price. But I love how woodsy they're keeping it and how far apart the houses are going to be. It feels like a serene vacation place. When I first bought the land, I had an architect do the blueprints for my dream house. Then I had some estimates done on building it, and I realized I'd dreamed too big and needed to scale back. So it's much smaller now, but I can't wait until it's done. It's about sixty percent there."

He smiled. "That's great. I'd love to see it."

"I like to drive over to the property every once in a while and check it out. Maybe next time you can take the ride with me, and I'll show you the lake and give you a tour of my half-built house."

"I'd like that."

. . .

Two hours later, Grant drove me home and parked in front of my apartment building.

"Thank you for coming with me," I told him. "I know it wasn't an ideal date, but I enjoyed it anyway."

"I did, too."

I definitely wasn't ready for him to leave. "Do you want to come in?"

Grant looked me in the eyes. "You have no idea how much I do."

I smiled, but as we got out of the car and made our way up the elevator, I became extremely anxious. When I went to put the key in the lock, Grant noticed my hand shaking.

"Are you cold?"

I shook my head. "Nervous, I guess. I'm just...I'm really attracted to you, and I like you, but I'm not ready to...have you spend the night. I don't want you to get the wrong idea because I invited you in."

Grant turned me around and put two fingers under my chin, lifting so I looked him in the eyes. "The choice is always yours. We can take it as slow as you want."

My shoulders relaxed, and I exhaled. "Thank you."

I felt much calmer after that. Inside, I went to my room to change and left Grant opening a bottle of wine. When I came back out, he was standing in the living room with a glass of wine in one hand and *Beauty and the Beast* in the other.

He arched a brow. "She wasn't joking."

I felt the heat on my face and snatched the box from his hand. "I went through a dry spell. Don't tell me you've never watched porn."

He grinned. "Of course I have. I just don't store mine in Disney DVDs."

I laughed, took the wine out of his hand, and guzzled half of it in one gulp. As long as we were on the subject, I figured I might as well see what types of things he liked to watch. Lord knows, I'd found I had a bit of a fetish. "Is your collection specific to any type of porn?"

Grant squinted. "Are you asking me if I like to role play or have any fetishes?"

"I guess. I just found certain things worked for me, while others didn't."

He took the wine glass from my hand and drank the other half. "I'm not particular. But now I'm desperate to know what you're into."

I let out a nervous laugh and took the empty glass from his hand. "I need more wine for this conversation."

After I refilled, I led Grant over to the couch. "Can you just pretend you didn't open *Beauty and the Beast*?"

Grant shook his head with a wicked grin as he lifted my feet onto his lap. He began rubbing. "Not a chance, sweetheart. Spill it. What's your kink?"

"It's not really a kink."

"So let's hear it. Or do I need to unveil your full Disney collection and figure it out for myself right now?"

I drank a little more liquid courage. "I found that I sort of like videos where the woman is pleasuring the man."

Grant stopped rubbing. "You like to watch a woman give head?"

It was the new millennium. I shouldn't be embarrassed by anything that empowered me sexually, yet I bit my lip and nodded.

"Jesus Christ," Grant grumbled. "You're fucking perfect. How the hell did you ever have a dry spell?"

I laughed. "My dry spell was self imposed. I have a pattern. I pick an asshole to date. Then I blame it on the entire sex and take a long hiatus."

"You're sitting here with me. Does that mean I'm an asshole?"

I sipped my drink. "I don't know, are you?"

His playful smile wilted. "I can be. But I don't want to be to you."

"It doesn't take Sigmund Freud to figure out where my issues come from. I have some serious trust issues, Grant. My dad used to accuse my mom of cheating all the time. I'll never know if there was any truth to his accusations. I like to believe there wasn't, and he was just irrational and unstable. But that's what they always fought about, and were fighting about the night he ended her life. When he panicked and took off, he left me handcuffed to a radiator where no one found me for two days. And yet I still have a tendency to be attracted to dominating, asshole men."

"And you see me as one of those?"

I shrugged. "I don't now. Though I never see it at first. I like confident men—ones who are assertive and exude a certain kind of energy. You definitely fit that bill. But in my experience, the men with the take-charge personality I find so attractive don't necessarily make the best partners. The last guy I dated was really controlling. He didn't like me hanging out with my friends, and when I did, he'd check up on me. When I told him to back off, he had a way of making me feel guilty for wanting my own space."

Grant took my hand. "I'm sorry. We all have past relationships that carry into how we deal with things in the future."

"You know how I finally decided it was time to get rid of Scott, my ex?"

"How?"

"Without even realizing it, I'd started to click my pen."

"And that means..."

"Scott had a pet peeve. He *hated* when anyone clicked their pens."

Grant squinted. "You said Bickman hated foot tapping and heavy perfume and you used to do those things to secretly annoy him."

I smiled. "Bingo. I was unconsciously doing things to annoy him. That's not a sign that screams stable relationship. So I broke things off."

"I'll have to remember that. When you type at me in all caps, I'll know what it means."

I laughed. "Is that your pet peeve? Not sure you should have shared that with me."

Grant smiled. "You have a wicked side, Saint James."

I felt like I'd shared a lot of my past, yet I didn't know too much about his. At least not the important stuff. I knew he was adopted from foster care, but I got the feeling his baggage didn't come from that.

"Can I ask what happened between you and your ex-wife?"

Grant's jaw flexed. He looked away for a minute and then stared down when he finally started to speak. "Lily had a similar background to me—an unstable mother with no father in the picture. Except her mother was mentally ill, not an addict like mine. When we first met, I was attracted to her because of how different she was than everyone else. I didn't know back then that mental illness was hereditary. I thought she was spontaneous and wild. And for a long time she was. But slowly, over time, the highs she ran on started to spiral into lows. There was no middle ground with her."

I'd learned a lot about mental disorders over the years. A part of me always wanted to believe there was something wrong with my father. I wanted to blame what he'd done on *anything* but him, because it would be easier to accept that he'd killed my mother if it wasn't his fault. So I knew bipolar disorder and other depression-related illnesses often started in a person's twenties.

"I'm sorry. That's tough."

Grant was quiet for a moment, and then looked up at me. "Thank you. Like you said, it doesn't take Freud to figure out why I haven't had many healthy relationships with women since then. I didn't lie. I made a point of making sure they understood I wasn't looking for love. I guess we both have trust issues."

I nodded. "I appreciate your honesty. But is that what you want from me, too? I'm incredibly attracted to you. I might be okay with a sex-only relationship if that's all you truly want. Though I could also see myself falling for you, Grant. So I'd appreciate you being up front about what you're looking for."

He tugged my hand and guided me to move from sitting next to him to sitting on his lap. He cradled my face between his hands and spoke into my eyes. "I want more with you. But I'm not sure what I'm capable of, Ireland. I won't promise you something I'm uncertain I can deliver. Yet I'd like to try to make this work."

His words weighed heavy on my chest. It made me sad for him that he seemed to think he was incapable of love.

I forced a smile. "Thank you for your honesty. I guess every relationship has a risk to it. So we'll just take it one day at a time and see where it goes."

Grant nodded, though he didn't seem too sure of himself.

"How did we get from porn to our fucked-up lives?" I asked.

He smiled. "I don't know, but I'd definitely prefer to go back to talking about how you like to watch a woman give head."

I play-smacked his chest. "Of course you would."

Grant crooked his finger at me. "Come here."

I'd been sitting on his lap and now lifted one leg to straddle him. Settling, I moved my face close enough that our noses were touching. "Where? Here?"

He gripped the back of my neck and spoke with his lips pressed to mine. "Right here. Exactly right here."

We made out like two horny teenagers after that. When our kiss broke, he tugged my hair to expose my throat and buried his face in my neck. He kissed and licked and bit his way up to my ear.

"Tell me, Ireland. Is it just women you like to see give oral? Because I can't wait to bury my face between your legs and have you watch me lick you."

"Oh, God." I loved the sound of that. My body was already on fire from this kiss, and I could feel his erection pushing against my swollen clit. I might only have to move back and forth a few times to get myself off if he kept talking like that in my ear. I was this close to doing just that...until a voice interrupted the moment.

"This looks better than the one I watched in *Aladdin*. Think I'll make some popcorn."

I jumped at the sound of Mia's voice. Literally. I jumped off Grant's lap, into the air, and landed on my ass on the floor. I rubbed my backside. "Jesus, Mia. You scared the crap out of me."

She chuckled. "I wasn't quiet when I came in. You were just too engrossed in what you were doing." She waved her hand at us. "Carry on. Pretend I'm not here. I'm going to bed, anyway."

Grant extended a hand and helped me from the floor.

"I assumed you were sleeping at Christian's," I said.

"Nah. I'm making him stay celibate for the two weeks before our wedding."

I laughed. "Poor Christian. A bridezilla that won't put out."

Mia stuck her tongue out at me. "Goodnight, lovebirds."

Once she was gone, I sat back down on the couch next to Grant. "Sorry about that."

"It's fine. Probably a good thing she walked in. You want to take it slow, and between the way you looked tonight in that dress, knowing you have a porn collection, and that kiss, I wouldn't have been able to control myself much longer. I think that was my cue to get going."

I wanted to tell him to stay in the worst way, tell him to come back to my room with me and I'd show him all the techniques I'd picked up from watching those videos. But he was right. If things didn't slow down, I would be the one to get hurt. That much I knew.

So I nodded. "Okay. Thank you again for coming with me. Would you...be my date for the wedding next Saturday night?"

He leaned over and planted a kiss on my lips. "I'd love that."

I walked him to the door and opened it, but stalled at saying goodbye. "Where is your trip this week?"

"The east coast."

"Okay. Text me if you have time."

His eyes roamed my face. "I'll make time."

My stomach did a little somersault. The oddest things gave me that warm, mushy feeling. Grant kissed me goodnight, and I smiled and shut the door. But a few seconds later, there was a knock again. Just like last time, I figured he'd forgotten something.

"Miss me already?" I teased.

"If you're free tomorrow afternoon, there's a party at Pia's Place."

"Oh? Your mom's charity?"

"Yeah. The main office is over in Glendale. They host a few parties a year for the kids and their Bigs. Tomorrow is Christmas in July. It's a holiday-themed carnival. My grandmother suckered me into working it, but I just found out I should be finished by about two."

I smiled. "That sounds great."

Grant nodded. "I'll text you the address."

After I shut the door again, I thought about the evening. One part stuck out. I'd told him I could see myself easily falling for him. Which was sort of a lie. I already was.

CHAPTER 19

Ireland

I hadn't expected a party this big. I'm not sure why, but I'd envisioned a few dozen people, a makeshift petting zoo, and a cotton candy machine. But there were hundreds of people milling around, a pretty big Ferris wheel, street-style vendor carts all over the place, and Christmas-themed performers.

I walked around for a while and checked things out, but Grant was nowhere in sight. A woman approached me holding literature. She smiled. "Are you a Big? I don't think we've met yet."

"Oh no. I'm not part of the program."

She held out a pamphlet. "I'm Liz, the director here at Pia's Place."

"Hi. I'm Ireland. I'm actually meeting someone here."

"Oh, okay. Well, it's a great program. Can't hurt to check out the information. I think you'd find it very rewarding."

I took the pamphlet. "Thank you."

"My number is on the back, if you have any questions. Have a great afternoon. Enjoy the carnival."

She started to walk away, but I stopped her. "Liz, is there any chance you know Grant Lexington?"

"Of course."

"Have you seen him around? I'm supposed to meet him here after two, but I can't seem to find him."

Liz smiled. "He got started late." She looked over her shoulder a moment. "But it looks like he'll be finishing up soon. The line is finally getting smaller."

My brows furrowed. "Line?"

She pointed. "For Santa Claus."

I looked over at the area I'd passed by twice and squinted, examining the people. Taking a long look at Santa Claus, my eyes widened. "Oh my God. Is that..."

Liz laughed. "Only his grandmother could get him into that getup. It's the first time he's playing Santa for us. His grandfather has played the part for the last twenty years. I guess they're passing the baton."

After Liz walked away, I stood watching from a distance. The man was certainly an enigma. He wore custom-tailored suits, made everyone sit up a little taller when he walked into a meeting, and had an abrupt, standoffish way about him. Yet here he was on a Sunday afternoon, wearing a Santa suit and lifting kid after kid onto his lap. The more I watched, the bigger my smile grew. Especially when they put a little girl on his lap— one about two or three—and she immediately started to cry. I actually chuckled to myself and watched how he handled it.

He tried in earnest to get her to calm down, even lowering his beard so she would see there was a man underneath, but the little girl wasn't having it. The look on Grant's face was pure stress until an elf finally helped him out. As I continued to watch, the line whittled down to only four kids, so I decided to join it.

Grant shook his head and laughed when he saw me waiting behind a five year old. Our eyes caught a few times as each kid ahead of me took their turn. I couldn't seem to get the smile off my face. The entire scene was just so amusing. When the other kids were done, I walked up and plopped my ass down on Santa's lap.

I wrapped one arm around his neck and patted his stuffed belly. "Big lunch?"

"I was supposed to be done with this shit before you got here."

I gave a little tug to his beard. "I kind of like it. You can pull off white hair. I bet you'll look hot when you get a little salt and pepper going."

"Glad you think so, because some of these kids gave me a few grays today."

I chuckled. "I saw the little girl in the pink dress. She wasn't a fan."

"I was doing fine at the beginning because I had a bag of candy next to me. When the damn thing ran out, I had nothing to bribe them with."

"You must be hot in that suit."

"I am. I should go get changed before any other little monsters get in my line."

I smiled and wrapped my other arm around his neck. "Don't I get to tell Santa what I want for Christmas?"

"He already knows. More Disney DVDs."

I laughed and went to get up, but Santa held me in place. "So let's hear it. What do you want for Christmas, little girl?"

"Hmmm." I tapped my finger to my lip. "Whatever package Santa wants to give me."

"Oh, Santa wants to give you his package, alright. Anything else?"

I'd been feeling kind of down before I got here today because of something that came in yesterday's mail. "How about a zoning variance?"

"Zoning variance?"

I sighed. "Yeah. I opened my mail this morning, and I had something from the City. They issued me a stop work order on my construction. Apparently an inspector came by and realized the contractor built my garage a foot too close to the road, and now I need zoning variance approval to keep it. Or I need to get rid of the garage. I called the architect to see what it would take to get the approval, and he said we should get it without a problem. But the City is backed up, and it will be a few months before we could get the required hearing. Oh, and I had a fight with the contractor over it, and he quit on me."

"That sucks. What will you do?"

"I don't know. I need to think about it." I stood. "But let's go get you changed. I can feel the heat radiating off your body."

Grant nodded and led me over to the main building. He waited until we were inside to take off the hat and beard. "I could use a shower, but I'll have to settle for a change of clothes for now."

We navigated through the building until we came to an office. Grant took keys out of his pocket and unlocked the door. Inside the large space was a duffel bag on the desk. He unzipped it and pulled out some clothes, then started to take off the Santa suit.

I leaned against the desk and watched him unbutton the red jacket. "I met someone named Liz who was giving out literature on the program. She said this was your first time playing Santa."

Grant peeled off the jacket and tossed it on the desk, then started to step out of the red wool pants. He shook his head. "My grandmother may look like a sweet, old lady, but negotiating with her is impossible."

He tossed the pants on top of the jacket. Underneath he wore a pair of gray sweats and white T-shirt. Thinking nothing of it, he grabbed the hem of his shirt and tugged it up and over his head.

"I think it's sweet you..." I stopped mid-sentence as my jaw dropped. *Holy crap.* I'd felt his arms and chest, so I knew he was physically fit, but my Lord, the man was ripped. His tanned abs were all carved muscle, and he had an eight-pack without even flexing.

Grant looked over and found me staring. Completely oblivious, he looked down to see what I could be gawking at. It seemed like he expected to find something wrong, as if he needed a big welt or something on his chest to make a person stop and stare. Confused at finding nothing, he looked up at me for an explanation.

I pointed to his chest. "Umm...that's just not fair."

His brows lifted, and he chuckled. "Are you saying you like what you see?"

Was he joking? I wanted to *lick* what I saw. "You're… just beautiful all over."

He'd gotten a clean T-shirt from his duffel bag, but he tossed it to the ground and walked over to me. Bare-chested, he put one hand on either side of the desk I leaned against and looked me up and down.

"I'm glad you feel that way, because the feeling is mutual." Grant wrapped a hand around the back of my neck, using it to bring my lips to meet his. He kissed me passionately, his warm, hard chest pressed up against my soft.

Things were really heating up when the door behind him abruptly swung open.

"What the hell?" a voice said.

Grant stopped the kiss, but stayed put and shut his eyes while shaking his head. "Shut the door, Leo."

"Who's the girl?"

"Leo!" he raised his voice. "Shut the door. We'll be right out."

I looked around Grant at a boy who seemed no more than eleven or twelve. He waved, flaunting an ear-to-ear grin. "She's too pretty for your ugly ass."

Grant's head dropped, and he chuckled. "Get out, Leo. And watch your language."

The door slammed shut, and I looked to Grant. "He could have come in."

Grant looked down, and my eyes followed to find a bulge in his sweatpants.

I covered my mouth and giggled. "Oh my. Yeah, I guess that was a good call."

He grabbed his T-shirt and pulled it on. "Leo's my Little."

"Oh, that's right. You told me about him. I can't wait to meet him."

Grant slipped the gray sweats down his legs and stood in a pair of black boxer briefs. The considerable bulge on display had my mouth watering. It had been a long time—too long, apparently. He pulled on his jeans, managed to zip up and over the swell, and then stuffed everything back into his gym bag.

"He was supposed to see his mother this weekend, but she canceled on him. Which is a good thing, if you ask me. He'll be back in here within two minutes if I don't go outside. He's as impatient as my dick feels tucked into these pants at the moment."

I laughed and planted a chaste kiss on his lips. "Okay, let's go."

Grant made the introductions in the hall, and Leo said Grant's grandmother had been looking for him because Pops needed to go to the bathroom and was kind of confused right now.

"She wants you to go with him," he said.

"Shit. Okay."

Leo smirked and pointed. "Language, Grant."

Grant shook his head. He looked to me. "I'll be right back. Why don't you two go grab something to eat, and I'll meet you at the picnic tables."

After Grant disappeared, Leo walked me to the food area. We decided to just get ice cream, so we got in line.

"So Grant's your Big Brother?"

"I guess so. But we see each other more than most kids see their Big in the program."

"How long have you two been paired up?"

"As long as I can remember. He used to watch me a lot when I was little. Before my sister got sick."

My smile fell. "Oh. I'm sorry your sister got sick."

Leo shrugged. "It's okay. She's a lot better now. It's not like when her and Grant were married."

The people before us in line walked away, and Leo moved up. I was still stuck in place. "Your sister was married to Grant?"

Leo nodded. "Yeah. My sister is Lily."

My eyes widened. Grant had mentioned Lily, and he'd mentioned Leo, too. But I guess the connection between the two hadn't come up. The times we'd spoken about his ex-wife, it had seemed like he wanted nothing to do with her. So I found it interesting that he was the Big Brother to her real little brother. From what he'd told me, their mother was mentally ill, so this little boy had at least two unstable women in his life.

When it was our turn to order, Leo chose a double twist cone of vanilla and chocolate dipped in sprinkles, and I ordered a single scoop of chocolate dipped in chocolate crunchies. We went to sit at a nearby picnic table, where Grant met us a few minutes later.

He straddled the bench, swiped the cone out of my hand, and took a big lick. "Chocolate on chocolate." He winked. "Good choice."

"Everything okay with your grandfather?"

"Yeah. He's just getting tired, so my grandmother is going to take him home. He seems to get more confused when he's wiped out."

"I'm sorry I didn't get to meet her or see your grandfather again. But I understand." I stole my cone back from Grant.

"She's not going to be happy when she finds out I brought someone to the carnival and she didn't get to meet you. But if I'd told her, she would've insisted on coming over. I figured Pops needed to rest more than she needed to interrogate you."

I smiled. "Maybe she won't find out I was here."

Grant looked over at Leo. "Not a chance."

The three of us chatted for a while, and then I noticed two women looking over. The first one I didn't recognize, but the other I definitely knew.

"Isn't that your sister, Kate?"

Grant looked over. "Yup. And my other sister, Jillian. If we get up and run the other direction, we might get out unscathed."

I laughed. "I'm sure you're exaggerating."

He shook his head. "You're about to find out."

The two women walked over. "Hi," Jillian said. "Aren't you Ireland Richardson, the early morning news anchor?"

"I am. And you're Jillian, right?"

"I am. It's nice to meet you."

Kate's eyes flicked to Grant and back to me.

"How are you, Ireland?"

"I'm good. Enjoying the carnival. Everyone looks like they're having such a good time."

"It's a fun day." She tilted her head. "Are you a Big Sister?"

"No, but I met Liz earlier, and she gave me some information on the program. It sounds amazing, so I'm looking forward to learning more. I just came to meet Grant."

Kate squinted at her brother before returning her eyes to me. "Business meeting on a Sunday?"

I shook my head. "No. Grant and I are...dating, I guess."

Kate's eyebrow arched, and she and her sister immediately sat down at our table. "Dating, huh? Grant doesn't tell us anything personal. How long has this been going on?"

Grant hung his head and mumbled. "Should have made a run for it while we could."

I elbowed him. "A few weeks."

"Interesting. And you're on the new committee Grant is spearheading, right?"

"I am."

"Were you two together before the new committee, or did that come about after?"

If Kate was trying to be discreet about digging for something, she wasn't doing a very good job. And I had a pretty good idea what she was getting at. I'd been suspicious of Grant's motives as well.

"After."

Kate deepened her squint and glanced over at her brother, who completely avoided any eye contact.

She smirked. "Such a coincidence. He formed a committee, and now you're dating."

I chuckled. "Yeah. A big one, isn't it?"

Kate and I laughed with an unspoken understanding that broke the ice. After that, we talked for almost an hour. Grant and Leo disappeared to go play some carnival games, and when he came back alone, Grant didn't take a seat.

He looked at me. "You ready to get going?"

"Ummm... Sure." I smiled at Kate and Jillian. "It was really nice getting to talk to you."

"Let's have lunch one day soon," Kate said.

Grant rolled his eyes.

"I'd love that."

"Want me to give Leo a ride home?" he asked Kate.

"No, I got him. You two go have a nice evening."

We went to find Leo and told him we were leaving. In the parking lot, Grant took my hand, which gave me that warm feeling in my belly again.

"Where are you parked?" he asked.

I pointed. "All the way in the back. It was packed when I got here."

He walked me to my car. Bringing our still-joined hands up to his lips, he kissed my knuckles. "Come back to my place for a drink?"

"Aren't you sick of me yet? We spent the last two evenings together."

Grant's face fell. "No. Are you sick of me?"

I squeezed his hand. "I was teasing. Not at all. And I'd love to come back to your place. Did you mean the boat?"

He nodded.

I pushed up on my toes and pressed my lips to his in a soft kiss. "I'll meet you there."

The entire drive over, I felt an excited sort of nervous giddiness. I knew Grant had said he wasn't sure how he'd be in a relationship, but he'd introduced me to his sisters and Leo, and I'd already met his grandfather. For someone who wasn't sure about where he thought things could lead, it sure felt like we were taking steps in the right direction.

Still, Grant made me nervous; he had from the very start. Which was why I'd said I wanted to go slow. I knew in my head that was the right thing to do. The only problem was, I wasn't sure my heart was listening.

CHAPTER 20

Ireland

66 I was beginning to think you were going to stand me up," Grant said from the back of the boat. He'd changed into shorts and a T-shirt, and his feet were bare. Something about him in bare feet just made me smile. It seemed very un-Grant-like.

I held up a white bakery box. "I have the worst craving for cheesecake. I had to get some. Wait. Do you like cheesecake? I'm not sure we can see each other if you don't."

He held out a hand for me to climb the stairs and board. "Cheesecake is good. Though I'm not a big dessert eater." After I was on the boat, Grant kept my hand and used it to tug me to him. He wrapped his other hand around my neck and pulled my lips to meet his. "Unless you're on the menu."

My body reacted to the intimacy with a flush. His kiss literally knocked the wind out of me. When his lips moved to my neck, I dropped the cheesecake on the ground.

His voice was strained. "It's not easy to move slow with you. You bring dessert, and all I can think about is smearing it all over your body and licking it off."

Oh. My.

I'd just arrived, and already he had my panties wet.

Grant devoured my neck. I wasn't even sure how I remained standing.

But then the sound of nearby voices made him groan and pull back. People had come outside on the boat next door. Grant dragged a hand through his hair. "Fuck. You better stay out here while I get some wine. Privacy might be dangerous for you."

I bit my lip. "Or...I could help you inside."

Grant's green eyes darkened to almost gray. They raked down my body and back up again. "You sure about that?"

I swallowed and nodded.

Grant bent to pick up the cheesecake and smirked. "We'll be needing this."

It was only a few steps to get inside the cabin of Grant's boat, but in the time it took to go from the stern to the door, all of my desire seemed to turn into nerves. Grant shut the door behind us, and the outside world went quiet.

I looked around and noticed the shades were drawn. I remembered he'd told me he had different shades. These were most definitely the blackout ones, though the lights were on inside.

Grant caught my eye. "I closed them before you got here because the late-afternoon sun heats up the inside, not because I was planning on luring you in here. I can open them if it makes you more comfortable. The view of the sunset is going to be nice soon anyway."

I thought about the sunset we'd watched a few days ago. The view was spectacular. But if I were being honest, the view standing before me was pretty incredible, too. I took a few steps toward Grant and fisted his T-shirt in both of my hands. "I think I prefer privacy right now."

Grant's pupils dilated as he looked down at me. "Oh yeah?"

I nodded.

He looked back and forth between my eyes. Seeming to find what he was looking for, he lifted his chin toward the couch. "Go sit. We'll have dessert."

Something in the tone of his voice told me he wasn't just planning on bringing me a piece of cheesecake. It made my entire body zing with anticipation. Taking a seat on the couch, I watched as Grant sliced open the red string on the box and cut two pieces of the creamy cheesecake. He put both on one plate, took a fork from the drawer, and walked over to me, offering it.

"Only one plate and one fork... Are we sharing, or are you giving me two pieces?"

Grant didn't answer. Instead, he lifted the fork from the plate in my hands and scooped a big piece from one of the slices. He brought it to my lips, and I opened for him. The cake was delicious, but the way Grant was looking at me had me more focused on him than anything. He had a devilish glint in his eye as he watched me chew and swallow. I licked my lips, even though he hadn't made a mess.

"Good?" he asked.

"Delicious. Try some."

His smile was positively wicked. He set the fork on the plate and used two fingers to swipe a big piece of the second slice. Slowly, he brought his hand to my mouth, but when I parted my lips for him to feed me, he shook his head.

"Don't be greedy. You already had some." He smeared the cheesecake on my neck, trailing a slow line down over my throat, continuing on to my chest and down into my cleavage.

I gasped when his mouth swooped down to lick the creamy mess. He took his time, starting at my neck and licking and sucking as he slowly glided toward my cleavage. When he got to the upper swell of my breasts, he teased and flicked his tongue. The rise and fall of my chest sped up in unison with my labored breathing.

Grant looked up at me with hooded eyes from under his dark lashes. "You're right. Excellent cake."

I somehow managed to restrain myself from shoving his head back down when he sat up and took the fork in his hand again. This was his game, and I certainly didn't mind playing. Grant fed me another spoonful of cheesecake and again watched me chew and swallow. His eyes never left my lips.

When I finished, he set the fork back on the plate and scooped another piece with his fingers. My legs were crossed, and he used his free hand to cup under my knee and uncross them. He gently pressed at my knee to guide them open.

My breathing quickened as he took the cake and smeared it from the inside of one thigh just above my knee, all the way up to the sensitive skin right below my shorts. He looked up at me with the sexiest damn smile as he leaned forward to follow the trail.

This time, he wasn't as gentle as he'd been with my neck. He sucked and licked and nipped. Each little bite sent a bolt straight to my clit. By the time he'd worked his way up to the hem of my shorts, I was wiggling in my seat. I wanted to take his head and move it straight between my legs.

The wicked smirk on Grant's face as he lifted to upright told me he knew exactly what he was doing to me.

I breathed out. "You're a tease. I wouldn't have taken you for one."

"A tease is when someone offers you something and doesn't give it to you. I'm happy to give you anything you want." He tilted his head. "Tell me what you want, Ireland."

A million things went through my head. I wanted him to not stop at the top of my breast. I wanted him to nip at my nipple the same way he'd just done on the inside of my thigh. I wanted him to suck on my clit like he did my neck.

"I...I don't want you to stop."

He smiled and took the cake plate from my hand. "Lean back, but bring your ass to the edge of the couch."

Grant got on his knees in front of me. He took his thumb and rubbed it over my clit through my shorts. "Let's take these off."

My hands shook as I undid the button and pulled down the small zipper to my shorts. He smiled. "Lift."

I did, and he slid my shorts and panties down my legs and tossed them aside. Sitting before him bare, I suddenly felt very exposed.

"Open your legs wide for me."

I hesitated, and he looked up at me. "I've wanted to taste you since the minute I laid eyes on you." He paused and looked down. "Wider, Ireland."

Ignoring the urge to do the exact opposite, I spread my legs as wide as I could. Grant flashed a cocky smile of approval and licked his lips before burying his face against me. He licked me from one end to the other and flicked his tongue over my clit in delightful torture. Whatever shyness had me keeping my knees close together went out the door when he sucked my clit. My hips writhed, and I dug my fingers into his hair and pulled. It felt so incredibly good that tears started to prickle at the corners of my eyes.

"Oh, God." I jerked when Grant thrust his tongue inside me.

"I want to drink every bit of your juices. Come on my tongue, sweetheart."

The vibration of his words against my tender skin made my body tremble. Grant licked his way back up to my clit and then suddenly two of his fingers were pushing inside me. It all became too much, too fast, and he groaned and coaxed me to come in his mouth.

When I lifted my ass from the couch and dug my nails into his scalp, Grant held me in place. He curved his fingers inside me while increasing the suction. "Oh God...oh...yes...yes."

My orgasm ripped through me almost violently. I thrashed my head from side to side as Grant massaged and stroked the tender spot inside of me until every last pulse rippled through my body. I felt boneless as I came down, panting and seeing stars through closed eyelids.

Eventually Grant stood up, only to lean down and scoop me off the couch, gathering me in his arms. He cradled me against him as he sat down where I'd been seated. I leaned my head against his chest, and a goofy smile spread across my lips.

"That was the best cheesecake ever."

Grant chuckled. He pressed his lips to mine. "You taste better than any dessert."

I blushed, even though the man's head had just been buried in the most intimate of spots. "I'm sorry I'm sort of useless at the moment. I just need a minute to get my bearings, and then I can take care of you."

Grant's eyebrows drew together. "This isn't tit for tat, Ireland."

"I know...but I haven't even touched you."

He pulled his head back to look in my eyes. "I'm fine. Don't get me wrong, I'll be taking a long shower later. But the first time I come with you, I want to be buried inside of you. I pushed my way to what just happened here, but I won't push for that. When you're ready, you'll let me know."

I sighed. "Honestly, I wouldn't have stopped you if that's where things had gone just now."

"Your body was ready," he paused and tapped one finger against my temple. "But how about this?"

I wanted to tell him he was wrong, but he was one hundred percent right. My body wanted him, but my head hadn't gotten there yet. The fact that he cared about the two being aligned meant a lot to me.

I smiled. "Thank you."

"For the orgasm or for not pushing you?"

"Both."

A little while later, Grant went to the bathroom, and I got myself dressed and lifted the shade to look outside. The sun was starting to go down. He really did get spectacular sunsets here at the marina. Grant came back and wrapped his arm around my waist. He kissed my shoulder. "Want to go outside and watch the sunset? I'll cut you a fresh piece of cheesecake and let you finish it this time."

I smiled. "Okay."

We sat on the bow of the boat in comfortable silence. Grant leaned against one of the mast poles with his knees bent, and I sat between his legs, leaning back against his chest. We sipped wine and pointed out things we saw in the clouds. We hadn't really talked about today at all, since we went straight to getting out some pent-up frustration when I arrived, and I was curious to learn more about Leo—though I didn't want to look like I was needling now that I knew Lily was his sister. So I started with something more playful.

"So...your sisters were really nice."

Grant sighed. "They're ball busters and were loading up with as much ammunition today as they could."

I smiled. "You mean like how your sister was suspicious that you'd created an entire committee so we would have a forum to spend time together?"

He shook his head. "I'm never going to live that one down. Honestly, I have no fucking clue what the hell came over me to pull that shit."

"So you're finally admitting you made up that committee just to have a reason to call me?"

"No. That committee wasn't even a thought when I called you. I just wanted to talk to you. I figured seeing how things were going your first day back would be reason enough to reach out. But you had to call me out on it, asking if I called any other employees to check how their days were going. So I panicked and made that shit up while I was on the phone."

I tilted my head up to look at him and smiled.

"Don't gloat, sweetheart. You're putty in my hands as much as I am in yours. I just don't lord it over you."

"I am not putty in your hands."

"No? Then give me that mouth, and let's see if you stop me when I'm feeling you up for all the neighbors enjoying the sunset to watch."

"You're an ass."

"Maybe. But I still would bet this boat that if we start kissing, you wouldn't stop me from slipping my fingers into your shorts and fingering that sweet pussy of yours."

My jaw dropped open.

Grant leaned down and kissed my chin. "Careful," he whispered in my ear. "You keep that mouth open too long, and I might fill it."

I wanted to tell him he was nuts, but honestly, even hearing him *say* "fingering that sweet pussy" had between my legs tingling again. So he wasn't that off base. Rather than challenge him, I turned my head forward and settled against his chest.

"So Leo and you have an interesting rapport."

"Kid's new hobby is being a pain in my ass."

I laughed. "He said you've been his Big for a long time."

Grant was quiet for a moment. "He's my ex-wife's half brother. They share the same mentally unstable mother. He was born in the hospital while his mother was a patient in the psych ward. Father is some guy she met when they were living in a halfway house. She went off her meds when she got pregnant and wound up back in a psychiatric facility. Kid was in foster care by the third day of his life."

"That's tough. And he's still in foster care?"

"He's living with his father's aunt, who's had temporary custody the last few years. But she's older and not really equipped for a teenager. I tried to get custody at one point a few years back when he'd gotten in trouble for stealing, but family trumps a single, non-blood relative who lives on a boat and works sixty hours a week."

I liked how honest he'd become with me, and that I didn't have to pry things out of him like at the beginning. But I really loved that he was the type of man who'd try to get custody of a troubled kid who was the sibling of his ex-wife. I turned around and looked into his eyes, pressing my lips to his.

"What was that for?" he asked.

I shrugged. "I just like you. The more I get to know you, the more I find to like."

Grant looked away for a moment. "You know how you said you don't always see things so clearly when you first date a guy, and you have a habit of picking assholes?"

"Yes."

He looked directly into my eyes. "You're doing it again."

My face wrinkled. "What do you mean?"

"Fairytales have a Prince Charming and a bad guy. Life isn't so black and white. Sometimes Prince Charming is both."

"I...I don't understand."

Grant shook his head. "I don't want you to be disappointed."

"But why would I be disappointed?"

"Ireland, I'm the kind of man who brings women to an apartment I don't live in to fuck them."

I blinked a few times. "Okay...well, you've mentioned that. But I'm here right now. And you know you could have pushed things and slept with me when we were downstairs. Yet you didn't."

He stared at me. "I don't want to hurt you, Ireland."

"Okay. I believe you. But I'm a big girl. If you do, I'll live. You don't need to keep warning me away."

Grant closed his eyes. After a solid minute, he opened them and nodded. "Okay."

The mood definitely changed after that little chat. I had to work early in the morning, so once it got fully dark, I told him I needed to get going.

Grant walked me to my car. "Thank you for coming to the carnival today," he said.

"I had fun. You're leaving for a business trip tomorrow, right?"

"Yeah. I have a seven a.m. flight."

"We'll both be up at the ass crack of dawn then," I smiled.

He leaned down and planted a gentle kiss on my lips. "I'll talk to you during the week."

"Okay."

The entire ride home, I went over everything that had happened that day. It had seemed like such a perfect afternoon, followed by a mind-blowing orgasm in the evening, and a picture-perfect sunset. Yet Grant couldn't seem to leave things that way. He had to tell me what a bad guy he was, even though everything I'd witnessed so far in my time spent with him had shown me just the opposite. I went round and round, analyzing and overanalyzing where things had taken that turn, and I came back to one commonality. Every time we talked about Grant's ex-wife, he took a step back.

There had to be a piece to the puzzle I was still missing.

CHAPTER 21

Grant – 7 years ago

"She's perfect." I kissed Lily's forehead and looked down at the tightly swaddled little princess. Eight pounds, four ounces of perfection. One little foot kept finding its way out of the blanket. It was hard to imagine how something so small could make such a big footprint on my heart so fast. But that's how it happened. I saw her face, and my heart immediately swelled inside my chest.

The last few months had been pretty damn amazing. Pregnancy seemed to agree with Lily—or maybe it was the therapist she'd been seeing. I wasn't sure, but she'd been so happy and excited through it all. We'd talked a lot about our own screwed-up home lives over the last nine months and how our personal experiences had taught us so much—what *not* to do. We were both excited to give our child the kind of life we'd dreamed of having with our own parents. We wanted the kind of life Pia and William had given me.

I pulled the blanket up and covered my little girl's foot. "Is it weird to say I feel different already?"

Lily smiled. "It's only been two hours. So maybe."

I couldn't describe what had changed the moment my daughter was born. I looked into her eyes and saw nothing but innocence, and suddenly the gravity of being a father hit me. I wasn't just here to change diapers and pay college tuition someday. My job was to protect her from all of the things in life that chip away at the innocence we're all born with. My mother's drugs and Lily's mother's mental illness had made us grow up too fast. But that wouldn't happen with my little girl. I'd protect her from the evils of the world as long as I could.

Lily rubbed her nose with the baby's. "How about Leilani?"

I'd wanted to pick out names over the last few months, but Lily said a child was like art. You didn't name it. It gave you its name when it was complete. To be honest, I'd thought that was a load of crap. But as I looked down at my daughter, my eyes roaming her beautiful face, I realized my wife had been right.

I nodded. "Leilani. That feels right, doesn't it?"

Lily looked up at me. "It's perfect. Just like she is."

I kissed the top of my wife's head. "Like you both are. My girls. Lily and Leilani. I'm going to take care of you two forever."

CHAPTER 22

Ireland

"Thanks, George." The guy from the mailroom had just come around and dropped off a package. On top was a legal-size manila envelope with my name across it.

I kicked off my shoes and sat down at my desk to slice it open. Inside was a Notice of Hearing for my zoning variance, and there was a yellow sticky stuck to the middle of the page.

Mr. Lexington asked me to pass this along when it came in. – Millie

At first I was confused. What in the heck was Grant doing with the paperwork for my house? Then I noticed the date of the hearing—a week from today. The architect had told me the building department was months behind. Had I even mentioned that to Grant? Ahhh... I'd told Santa Grant. How the hell had he done this?

I picked up my phone and started to text him, but decided to call instead. I wanted to remind him about something else anyway.

Grant picked up on the first ring.

"Are you really Santa Claus or something?"

He chuckled. "Hang on a second." I heard the sound of the phone being covered and then a muffled *"Excuse me for a minute, gentlemen,"* before a door opened and shut and Grant returned to the line.

"I'm guessing you got the paperwork from the City."

"Yes. But how?"

"I have a friend at the building department who owed me a favor. I called it in and asked him to prioritize whatever you needed."

I shook my head. "I can't believe you did that. Thank you so much."

"Can't have my employees homeless, now can I?"

"Is that why you did it? Because I'm your employee? If that's the case, I think I overheard Jim in Accounting say his landlord was kicking him out of his apartment so his daughter could move in. I'll stop over and tell him you're on it and will be finding him a new place to live."

Grant chuckled. "Can't let one slide, can you?"

I leaned back in my chair. "Thank you so much for doing that. It was really sweet. And here I was, thinking it was already Wednesday and I hadn't heard from you, so you might be blowing me off."

Grant was quiet for a minute. "Figured it might be best to give you a little space."

"Is that what *you* want? Space?"

"What do you want me to say, Ireland? That I haven't been able to get you out of my mind since the day we met? That I've jerked off every day this week to the way you looked when you came on my tongue the other day?"

"If that's true, then yes."

He blew out a breath, and I pictured worry lines on his forehead while he raked a hand through his hair.

When he went quiet again, I got up and shut my office door. "Would it help if I shared, too? You aren't alone in this. I haven't been able to stop thinking of you either. In fact, I thought of you last night while I was in the bathtub."

Grant's voice was gruff. "Ireland..."

"Remember when you told me you thought you could slip your hand into my shorts while we were outside on the boat and get me off while people watched? That I basically couldn't control myself once we started kissing?"

He grunted a yes.

"Well, I shut my eyes and imagined that. You slipped your fingers in...but since you weren't around, I had to use my own and pretend they were yours."

"Ireland..."

"It's funny—the tone of my voice while I was saying your name over and over last night was about the same as yours is right now. Almost sounds painful, doesn't it?"

"Fuck...." He let out a loud exhale.

I smiled. "Anyway, I think I interrupted a meeting when I called. I'm sure you're really busy. I just wanted to say thank you to Santa Claus and remind you about the wedding Saturday. I'll let you get back to work."

Grant groaned. "You don't really think I'm going to be able to walk back into my meeting after you just told me you masturbated while pretending your fingers were mine, do you?"

"Oh." I giggled. "I guess it is a little easier for me to hide my arousal than you."

"Yeah, thanks."

"If you want, I'll stay on the phone and tell you more about my bath last night while you slip into the men's room and take care of business."

"As tempting as that may be, I think I'll just take a quick walk."

I smiled. "Okay. Well, thank you again for pulling the strings at the Building Commission."

"No problem."

"Have a good afternoon. Hope your meeting isn't too *hard*."

"I look forward to repaying the torture, Ireland. Very soon."

After I hung up, I sat in my office smiling. I felt better than I had in days. Grant might not have called because he was trying to give me some space, but what he'd done to get my zoning variance told me lack of contact hadn't stopped him from thinking about us. Not to mention, I was giddy hearing him say he'd done the same thing as I had during his shower.

I left for the day around one, which was technically the end of my workday since I started at five, though I rarely left before three. I needed to pick up my dress from the tailor for Mia's wedding this weekend and run a bunch of errands. Since my workday ended when most people were heading to lunch, the lobby was bustling. Just as I was about to walk out, Grant's sister Kate happened to be walking into the building.

Seeing me, she smiled. "Hey. I was going to call you. I enjoyed torturing my brother at the carnival, but I wasn't kidding when I said I'd love to have lunch."

I smiled. "I'd like that. When did you have in mind?"

She shrugged. "I'm just coming back from a meeting and haven't eaten yet. Now, if you're not heading somewhere else?"

I had a mile-long to-do list, but...I hadn't eaten anything other than a power bar on the way to the office at four o'clock this morning. Plus, I had so many unanswered questions about Grant, and who better than his sister to shed a little light on the enigma? So, screw it. *Why not?* The tailor would still be open in an hour or two.

"Sure. Let's do it."

• • •

"So...my brother really likes you, I can tell," Kate announced.

She and I had made small talk through most of lunch. I was relieved when she not-so-subtly brought our conversation around to Grant during coffee.

I smiled and lifted my cup to my lips. "I like him, too. Though sometimes he can be..."

While I was thinking of the right words—maybe *difficult, hard to read, abrupt*—Kate filled in the blank.

"A total jackass."

I laughed. "Yeah, that."

She smiled warmly. "He doesn't often bring women around, not casually anyway. He'll bring a date to something formal that requires one, but it's been years since I saw him with a woman while he was dressed in a pair of jeans. It's like women became necessary companions for social functions and, well, I'm sure for other purposes we don't need to discuss unless you want to see my lunch all over this table. But they aren't really a part of his life anymore."

From what Grant had told me about his dating, his sister's assessment was on point. He kept women very separate and distant from the things that mattered in his life. But while Kate's comment wasn't a surprise, I hoped she could shed light on *why* he was that way.

I nodded. "When we've talked about his previous relationships, that's pretty much what he alluded to. Actually, he didn't allude. He came right out and said he was upfront with the women he's dated the last few years—he wasn't looking for a long-term relationship."

Kate frowned. "You two seemed pretty relationship-y on Sunday. Something's different than the way I've seen him with other women. He's warm, not cold. I watched you guys walk out to the parking lot; he even took your hand."

"He's trying. But we take a step forward, and then he retreats."

Kate sighed. "My brother has trouble letting people in."

I wasn't sure I should be discussing the things Grant had confided in me about his marriage. But I knew that had to be the root of all his cynicism on relationships. He'd been burned badly and was afraid to get too close to the fire again.

"His marriage obviously had a profound impact on who he is today."

"Has he...opened up to you about his marriage?"

"Somewhat. He's told me about Lily's mental health issues."

Kate was quiet for a moment. She seemed to be debating something or lost in thought. Finally she said, "Did he...go into detail about how it ended?"

"Not really. It was more general, I guess."

Kate nodded. Again she was quiet as she considered her words. Then she reached across the table and covered my hand with hers. "My brother is like an oyster. He's shut tight, and he might never open, or you just may be the one who pries him loose. If that happens, I promise you'll find a pearl waiting for you."

• • •

On Thursday morning, Grant called and said he was taking an earlier flight home than expected and asked me to meet him for dinner. He said he would come straight from the airport because he knew my routine included being in bed by eight o'clock on weeknights.

I agreed to meet him at a restaurant not too far from my house, and when I arrived, I found him already seated at the bar. A woman in a tight green dress stood next to him, talking, and her hand rested on his back as she spoke.

"Hey. Sorry if I'm a few minutes late," I said as I approached.

Grant stood and kissed me on the lips. "Flight landed early. You're not late." He kept his hand on my back, and the woman stood there waiting to be introduced.

Grant cleared his throat. "Ireland, this is Shannon. She's the hostess here. She used to work over at the steakhouse next to our office."

I smiled. "Nice to meet you."

Though she showed me her pearly whites with a full, plastic smile, the quick drop of her eyes to assess me said a lot. When a woman is standing with a man and another woman approaches, she sizes her up for one of two reasons—to see who her competition is or to see who the man she's lost has moved on to. I wasn't sure which this was.

"You, too," she finally said. She reached out and touched Grant's arm. "I'll check to see if your table is ready."

When she walked away, Grant buried his face in my hair. He took a deep breath in. "Mmm... I missed you."

"Really? It seemed like you had good company..."

Grant arched a brow. "Do I detect jealousy?"

"Do I have a reason to be jealous?"

He shook his head. "Not at all. But full disclosure, Shannon and I did go out a few times."

I frowned. "Did she visit your apartment?"

Grant looked down. "I know you didn't think I was a virgin. Though if I'd known she worked here, I wouldn't have picked this place." His eyes rose and locked with mine. "I get it, though. I wouldn't be happy in the presence of anyone you've been with."

His not belittling how I felt made me feel better. Besides, I was being silly. We both had pasts. I shrugged. "It's fine. I'm a big girl."

Shannon walked back over to us. "Your table's ready."

After we followed a woman he used to sleep with back to the table, it made me realize we'd never spoken about seeing other people. The thought of him with anyone else made me crazy. Though, I suppose technically, we both had the right to do it.

Grant pulled out my chair, and once we were both seated, Shannon said she'd send the waiter over to take our drink order. I shook out my cloth napkin and laid it over my lap.

"We've never spoken about seeing other people."

Grant had picked up a glass of water and froze with it halfway to his mouth. "I assumed we were exclusive at this point."

"Oh. Okay."

"The thought of you with another man makes me feel irrational."

I smiled. "I feel the same way."

He leaned across the table. "I'm glad we've had this talk. I thought it was torture to be near you and not know what it feels like to be inside you. But apparently there are way worse things than not fucking you, such as imagining that someone else is."

I laughed. "Well, put that thought out of your head. How was your trip?"

Grant shook out his napkin. "Productive. We're buying a building on the east coast and going to relocate a few of our smaller businesses' headquarters around the city into one building. It's a good time to buy."

"Oh, that's exciting."

"I thought it was. Though I'm realizing how much time I'm going to have to spend out there to get it done. I like New York, but it's a long trip."

"I haven't been there in years. I'd like to go at Christmas. I'm sure it's touristy, but I think it would be nice to skate at Rockefeller Center and wait in line to see the windows at Bloomingdale's."

"You sound like Leo."

"He wants to go to New York at Christmas?"

Grant nodded. "Maybe we'll take him."

I got that warm, fuzzy feeling in my stomach again. He didn't hesitate when he spoke of things in the future, like it was a given we'd be together.

The waiter came over to take our drink order. I loved that Grant remembered the wine I liked, yet looked to me for approval when ordering it. I also really loved the five o'clock shadow lining his masculine jaw, and the blade of a nose that was his profile when he handed the wine menu back to the waiter.

I'd been hesitant to mention that a bunch of us had booked hotel rooms down the block from Mia's wedding. It would be odd to not stay in the same room, and yet I hadn't been sure I was ready for that. Though we'd just confirmed we were in an exclusive relationship and were talking about plans a few months away, so what was I waiting for? God knows desire wasn't the problem. I only had to look across the table to get my feathers all ruffled.

So when the waiter walked away, I decided to go for it. "Umm...this weekend... Most of the wedding party is going to stay at the Park Place Hotel down the block from the restaurant. This way everyone can indulge and not have to worry about getting home. And Mia is having a brunch the next morning at the hotel restaurant. I have a room booked, if you would want to stay."

"Is that really a question?"

I laughed. "I guess not. But I wasn't going to assume."

"Let me make it easy for you in the future. If the invitation involves you and the potential of you being naked, count me in."

What had started as an awkward arrival with the green dress now turned into a fun and comfortable dinner. Shannon passed by a few times, and I could honestly say Grant didn't notice. He had a way of making me feel like the only woman in the room without even trying. I *felt* all of his attention, because I actually had it.

I needed to use the ladies' room, so I excused myself after Grant ordered a slice of cheesecake for us to share with a wink. When I finished up in the stall, I opened the door to find Shannon lining her lips in the mirror. Her eyes slanted to mine in the reflection. She wasn't surprised to see me.

"How long have you and Grant been together?"

I stepped to the sink to wash my hands. I had no desire to chitchat with this woman, or any woman Grant had slept with. But a sadistic part of me was curious.

"Not too long." I tilted my head and flashed an insincere smile. "He mentioned you two were...friendly."

"Is that what he told you? That we were friends?"

I dried off my hands. "No. But I thought it sounded nicer than fuck buddies."

She squinted at me. "We were together for about six months."

That surprised me. Though I wouldn't give her the satisfaction of seeing it. Instead, I followed her lead and started to line my lips in the mirror. She watched me in silence.

I blotted and looked at her pointedly. "Did you want to tell me something else?"

"I thought I'd give you a little woman-to-woman advice. When he tells you he's not cut out for a relationship, believe him. He says one thing and acts another way. It'll make you think you're different than the rest. He's very convincing. I remember one time my car had gotten towed, and I asked him if he could take me to grab it after work from the impound lot. When I walked out of work, my car was parked in my usual spot in the parking lot. He'd even gotten it washed for me. He's very sweet when he wants to be. Took me a year to get over him."

Even though my insides were freaking out, I kept my face stoic. I dropped my lipstick into my purse and walked behind her. Catching her eye in the mirror, I said, "Thanks for the advice. But you're fooling yourself if you think it took a year for you to get over him. Obviously, you're still not."

I walked out of the bathroom and stopped in the hall to catch my breath, feeling completely rattled.

Clearly, the woman was still hung up on Grant and wanted to shake things up between us. Oddly, that isn't what upset me. It was what she'd said about him getting her car for her. For the last few days, I'd been feeling like everything with Grant was good, feeling the first sense of security that maybe he wouldn't rip my heart out. And why? Because of the simplest thing—he'd done something thoughtful by taking care of my problem with the Building Commission.

Not all that different than getting Shannon's car out of impound, was it?

CHAPTER 23

Grant

Something was off with Ireland. I'd sensed it the other night during dessert, but chalked it up to her being tired since she got up so early in the morning. Yesterday I'd texted to ask if she wanted to catch lunch, and she didn't respond until long after she was home, claiming she'd been swamped at work. Now today, I could see she had read my message, and yet an hour later, still no response.

So against my better judgment, I walked my ass across the street and took the elevator up to the News floor.

Ireland was standing while talking on the phone when our eyes caught. The change in her expression confirmed my suspicion that something was off. She hung up just as I entered and closed the door behind me.

"I don't like to come over here because I don't want to make things difficult for you at work."

She forced a smile. "I appreciate that."

"But you leave me no choice when you avoid me."

"I'm not avoiding you."

I made a face that said she was full of shit.

Ireland sighed and sat down. "Fine."

"What's going on?"

"That woman the other night just freaked me out, I guess."

My brows drew together. At first I wasn't even sure who the hell she was referring to. "Shannon?"

She nodded.

"We stopped seeing each other probably two years ago. I had no idea she worked there."

"I believe you. It's just something she said."

I tried to think back, but I couldn't remember Shannon saying much of anything once Ireland had arrived. "What did she say?"

"She came into the ladies' room when I was in there and said you guys had dated for six months, not just gone out a few times."

"I honestly have no idea how long it lasted... Maybe we went out six times over four months, at the most. It sounds like she was trying to make it out to be something more than it was."

"She also said it took her almost a year to get over you."

I frowned. "I had no idea she followed you into the ladies' room. I'm sorry if she felt that way. But like I told you, I was honest with women I had any type of arrangement with from the start."

"I know. And she said that, too. But..." She shook her head.

This was all my fault. I was fucking things up. Ireland was afraid to be with me because I'd given her no reason to feel secure. The best I'd offered was that I wasn't sure what I was capable of. If it wasn't me pulling back, it was her. The two of us were playing a game of perpetual chicken, and it was time for me to either get the hell off the road or say fuck it and crash into her and hang on.

I leaned forward. "I'm crazy about you, Ireland. The only other woman I told that to, I married. I'm sorry for giving you doubt. I know I've done that. But..." I made sure to look directly into her eyes. "I want to make it work with you. For the last seven years, I didn't *want* to make anything work. I think about you at eleven a.m. when I'm busy in a meeting. The last seven years, I only thought about women at eleven p.m. when I was lonely. There's a big fucking difference."

Ireland's eyes started to water. "I want it to work, too."

I smiled. "So let's do that, sweetheart. Let's just let it work."

She took a minute, maybe to digest everything I'd said, I wasn't sure.

But then she smiled. "Okay."

I let out a breath. "Do you want to get some lunch or what?"

She nodded. "I need about twenty minutes to finish up."

I stood. "I'll order us something. Meet me over in my office when you're done."

"Okay."

I turned around to open the door, but I stopped with my hand on the handle. "Take off your underwear before you come. Because when we're done with lunch, I'm going to eat you on my desk."

• • •

The bride is supposed to be the center of attention at a wedding, but I couldn't keep my eyes off of the woman in royal blue. The sexy spaghetti-strap dress hugged every one of Ireland's luscious curves, and her pinned-up hair showcased a long, delicate neck and that collarbone I loved so much. Her skin was creamy and smooth, perfectly unblemished, and I sat in my seat salivating at the thought of sinking my teeth into it tonight while I tore that pretty dress from her body. She squinted and smirked as she walked toward where I sat watching her from across the room.

"You look devious right now," she said, arriving at the table.

I took her hand and tugged her to sit on my lap. "That's because I'm thinking devious thoughts."

She giggled. "Oh yeah? Tell me about them on the dance floor. I think I'm done with wedding party duties, so I'm all yours for the rest of the night."

"I like the sound of that."

Out on the dance floor, I pulled her close and rested my cheek against hers. I used the opportunity to whisper in her ear. "Have I told you how beautiful you look tonight?"

"You did. But that's okay. I don't mind hearing it again."

"Women don't usually wear dresses from a wedding party a second time, right?"

"Usually, no. But I think I might get use out of this one. It's so pretty and simple. It doesn't look like a typical maid-of-honor dress."

I spun us around. "I'll buy you a new one."

Ireland's cute little nose wrinkled. "Oh my God, did I get something on it?"

"No, but by morning it's going to be shredded."

Her eyes widened. "It's ripped? Where?"

"Relax. It's not ripped...yet. But I'm literally going to tear it from your body later."

She smiled. "Is that what you were thinking when I walked over? You had such a devilish face."

"It's the only thing I've been able to think about since I picked you up tonight."

She tucked her head in so we were cheek to cheek again and whispered in my ear, "Remember when we danced at the fundraiser?"

"I do."

"My entire body was tingly while I was in your arms, and I had to pretend to be unaffected while we danced."

I smiled. "And I had to keep my hips at a distance so you didn't feel how hard you were making me."

"I guess we've both been attracted to each other from the beginning."

"Sweetheart, you have no idea. You had my curiosity piqued with a drunken email that told me to go to hell."

We danced in comfortable silence for a minute. One song ended and a new one began. I was grateful it was another slow song so I had a reason to keep Ireland in my arms. I shut my eyes and enjoyed the moment. Though the woman in my arms must've been looking around.

"I don't want a big wedding like this," she said.

Normally, a woman even mentioning the word *wedding* had me running for the hills. But not this time. I wanted to hear more.

"Were you one of those little girls who played bride when you were a kid? When I was little, my sisters used to spend an entire day making decorations for the living room for their pretend weddings. They'd take turns wearing our mother's wedding dress, and my mother would make me stand in as the groom. I hated it."

She laughed. "That must've been adorable."

"It was more like torture."

She sighed. "I didn't have any siblings, and my parents had a screwed-up relationship. So maybe that's why I never really imagined my wedding as a little girl."

That made me hold her tighter. "I'm sorry."

"It's okay. I'm not sure if little girls dreaming about weddings is so healthy anyway. I didn't play bride, but I definitely played news anchor. I spent hours in front of the mirror talking into my hairbrush handle. At least I didn't grow up chasing some fantasy of what a wedding is supposed to be."

"So no big white dress and three hundred people at a catering hall then?"

She shook her head. "Nope. I want to be barefoot on a beach somewhere. Maybe at sunset with a few friends and close family, and lights hanging from palm trees while a local calypso band plays."

I smiled. "That sounds nice." It was the first time in forever that I'd discussed anything to do with a wedding without comparing it to my and Lily's fiasco. I had no desire to think of my ex-wife when Ireland was in my arms. With every woman I'd been with since my divorce, I'd wanted that constant reminder—wanted to remember why I needed to keep my distance. Yet with Ireland, I wanted to forget it and move on.

The rest of the evening, we alternated talking to her friends, hanging out with the bride and groom, and dancing together. She even made me dance to some pop music, which I never did. But it was worth it to watch her tits bounce up and down while she jumped. By the end of the night, I couldn't wait to get her back to the hotel alone. I'd admitted I couldn't wait to rip the dress off of her, but I knew I would follow her lead as to where she wanted things to go. She'd invited me to stay the night, but I still wasn't sure if she was ready to take the next step.

So I slowed things down once we were in her suite. I opened wine and handed it to her while she looked out at the water from the bedroom window.

"Thank you."

I had to shove my free hand into my pocket to stop myself from touching her. One touch while we were alone in a room with nothing but a bed, and I could be done for. So instead, I sipped my wine and stared out at the sea with her.

She turned to look at me. "You're awfully quiet since we got here."

"Am I?"

She nodded. "Mmm-hmm. And you're awfully... far away. For a man who told me my dress was going to be shredded by morning, I figured any quiet would be because your tongue was down my throat, and the farthest we'd make it into the room would be my back against the door."

I turned to look at her. "I'm trying to be a gentleman."

She tilted her head. "Why?"

"Because I wasn't sure of your expectations for the evening. I didn't want to assume that your invitation to stay tonight meant you were ready for anything more than sharing a room."

Ireland set her wine glass on the table next to her. She reached up and started to unfasten an earring. "If you weren't feeling uncertain, what would you want?"

She set the earring down on the table next to her full wine glass and began to unfasten the second one.

"What do you mean? What would I want how?" I needed to be sure what she was asking, even though it sounded pretty clearly like she wanted to know what we'd be doing at this very moment if she were game for anything.

"To happen this evening between us. Sexually, I mean."

I drank a big gulp of my wine while she set the other earring on the table. "You sure you want that answer?"

"I do. I want to hear your honest answer." She smiled, turned around, and gave me her back. "Would you mind unzipping me?"

Fuck. I swallowed. "Well, I want to spread you wide on that big bed and eat your pussy for starters. Make you dripping wet."

Ireland's voice became huskier. "Anything else?"

I reached for her zipper. My hand shook because of how much effort it took to keep my physical self-control. The sound of the teeth slowly coming apart echoed throughout the quiet room.

"Plenty else. I'd lift you up onto the dresser behind me. I've already scoped it out, and it's the perfect height to fuck you while standing up. I want to watch you come and look into your eyes while I plunge as deep as I can and fill you with my cum."

She laughed nervously. "That's pretty specific."

"I'm not done." I reached the bottom of the zipper and couldn't help myself. I slipped my hand inside her dress and ran my fingers up her spine. "Then we'll take a shower together, and I'll hold your ass in my hands with your legs wrapped around my waist and your back against the tile. When you start to come on my cock, I'll slip my finger into your ass so you feel me inside of you in every way possible."

She shivered, so I took that as a sign she wanted to hear more. "After that, I'll let you get some sleep, and in the morning, we'll have breakfast together. And by that, I mean, I'll fill your mouth with my cock while I eat your pussy. You'll be on top, so you'll think you have control. But when you start to come on my face, I'll lift my hips and push into your throat a little farther, then I'll fill it with my hot cum."

I used my hands to guide Ireland to turn around. The look on her face was a mixture of shocked and aroused. It was sexy as all hell.

I cupped her cheeks. "Too much?"

She let out a shaky laugh. "I can never accuse you of holding back, can I?"

"What about you?" I ran my fingers along her collarbone. "What do you want?"

She held my eyes while she reached up and pulled the straps from her dress and loosened it from her shoulders. With the back undone, she let go and the material fell to the floor, into a puddle of blue at her feet.

"I'm game for everything you mentioned—except I'd like to add one thing I haven't been able to stop thinking about."

She looked so gorgeous standing before me in nothing but a lacy, royal blue bra and panties. Her ample tits practically spilled over the little cups. Distracted, I'd heard her speak, but didn't really comprehend a word of what she'd said.

I shook my head. "I'm sorry. What did you say?"

Her lips curved to a wicked grin. "I said I wanted to add one thing to your plans. Is that okay?"

"Whatever you want."

Ireland's eyes sparkled, right before she dropped to her knees.

Oh shit.

I had the strongest desire to close my eyes and thank the dear Lord for getting this woman drunk enough to write a scathing email, but I couldn't take my eyes off the sight of Ireland on her knees in front of me. She unbuckled my pants and unzipped me while I stood, unable to form words. When her little hand reached in and squeezed my already hard cock, I thought I might come then and there.

I hissed. "I'm not going to last, sweetheart."

She looked up and smiled as she fisted my dick. "It's okay. We have all night."

She pumped my cock twice, slowly, while she wet her lips, and then she lowered her jaw and slid me inside. There was no preamble, no licking my head and swirling her tongue around my crown, the way most women seemed to like to do—which was nice and all, but totally unnecessary when a man is raring to go already. I wasn't sure if I should appreciate that Ireland seemed to know that, or if it should bother me that she did, but as she started to bob her head, I couldn't even remember what I'd been considering debating.

Once my cock was inside her beautiful mouth, she lowered her jaw a little more and shocked the crap out of me by swallowing.

Fuck me. She can deep throat. I'm done.

Just as fast as I was down her throat, she pulled back and let her flattened tongue glide along the underside of my dick as it slid almost all the way back out. Her eyelashes batted, and as she looked up at me, I could see the mirth in her gaze.

"Jesus Christ, Ireland."

She slid back down and again took me all the way into her throat. I had to look up at the ceiling to keep myself from being a two-pump chump who finished before she'd really started. Watching her on her knees, swallowing my cock, was too much to handle. I groaned and reached down to tangle my fingers in her hair.

I tried not to look down, or watch her head as it bobbed up and down each time my cock went in and out of her throat, but I couldn't fucking help myself. The sight was just too incredible to miss. Ireland took me deep a few more times and then switched from long, deep sucks to short, fast pumps with her mouth and hand.

It was seriously the most brilliant thing I'd ever felt. It was like I'd died and gone to porn star heaven.

I tried to hold back, but she made it damn near impossible. Especially when she reached up and urged my hands into her hair to guide the rhythm. She'd basically given me license to fuck her face. As much as I would have liked to stand here and do that all day long, I only made it three pumps more. The urge to finish was too strong, no matter how hard I tried.

I'd told her I wanted to come down her throat, and I did, more than anything, but I also wasn't an asshole. She might deep throat like a porn star, but she was a woman I respected. So I had to warn her.

"Ireland...baby. *Fuck*. I'm gonna...come."

But she didn't move away. I was just about to warn her again, just in case she hadn't heard me. When I looked down, Ireland's eyes were shut, but sensing me, she opened them and looked up.

"Babe, I'm gonna come."

She responded by sucking me in so deep, I thought I might never come out—not that I wanted to. Ireland

Saint James's throat was my nirvana, and I never wanted to leave. But she'd heard me loud and clear that time, and she made sure I knew it. She wanted me to come down her throat, and I was fucking thrilled to oblige. With the groan of her name and one more thrust, I stopped moving my hips and let go, filling her throat with a never-ending stream.

I barely had the strength to pull her to her feet when she was done.

"Jesus Christ, Ireland. How the hell did you learn to do that?" I shook my head, still lightheaded from my release. "Forget it. I don't want to know."

Ireland giggled. "I told you I liked to watch men being pleasured. Might have picked up a thing or two."

I looked up at the ceiling. *Thank you, Lord.* Any answer other than her learning it by watching a *video* would have been totally unacceptable.

I smiled. "You couldn't be more perfect if I'd made you myself."

"By the way, I'm on the pill."

It was going to be one hell of a long night.

CHAPTER 24

Ireland

I once read an article that said the average time spent on foreplay was fourteen minutes. Obviously in the beginning things usually went a little longer for a couple, but I'd never spent two hours fooling around with a man without getting to sex—even when foreplay was all that was going to happen.

But Grant took his time, and I really, really liked that. After I went down on him, he repaid the favor by giving me two orgasms with his mouth. Then we talked while he caressed my body. I thought he needed some recovery time, but when I snuggled closer and felt him fully erect already, I found that was definitely not the case.

He studied my face as he touched my body and told me all the things he wanted to do with me—slide himself between my breasts and come all over my neck, take me from behind, blindfold me, tie me to the bed. I should've been satiated after two powerful orgasms, but the more he talked, the more I wanted him inside of me.

Grant started at my ear and kissed his way down my body to my toes. Then he licked and sucked his way back up. I was frenzied by the time he finally began to kiss me again. It made me crazy that he didn't seem as desperate as I felt. So I made it my personal mission to make him feel the same way I did.

When he kissed my neck, I nudged him a little, encouraging him to roll onto his back, and I climbed onto him. I took his mouth in a kiss as I slid my hips down so my wet center lined up over his erection. Then I started to grind against him as the kiss heated. That did the trick. In one swift move, I was on my back, and Grant was hovering over me again. Only this time, he looked a lot more impatient. The victorious smile I flashed was met with a growl.

"I was trying to go slow."

I cupped his cheek. "I don't want slow. I want *hard*. Now."

Grant grumbled a few curses as he reached for the nightstand. He grabbed his wallet and ripped out a condom, tossing everything else to the floor. Then he sheathed himself in record time.

Reappearing over me, he looked deep into my eyes. "You are..." He shook his head. "...incredible."

I pulled him down so our lips met and spoke against them. "Every time I look at you, I feel equal parts excited and terrified. But right now, I just want the excitement."

Grant never broke our gaze as he pushed inside of me.

"Fuck." He swallowed. "You're so wet."

He moved in and out slowly, stretching me a little at a time. Even though I was prepared for him, and I obviously knew how thick and long he was since I'd had him in my mouth, it had been a while since I was with a man, and my body needed some encouragement to accept his full girth. His arms shook as he took his time, and when he was finally seated inside me, he groaned. The sound was so guttural and raw, it sent chills down my arms and legs.

He stilled and kissed me gently before he looked into my eyes and fucked me the way I needed it—hard, raw, rough, and real. Each thrust went deeper and harder until the only sounds in the room were my moans and the wet slapping of our bodies against each other.

I dug my hands into his hair and tugged, saying his name over and over. The pulsing wave began to roll through me, and Grant's breaths became uneven. We were both losing control at the same time.

"Fuck. You feel...so fucking good. So fucking good." Grant gritted his teeth.

"Don't stop. Yes. Just like...oh...oh..." My orgasm hit me like a punch, and whatever words I'd been trying to form were swept away, along with any fear I had.

Grant closed his eyes. The muscle in his jaw flexed and the veins in his neck bulged. He sped up his pace and kept going while I rode the wave. As I pulsated all around him, he let out a roar. "Fuuuck!" His hips bucked, and he planted himself deeply inside of me.

After a moment, he kissed my neck and continued to move in and out at a leisurely pace. Pushing the sweaty hair from my forehead, he smiled down at me. "I'm done for after tonight, sweetheart. Now that I know how good it feels inside you, I'm never going to *not* want to be here."

I smiled. "That's okay. I like you here."

He kissed my lips softly and nodded. "Yeah. I like you here, too."

• • •

We overslept the next day. I guess technically we didn't, since oversleeping implies that we slept for a long period of time. But since we didn't fall asleep until the sun came up and woke up to the sound of my cell phone only two hours later, we really sort of underslept.

I cracked one eye open to slide my phone on. "Hello?"

"Why aren't you down here?"

Shit. Mia. I pushed up on one elbow. "What time is it?"

"Twenty minutes after brunch started."

"Oh. Crap. I'm sorry. I guess I overslept."

"You overslept or someone kept you up all night?"

"Both."

Mia squealed, and I had to pull the phone away from my ear. Grant squinted his eyes open, so I covered the phone.

"It's Mia. We're late for brunch."

"Tell her we're skipping and I'm going to eat you again instead."

Of course Mia heard that even though I'd had the phone covered. She squealed again. "Get down here now. I want to hear all the details."

Grant took the phone from my hand and looked at me as he spoke. "We need twenty minutes to shower."

His eyes dropped to my exposed breast. "Make that thirty."

I had no idea what she said, but he swiped the phone off and buried his head in my neck. "Morning."

I was positive I had the goofiest smile on my face, though I didn't care. "Good morning."

His hand slipped between my legs, and he ran his fingers over my swollen flesh. "Sore?"

I was, but I downplayed it. "A little."

He caught my gaze. "You sure?"

I nodded.

Grant plucked one nipple, and it stiffened to a peak. "Good," he said gruffly. "I want to fuck you from behind in the bathroom, with you bent over the sink and watching in the mirror."

My muscles ached, and between my legs was tender from how many times we went at it last night, yet thinking about Grant standing behind me while I was bent over already had my body thrumming to life.

I bit my lip. "Then why are we still in bed?"

A few heartbeats later, Grant lifted me from the bed and cradled me in his arms. I yelped in surprise, but truly I loved it. I loved the feeling of being in his arms, and the way he could toss me around like I weighed nothing.

He carried me into the bathroom with a condom between his teeth, and then we did exactly what he'd said he wanted to do. He fucked me from behind over the sink while I watched. It was fast and furious, but no less satisfying. We both came hard, and it was a perfect way to wake up. After, we got ready quickly and went downstairs to join the rest of the wedding party for brunch.

Mia's eyes lit up when she saw us. My hair was tied back in a wet ponytail and Grant's was slicked back from the shower. She pointed to the empty seat next to her as we approached the table. "Get your butt over here."

I looked at Christian. "Your wife is very bossy."

He smiled and looked at Mia with admiration. "My wife...I like the sound of that."

Grant took the seat across from Christian, and the two of them fell into easy conversation. The newlyweds were going to Kauai for their honeymoon, and apparently Grant had been there before, so they spoke about what boat tour to take and some helicopter ride.

Mia attempted to grill me on how things had gone with Grant, but I would only say we had a good night together. Though the smile on my face and the flush still on my cheeks from an orgasm twenty minutes ago probably told her a lot more than what came out of my mouth anyway.

Overhearing Grant and Christian talk about where Grant had stayed in Kauai, Mia interrupted, "Oh. I saw that place online. It looks gorgeous. But they were sold out. Apparently they lost more than half of the resort in a storm a few years back."

Grant nodded. "Didn't know that."

"How long ago were you there?"

Grant's eyes flickered to mine for a moment. "Eight years ago."

I felt a stab of jealousy, though I knew that was stupid. Grant had probably gone to Kauai on his honeymoon. His marriage was long over, and we'd just spent an amazing night together growing closer, yet I still felt jealous. I tamped down my silly emotions and tried not to let them spoil the euphoric feeling I'd come in with.

"So, Grant..." Mia pointed her fork at him. "Now that I'm an old married woman, I think I should warn you that I've mapped out my friend's future. Ireland and I are going to be neighbors with white picket fences and little boys born within a week of each other named Liam and Logan."

I laughed. "Mia decided this in fifth grade. We used to walk by these adorable matching houses on our way home from school every day. Two sisters owned them, and they sat on one porch every day on our way to school drinking coffee, and on the way home they were always seated on the other porch drinking iced tea. We used to wonder if the tea was spiked."

Mia bumped her shoulder with mine. "Ours will definitely be spiked." She looked at Grant. "So which name do you want? Liam or Logan?"

Obviously it was too soon to be talking about anything serious between Grant and me, but the entire thing was said in good fun.

Only Grant's answer was serious. "I don't want children."

All of our smiles and laughter disappeared.

"Really?" I said.

Grant nodded.

A horrible feeling settled in the pit of my stomach. I knew it wasn't the time or the place for this discussion.

Unfortunately, Mia wasn't going to let go so easily. She waved at Grant. "Lots of people say that—until they meet the right person. You'll change your mind."

Grant's face remained stoic. He looked at me and then down at his breakfast.

There were a few minutes of awkward silence after that. Mia knew I wanted children. And I didn't just want one; I wanted a few. I'd grown up an only child and always longed for sisters or brothers. Eventually Christian changed the subject back to sports, and he and Grant returned to light conversation. Mia and I exchanged a few glances, and though I joined in the discussion around the table, I couldn't really get past what I'd learned.

Grant and I hadn't even been seeing each other long, so I didn't think it should bother me so much. But the bottom line was, I really liked Grant. Most other ideals and values had a workaround for couples. If one wanted to live in the city and the other the country, you could compromise and have two homes or live on the outskirts of the city where it was a little more suburban. If a husband wanted a stay-at-home wife, and the wife wanted to work, they could compromise on a part-time job. But there wasn't any middle ground when it came to having a family—you either had one or you didn't.

I tried my best to put a smile on through the rest of brunch, but Grant's comment was like a nagging, dull toothache. When it was time to say goodbye, Mia and I hugged.

"Have a great time," I said. "Send pictures."

She smiled. "I will. And don't worry about what Grant said. I'm sure he'll change his mind. Men don't know what they want until you show it to them. Well, except a blowjob. They always want a blowjob."

I smiled back. "You're right." Though inside I wasn't so sure. Something about the way Grant had said the words made him seem pretty sure.

Grant and I had to go back to our room to get our luggage. I hadn't even realized how quiet I'd been on the elevator ride up or while I packed until he came up behind me in the bathroom. He rubbed my arms as I grabbed my toothbrush, and spoke to my reflection in the mirror. "I didn't mean to catch you off guard or upset you. I'm sorry."

I shook my head. "It's okay. There's nothing to be sorry about. Mia put you in that position by talking about her life plans."

Grant nodded, but our eyes stayed locked. I got the feeling he was waiting for me to say more. So I did.

"Do you...really not want children?"

He nodded.

"Are you sure?"

He frowned and nodded again.

"But you're so great with Leo."

Grant guided me to turn around and tilted my chin up so our eyes met directly, rather than through the mirror. "I don't want children, Ireland."

"Is it because you were in foster care? Do you mean you don't want biological children because there are so many kids who need homes?"

He stared into my eyes. "No, I don't want children at all."

It felt like a hit to my gut. Because I somehow knew by the look in his eyes that his decision hadn't been made lightly. We'd had *such* a great night, and I'd never expected that a moment of teasing this morning at breakfast would bring such an immediate and sudden halt to the excitement of what was growing between us. It was shocking, really.

I looked down. "Okay."

"I'm sorry."

"No, it's fine. I guess it's better that we have this discussion now than down the road. It's just that..." I looked up and felt my eyes well. Which seemed ridiculous. This relationship was so new, yet it felt like I'd suffered a loss. "I really want a family someday. Two or three little ones close in age, maybe a golden retriever named Spuds—a real full house. Not tomorrow or anything. But when the time is right."

Grant nodded. "Of course." He pushed a lock of my hair behind my ear. "And you deserve to have everything you want."

I needed some time to think about this. "We should probably get going. We're past the late checkout time they gave me."

We packed the rest of our stuff and headed to the car. Both of us were quiet as we got on the road. Grant took my hand and weaved his fingers with mine before lifting it to kiss the top.

"I have to head to the office for a few hours," he said. "You want me to drop you off at home?"

"Yeah, please."

At my apartment, Grant unloaded my suitcase and walked me to the door. "I'll call you later?"

I nodded. He gave me a soft kiss and waited until I got inside.

Leaning against the door, it felt like I'd been whiplashed. One minute, I was falling for a great guy, and we couldn't get enough of each other. The future was so bright. And the next, I needed some time alone to think, and I wondered if we had a future together at all.

CHAPTER 25

Grant

I leaned back in my chair and whipped the pen in my hand across the room. It hit the corner of the credènza and boomeranged back at me, landing on my desk right on top of the most recent letter. Figures. I can't even get that shit right today. Stewing, I picked up the envelope, angrily shredded it into twenty little pieces, and threw them all in the direction of the wastepaper basket. Half wound up on the floor.

I'd come to the office right after dropping off Ireland, thinking I could knock out a few hours of work. But four hours had passed, and I'd only managed to get about five minutes of business done. I couldn't fucking concentrate.

Of course Ireland wanted kids. She was a loving person with so much to offer. It wasn't the first time the subject had come up with women I'd dated. Hell, before Ireland, just having the subject raised by a woman had been a red flag. The mention of any long-term plans meant their expectations were too much, and it was time to call it quits. But Ireland wasn't some fuck buddy I wanted to run away from.

I picked up my phone and debated sending her a text. Should I give her some space? Bring it up again? Pretend it never happened and move on? I decided to stop acting like such a pussy and just send a damn text without overthinking it. I'd overthought enough for one day.

Grant: Dinner tonight? I could swing by on the way home from the office, and we could have Chinese on the boat and watch the sunset.

I watched as the little dots jumped up and down. Then stopped. Then started again. It was a long-ass few minutes waiting while she deliberated over her response.

Ireland: I'm actually pretty wiped out. Think I'm just going to crash early.

Fuck. I wanted to be with her, even if it meant just sleeping with her in my arms. But she wasn't offering. And I couldn't be a dick and bulldoze my way in with her. So I let it go.

Grant: Okay. Sleep well. I'll catch up with you tomorrow.

She sent back a happy face. Though I was sure neither of us was smiling right about now.

I managed to answer a few emails and approve a marketing budget before I called it a day. The work would be here when I was in a better frame of mind. Neither of us had gotten much sleep last night, so I convinced myself Ireland was right: going home and crashing was for the best. Though halfway through my drive, I found myself getting off the highway two exits before the marina. Pops had been like a second father to me my entire life, even more so since my dad was gone, and he was the one person I knew would give me the truth—even if it wasn't what I wanted to hear. I just hoped today was a good day for his memory.

• • •

"Grant, what a nice surprise. Come in. Come in."

My grandmother stepped aside for me to enter, and I kissed her cheek as I went through the doorway. "How's the alarm system doing?"

"It's fine. But your grandfather has slept like a baby since it was installed."

"Good." I looked around the living room. The house was quiet. "Is Pops around?"

"He's downstairs tinkering in the basement. Last I looked, he was making a miniature coffin for that crazy dollhouse he and Leo love so much. I try to keep away when he's doing the woodwork. The pieces are so small, and I get nervous he's going to cut his fingers off sawing them."

I smiled. Pops had started to forget a lot of things, but using tools wasn't one of them. Though dementia affects the memory, his woodworking skills were more second nature to him than learned. I couldn't imagine there would ever come a time he couldn't make things, whether he knew the name of the person he was making them for or not.

"I'm going to go down and visit him."

"I'll make you some snacks and bring them down in a bit."

"Thanks, Gram."

I found Pops in his pjs and a bathrobe, with a toolbelt wrapped around his hips. He had on a pair of goggles, and his gray hair was littered with wood shavings as he planed down the rough sides of a tiny coffin to make them smooth.

He smiled when he saw me, lifted the goggles to rest on top of his head, and held up three fingers with Band-Aids. "Mousetraps," he said.

My brows drew together. "You have mice?"

"Not that I'm aware of. But I used the little old wooden traps to make floorboards for the bedrooms and the hinges to attach the coffin doors. Leo set one up with cheese while we were working last week to see if he could catch a mouse. I picked it up this morning. Cheese is still there." He wiggled his fingers. "Now some of my skin is, too."

I chuckled. "Gotta be more careful, Pops. Grams is already worried about you using power tools. Cut off a finger, and you'll come back from the hospital with an empty workshop."

Pops muttered, "She worries like a rocking chair. Gives her something to do, but it never gets her anywhere."

I walked over to the creepy dollhouse and checked out the new pieces he'd made this week. There were tiny wood-framed mirrors with scary faces painted in them, a few hanging ghosts, and a fireplace carved with an ornate, angry wolf's head. Picking up the fireplace, I admired the workmanship that had gone into it. Pops was truly gifted.

"So what's new?" I asked as I set the fireplace back down in the dollhouse.

"Nothing. And that's exactly how I like it at my age. Every time I get something *new*, it's a pill, a pain, or prostate exam I don't enjoy." He looked over at me and set down his tool and the wood he'd been sanding. Under his woodworking table were two stools. He pulled one out and slid it over to me before taking a seat on the other.

"Have a seat. Tell me what's bothering you."

"How do you know something's bothering me?"

Pops lifted his chin and pointed to my pants. "Your hands are shoved in your pockets. Always a dead giveaway with you. Remember the time you cut off your sister's ponytail while she was sleeping because she left your bike outside and it got stolen?"

I laughed. It never ceased to amaze me how far back he could remember, even in stage one of dementia, yet sometimes he forgot the simplest things right after he heard them.

"I remember. Someone found the bike the next day and returned it, but Mom didn't let me ride it again for months."

"You had your hands in your pockets that day. Probably because you also had her damn ponytail shoved in there. You have done it every time you were worried about something since."

I wasn't so sure he was right, yet I made a conscious choice to remove my hands from my pockets before I sat down.

I sighed. "Am I a selfish person?"

Pops frowned. "You mean because you hold the reins at work and boss around your sisters?"

That hadn't been what I was referring to, but *thanks, Pops.* I shook my head. "I met a woman."

Pops nodded. "The looker? Charlize?"

I chuckled. "Yeah, that's her."

"Good choice. She seems like a woman who won't put up with your shit." Pops wagged a finger at me. "That's the key to a happy marriage. Marry a woman who scares you a little, one who makes you think *what the hell is she doing with a jackass like me*? Then spend the rest of your life trying to live up to what you think she deserves."

Pops had a lot of wisdom, and I knew he was right, but I wasn't asking the question I really wanted answered. So I took a deep breath and spit out what was really bothering me.

"It's new. But I really like her...and...she wants kids."

Pops held my eyes as so many unspoken words passed between us. He didn't need any more of an explanation about why that was an issue for me.

His face saddened, but he nodded. "So you think you're selfish for not wanting kids."

I nodded.

"You're not selfish, son. You just don't know how to deny someone you love anything. That's an admirable quality in a man. Your situation is different than a man who doesn't want children because he likes his lifestyle. I could see how that might seem somewhat selfish, though it's still a person's choice. It's their life. But you...it's not about that. I'd guess that down deep you even *want* to have children, that your reasons are more of a protective nature—for a future child, and maybe even a little for yourself."

I felt a heavy weight on my chest and looked down. "I don't know about that, Pops."

When I looked back up, he caught my gaze. "Do you trust me?"

"Of course I do."

"Then trust me when I say you're not selfish. That's not what this is about." Pops sighed. "Have you spoken to your lady about your reasons?"

I shook my head.

"Well, that's where you need to start. If nothing else, at least she'll understand your position better."

"It's not something that's easy to explain."

"Of course not. But I think you need to tell your story. It's been a long time coming. And even if you two can't work out your differences, it's important for you to come clean with her...and yourself."

• • •

Ireland blew me off again on Monday. By Tuesday morning, I was feeling restless and snapping at my staff. Even Millie was keeping her distance. But then my desk phone rang in the early afternoon, and the caller ID flashed the name Ireland Richardson.

My heart was pumping before I even lifted the receiver. "I got my zoning variance!"

I smiled at the sound of her voice. I'd forgotten her hearing was this morning. "That's great news. I'm glad it worked out."

"It didn't work out. You *made* it work out. Thank you so much, Grant. I owe you one."

My normal response would've been *Why don't you bring your sexy ass up here to my office, and I'll cash that chip in after I lock my door,* but things still felt off. So instead I said, "You're welcome. But it was really no trouble at all."

"I think I might have even found a new contractor to finish the bathroom. He said if I could get someone in to sheetrock by midweek, he could tile the shower and floors. Then the plumber would just need to come back to set the sink and toilet and I'd at least have one working bathroom. If I can get that and a bedroom done, I could move in when my lease is up and get the kitchen and other rooms done slowly."

"Do you have a drywaller lined up?"

She sighed. "No. But I'm going to start searching as soon as we hang up."

"You just need the bathroom done this week?"

"Yeah. So hopefully it won't be too hard to find someone."

I remembered all the house construction Pops and I had done over the years. They were actually some of the best memories of my life. We'd spend the day bullshitting and laughing, and things would somehow get done. Which gave me an idea...

"You don't have to call around. I have someone for you."

"You do?"

"I do."

"Oh my God. I wish I could climb through the phone and kiss your face right now."

I grinned. "Save that thought. Because that's how you'll be paying the contractor who's going to do your work."

"Did you just tell me I have to make out with the contractor?"

I chuckled. "I most certainly did."

"Now I'm lost. Who is this contractor?"

"Me."

CHAPTER 26

Ireland

God, *I like that toolbelt.*

I leaned against the doorframe, watching Grant work in the front yard. He had a piece of sheetrock set up on two sawhorses and was running a saw over it to fit into an area of the bathroom he'd just measured. He had on a pair of jeans, work boots, a T-shirt, and a ratty old toolbelt. And he looked ridiculously hot. I mean, I loved him in a well-fitted suit, and I loved him with a pair of board shorts on his boat, but this... This made me want to get sweaty and dirty.

"Keep looking at me like that, and nothing is going to get finished."

His head had been down, and I hadn't even been aware that he knew I was watching. I sipped water from a plastic bottle. "Pay attention to the saw in your hand. I wouldn't want you to cut off anything important."

Grant lifted the cut sheetrock upright, pulled the goggles from his head, and hung them on the end of one of the sawhorses. He carried it up the steps and stopped in front of me, in the tight space of the doorway, to plant a chaste kiss on my mouth. "Let's get finished. Every time I pass the frame where the kitchen counter will be, all I can think about is how it's the perfect height to fuck you."

Despite my confusion about our future, I seriously had it bad for this man. One kiss and the mention of sex, and I could feel my nipples harden and a tingle between my legs. I had to clear my throat to not show how affected I was. "Better get back to work. Or I won't pay you later."

His eyes darkened. "*Try* not to pay me later, sweetheart."

While Grant went back to the bathroom, I sat down on the steps of the porch. I wanted things to truly be as light and easy as they'd felt for the last few minutes. I'd avoided Grant since my discovery that he didn't want children. I'd given a lot of thought to breaking things off with him. I already had strong feelings, and spending more time together would likely just make it worse when the time came. But that was logical, and the heart doesn't do logic. So for now, for the short term anyway, I'd decided to stay in the moment.

I wasn't ready to give up Grant, and I wasn't ready to accept that I might not have a family someday. Basically, I'd decided avoidance was my current tactic. I also needed to understand why Grant was so adamant about not having children, and if there might be some compromise on that someday.

On that thought, I went back to the bathroom to be in the moment with my sexy construction worker. Grant was screwing in the drywall he'd cut.

"What can I do?" I asked from the doorway.

"If you're good at measuring, you can take that tape measure over there and figure out the dimensions of the last piece we need to cut."

I smiled. "I can do that."

He looked over his shoulder at me. "You've measured before, right?"

"Of course." I actually hadn't, unless you counted slipping the tailor's measuring tape around my waist when I was on a kick to lose an inch. But how hard could it be?

After I measured and typed the dimensions into my phone, I waited for Grant to finish. He lifted his chin to the area that still needed drywall. "Want me to double check what you came up with?"

I put my hands on my hips. "Do you think I'm incompetent because I'm a woman?"

Grant raised his hands in surrender. "Nope. I'm sure you did fine. It's just that we only have one piece of sheetrock left, so if we screw it up, we'll have to make another run to the store."

"I didn't screw it up." *I really, really hope I didn't anyway...*

Back outside at the saw, I enjoyed the way Grant's muscles bulged as he held the sheetrock in place. "How often do you work out?"

Grant looked up at me. "Five days a week. More if I'm frustrated and need to burn off some steam.

Needless to say, it was seven days a week for a while there after I ran into you at that coffee shop."

I tilted my head. "So now I don't frustrate you?"

He smirked. "Didn't say that. But now I have a much better way of working that frustration out—on you."

He finished cutting, and I followed him to the bathroom to put up the last piece. Only when he raised the sheetrock to the wall, it was a few inches too small. My eyes bulged. "You cut that wrong."

Grant's brows shot up. "Me? Pretty sure it's your measurement that's off."

I squinted. "It is not." *Uh-oh...*

Grant looked up at the ceiling and mumbled something, then took a deep breath and exhaled. "Care to put a little wager on who's right?"

"What did you have in mind?"

He looked down at the kneepads he'd been wearing all day. "My cut matches your measurements, and you'll be wearing these."

Oh. Well, it wasn't like it was a hardship if I lost. I reached out to shake on the deal. "Fine. But if I win, you're going to take off all your clothes, *except* the toolbelt, when you're on your knees."

Grant reached around me to grab the tape measure and lowered his face to mine for a kiss. "You like the toolbelt? I'll wear it every fucking day."

I smiled. "Pretty sure people at the office would think you'd lost it."

Grant measured the open space on the wall and showed me the width. "Thirty-two and three quarters, do you agree?"

I leaned in and checked. "Yup. Thirty two and three quarters."

He pointed to my phone. "Read me the dimensions you called out."

I held my breath as I swiped my cell alive. I hated to be wrong, but the way Grant was all bossy in his construction worker outfit really worked for me, and I secretly hoped I was this time. Dropping to my knees sounded pretty good right about now. I looked at my phone and smiled broadly as I turned it around to show him what I'd typed in.

Grant's face wrinkled. "You do know that says twenty-two and three-quarters, right?"

"I know." My smile widened.

"That means you lost the bet."

I bit my bottom lip and dropped to my knees. "I know. You can keep the knee pads on...and the toolbelt."

• • •

An hour later, Grant was a lot more relaxed as we walked around Home Depot. Since we were here anyway, I wanted to show him the two tiles I was considering for the bathroom. But the aisle was closed off while they used a forklift to take a pallet down from the top shelf, so Grant said he'd go get a cart in the meantime. When they opened the aisle, a construction worker struck up a conversation with me.

"Trying to decide between the two? Go with natural stone, rather than the ceramic."

"Oh really? Why?"

"Ceramic chips easily. Stone doesn't. And if you like that one in your left hand, they make it in a tumbled version, too. Stone doesn't chip easily, and tumbled stone you can't even tell when it does chip."

"Oh, that's great to know. Thanks."

He smiled. "No problem."

"Are you a tile contractor?"

"Nah. Not by trade. I'm a drywaller."

Grant walked up the aisle, pushing one of those tall carts you put big items on. He stopped next to me and eyed the guy like a suspect.

"I was actually looking for a drywaller. Never thought of trolling the aisles at Home Depot to find one."

The guy dug his wallet from his back pocket and slipped out a business card. Offering it to me, he smiled. "If you need help again, give me a call."

I took the card. "I will. And thanks for the education on tile."

When the guy walked away, I looked at Grant. "I found a drywaller."

He plucked the card from my hand. "Who wants in your pants. I'll file this for you." Grant crumpled up the card.

"Oh my God. You're jealous?"

"No, I'm not. I'm territorial."

"That's the same thing."

"Whatever. Show me the tile."

I grinned and sing-songed, "*Gra-ant's jeal-lous.*"

He shook his head. "You're a pain in my ass, you know that?"

I pushed up on my tippy toes and brushed my lips with his. "You'd be bored with easy."

After looking at the tumbled-stone tile, I still couldn't decide. Grant loaded a box of each onto the cart and told me he'd lay them out on the floor when we got home so I could decide, then return the one I didn't pick. Outside, he had to leave his trunk open and tie the big piece of sheetrock in place so it didn't fall out. It was a pretty funny sight—Grant's expensive Mercedes with a piece of rope keeping construction materials inside.

"Something tells me this is the first time this car has ever had sheetrock in it."

"I hire people because I'm busy, not because I'm incapable of doing it myself."

"I know. And the fact that you made time for me means a lot."

Grant looked back and forth between my eyes and nodded. "Come on. Let's get this stuff back, and this time, we'll use *my* measurements."

CHAPTER 27

Ireland

A week later, Grant and I seemed to have settled back into the comfort we had before Mia's brunch. We ate lunch in his office most days and took turns staying at each other's places. But we still hadn't had any more conversation about having kids someday. We'd just moved on.

I'd mentally made a decision that I wasn't ready to make a decision about whether having children meant more to me than having Grant. I guess I just hoped things would work themselves out. Maybe I'd discover Grant wasn't Mr. Forever, or he'd soften on his position. Either way, it kept me from having to make the decision to walk away—which I definitely wasn't ready for at the moment.

On Saturday morning, I woke up from the rocking. It was the first time I'd slept on Grant's boat and felt more than a light sway. Patting the bed next to me, I found cold sheets instead of a warm body. So I pulled on the dress shirt Grant had worn to work yesterday and went searching for its owner. I found him outside on the back deck.

The wind blew, sweeping up the bottom of the shirt, and I caught it just as it was about to flash my ass. "It's so windy."

Grant nodded. "Storm's brewing."

The sun looked like it was trying to come out, but the sky was so cloudy, it just turned everything an ominous dark gray color.

Grant held out his hand and guided me to sit in front of him, between his open legs.

"Do you stay down here during a storm?"

"Sometimes. Depends on how bad it is. We don't really get too many days where there are whitecaps in the inlet."

"How long have you been awake?"

He shrugged. "I don't know. A few hours."

I turned my head and looked up at him. "What time is it?"

"About six."

"And you've been up for a few hours?"

Grant nodded. "Had trouble sleeping."

"Is everything okay?"

"Just some work stuff on my mind."

We sat quietly watching the sky for a little while.

Then Grant spoke again. "I'm full of shit."

My forehead wrinkled. "About what?"

He shook his head. "It's not work that's bothering me."

I sat up and turned around to face him. When I'd walked out, I hadn't really taken a good look at him, but now I could see his face was etched with tension. "What's going on? Talk to me."

He looked down for a long time. When he looked up, his eyes were watery. "Today is Leilani's birthday."

I was confused. "The boat?"

Grant shook his head. He looked over my shoulder at the sky and swallowed before his eyes met mine again. "My daughter."

"What?"

He closed his eyes. "She would've been seven."

Would've been. I clutched my chest. "Oh my God, Grant. I had no idea. I'm so sorry."

He opened his eyes and nodded.

My daughter. Two simple words that explained a whole lot. The name of the boat, obviously the reason he didn't want to have kids... It was like the missing puzzle piece of Grant Lexington swirled around in the air and clicked into place.

"Was she...sick?"

Grant kept staring out at the turbulent sky. He shook his head.

My eyes widened. "What happened? An accident of some sort?"

A tear rolled down his cheek as he gave the slightest nod.

I wrapped my arms around him and hugged as tight as I could. "I'm so, so sorry. So very sorry." Grant's pain was palpable, and my own tears started to flow.

I have no idea how long we stayed like that, clinging to each other, but it felt like hours. So many questions swirled around in my head. *What kind of accident was she in? Why didn't you tell me until now? Is that why you spent the last seven years keeping women at a distance? Have you been to therapy? Did she look like you?* But obviously the subject wasn't an easy one for him to talk about. So I needed to let him decide what he was ready to share.

At one point, someone yelled hello to Grant from the dock, and he raised a hand to wave. I took the opportunity to sit up and look at him.

"Do you...want to talk about it? I'd love to hear all about her."

Grant looked me in the eyes. "Not today."

I leaned forward and pressed my lips to his. "I understand. And I'm here whenever you're ready."

The first raindrops started to fall a few minutes later, so we went inside. Grant looked exhausted, so I led him back downstairs to the bedroom, and we got back into bed. He wrapped me in his arms, spooning me from behind and gripping me so tightly it bordered on painful. But it didn't matter. If holding me gave him even one ounce of comfort, I'd let him crush me. At some point, I felt his grip loosen, and the sound of his breathing slowed. He'd fallen back asleep. Though I couldn't. There was way too much to go over in my mind.

Grant had a daughter.

Who would have been seven today.

Her name was Leilani, and she had a boat named after her.

And Grant lived on this boat—seeing his little girl's name in big bold letters every single day when he came home.

My aunt used to say grief was a lot like swimming in the ocean. On the good days, we could float on top with our heads above water, feeling the sunshine on our faces. But on the bad days, the water grew violent, and it was difficult not to get sucked under and drown. The only thing we could do was learn to be stronger swimmers.

But I knew there was another way to keep afloat—find a life raft. I'd been young when I lost my mother so tragically, and my aunt had become just that for me. I didn't know if Grant had a life raft, but I felt like maybe, just maybe, everything happens for a reason, and I was here to pay it forward and be that for him.

CHAPTER 28

Grant – 7 years ago

All good things must come to an end.

Whoever coined that phrase must've been a goddamned genius. I was an idiot for thinking the normalcy that lasted while Lily was pregnant would continue. It had hung on a little while after she gave birth, and two months ago, we'd left the hospital practically floating. In the weeks that followed, though, things started to break down a little bit each day. Lily had trouble sleeping and was irritable. But we had a newborn, and after I went back to work, she did most of the getting up at night. So who wouldn't be tired and cranky?

At six weeks, we went to her postpartum checkup. When the doctor asked about mood swings and depression, *I* mentioned the changes in Lily, since she'd answered that everything was great. But Dr. Larson only patted my hand and told me an adjustment period was normal. Lily's hormones were going back to normal, she had the stress of new motherhood, and Leilani seemed to have her days and nights mixed up. I left feeling hopeful that I'd been overly concerned.

Things started to go downhill pretty steeply the next few weeks. Lily became almost paranoid that something bad was going to happen to the baby. She didn't even want the nurse to hold Leilani at her two-month checkup, claiming she wasn't supporting her head enough. Everyone seemed to chalk the behavior up to motherly instincts—a hyper-protectiveness that stemmed from her trying to be the best mother she could. Again...it made sense.

But in the last week, everything had begun to unravel. Lily couldn't sleep—like, at all. She was physically exhausted, yet barely allowed me to touch the baby. She claimed Leilani liked things a certain way, and I wasn't doing it right. But I had the feeling she didn't trust me around my own child. Her paranoia seemed to spread wider and deeper each day, and we argued about it. In fact, lately it seemed like all we did was argue.

Saturday night, I was intent on making things between us better. I made Lily's favorite dinner, it was a beautiful night, and she sat on the back deck with the baby cradled in her arms, looking peaceful for a change.

"Do you want to eat outside?" I asked, poking my head out from the cabin. "Or should I set up dinner in here?"

"I'm not hungry."

I frowned. "You didn't eat anything today."

"I can't help it if I'm not hungry."

"You need to eat, Lily."

"Fine. I'll have a little."

"Inside or outside?"

She shrugged. "Wherever."

I sighed and went inside to plate the food. Since we had Leilani's bouncy chair and a dozen other contraptions inside the cabin, I figured it would be easier to eat there. I set everything up at the table and lifted the baby's favorite vibrating chair onto the bench seat between where we'd sit.

"Come inside. Dinner's on the table."

Lily took her seat with Leilani still cradled in her arms. I reached to take her, and she abruptly twisted her body so I couldn't touch the baby.

"What the hell, Lily? I was just going to put her in her seat so we can eat."

"I can eat while I hold her."

"I didn't say you weren't capable. But there's no reason you can't take a few minutes to have a meal in peace. We'll put her right here between us."

"That chair is too bouncy. It's not safe. What if we hit a wave and it flips over?"

My forehead wrinkled. "A wave? We're docked, Lily. In the inlet. And it's flat as a lake outside today."

"You don't care about us."

"You know that's not true. I just want to be able to eat a meal with my wife for a few minutes. Is that asking too much?"

Lily looked down at the baby and ignored me.

I sighed. "How about if I hold the baby while you eat. I'll eat when you're done."

"No. I got her. Go ahead and eat."

I felt the last few weeks coming to a boil. I lost my patience. "Give me the baby, Lily."

"No."

"This is ridiculous. You're not the only one capable of taking care of her. She's both of ours, you know."

Again my wife ignored me. I threw the napkin on the table and stormed out toward the deck. "Enjoy your meal with our daughter."

Later that night, I felt bad for walking out and yelling at Lily. The baby was sleeping in the bassinet in our bedroom, and Lily was in the shower with the door open *and* the monitor on the sink, which was only five feet away. When she emerged from the steamy bathroom, I was sitting on the bed waiting to apologize. But two things snagged my attention first—the deep dark circles under Lily's eyes, and how thin she looked wearing just a spaghetti-strap nightgown. She had lost a hell of a lot more than baby weight.

Shit.

I took Lily's hand as she went to pass by. "Come here."

She glanced over at the bassinet and hesitated. The baby was sound asleep, so I gave her a little tug and guided her onto my lap. "I'm sorry for yelling at you earlier."

She shook her head and looked down. "It's fine."

"No. It's not. I just...I miss you, Lily, even though you're right here."

"I'm taking care of the baby. What do you expect?"

I sighed. "I know. And I want to help more. But you won't let me."

"I don't need the help."

"It's not about you needing help. I believe you could do this all on your own if you had to. But you don't have to. I'm right here. And I want to help. I miss holding Leilani and spending time with her. And I miss you, too. You haven't kissed me in months. Every time I try to give you even a peck on the lips, you give me your cheek or your forehead."

Lily's eyes started to fill, and she looked down, twisting her hands. I cupped her chin and gently guided her so our gazes met. "I miss you, babe. You're right here. But you're a million miles away at the same time. I wish you'd talk to me. Tell me what's going on in your head."

I'd been doing so well—it seemed like I might've been getting through to her. Until...I questioned what was going on in her head. That was it. I saw the fire ignite in her eyes.

She jumped off my lap. "I'm not *fucking crazy*."

"I didn't mean to imply you were."

"Get out!"

"Lily. I—"

She pointed to the door and screamed louder. "Get out!"

I stood and put up my hands, showing her my palms. "Lily. Stop. I didn't mean—"

Leilani let out a wail. Our yelling had startled her awake. Lily marched across the room to the bassinet and scooped our daughter into her arms. She immediately stopped crying. Yet Lily said, "Now look at what you've done."

"She's fine, Lily. Look. She's falling back asleep already."

"Leave, Grant! Just get out!"

I looked my wife in the eyes, the girl I'd known since we were fourteen, and what I saw scared the shit out of me. No matter how deeply I searched, I couldn't find any sign of sense. She looked almost deranged. "I'm not going anywhere without Leilani."

Lily's eyes widened. "You're not taking her anywhere."

I raked a hand through my hair. It was pointless to try to talk to Lily when she was in this frame of mind. But the look in her eyes made my blood run cold. I wasn't leaving my daughter alone with her in this condition. Blowing out a ragged breath, I shook my head. "I'm going next door to sleep in the guest berth. I'll talk to you in the morning when you calm down."

· · ·

I couldn't sleep. I tossed and turned half the night, hating what things had turned into between Lily and me. But even more than that, I was worried about my wife. Being a foster care kid, she'd bounced around a lot, so she didn't have too many friends. And since she'd aged out of the system and my mom was gone now, no one was keeping an eye on her—no one except me. So it was up to me to push when I thought she needed help. The problem was, when anyone pushed Lily, she pulled away. Lately, it felt like my choices were to be her caretaker or her husband. Being both wasn't really possible.

But things had deteriorated to a point where she was at risk and needed help more than she needed a husband. And taking care of her and the baby was more important than her being pissed off at me.

Feeling the need to check on her, I climbed out of bed and went to our bedroom. The door was closed, and I tried to creak it open quietly so I wouldn't wake either of them. I just wanted to see that she was sleeping soundly. The lower level of the boat was a lot like a basement when things were shut tight, so I couldn't make out anything in the pitch dark, even once I'd managed to open the door wide enough to see inside. Everything was so still, and I couldn't hear either of them snoring or breathing. So I walked in and went to the bed for a closer look.

There was a lump on the bed, though I couldn't be sure if it was the blanket or Lily. Leaning down closer, I still couldn't hear any signs of breathing. So I gently felt around, still expecting my hands to hit a warm body. But the only thing I found was a pile of cold covers.

I froze. A shiver ran down my spine while my heart leaped to my throat. Rushing to the wall, I held my breath while I felt around for the light switch. A horrible dread washed over me when I found the bassinet was empty, too.

"*Lily!*" I yelled.

Feeling desperate, I swung open the bathroom door and yanked at the closet doors, too. Of course, she wasn't hiding in either. I bolted out of the bedroom and up the stairs, yelling with every step. "*Lily!*"

No answer.

The kitchen and living room were empty. I banged on the upstairs bathroom door. "Lily!"

No answer.

My heart was beating so fast. An overwhelming sickening feeling came over me, and for a second, I thought I might throw up all over the place. *What the fuck?*

I ran to the cabin door leading to the deck and whipped it open.

Thank God!

I shut my eyes and let out a huge exhale. Lily was standing on the back deck at the railing, but she didn't turn around upon hearing the door open. It took me a few heartbeats to pull myself together enough to step outside. It was still dark, but I could see her arms in the cradling position they'd been in every time I'd looked at her for the last few weeks. They were safe at least.

I didn't want to startle her, so I whispered, "Lily."

When she didn't respond or turn around, I took a few steps toward her. It was then that I heard her crying.

Shit.

I put my hands on her shoulders. "Don't cry, Lily. I'm right here."

She started to sob harder, so I guided her to turn around so I could hold her in my arms.

But when she did...

...I saw the blanket she had cradled in her arms was empty.

A shiver ran from the top of my head down my spine and into my toes. "Lily, where's Leilani?"

She started to cry harder.

My voice rose. "Lily, where the hell is she?"

I ran around the back deck and then returned to Lily. Grabbing both her arms, I shook her. "*Where the fuck is she, Lily! Where is she?!*"

Lily turned to look out at the water. "She's gone."

CHAPTER 29

Ireland

Sometimes you chip and chip at a brick wall until you're exhausted and still make no progress bringing it down. And other times, you pull out one brick and the entire thing starts to crumple. Leilani was the brick that had kept Grant's wall standing. Everything seemed to have changed since sunrise this morning. It wasn't anything you could tell from the outside, but it was in the way Grant showed me himself.

After he woke up, he'd driven me home and said he needed to run a few errands. But he'd asked me to pack an overnight bag and be ready when he came back in a few hours. To my surprise, he took me to his condo downtown. The building was a fancy high-rise overlooking the waterfront, with a doorman and security desk.

The uniformed guard nodded as we walked in. "Both your deliveries came and the crew just left, Mr. Lexington."

"Thanks, Fred."

I waited until we were in the elevator to quiz Grant. "You have a crew?"

Grant chuckled. He intertwined his fingers with mine. "You'll see." He slipped a card into a slot on the elevator panel and pushed a button: PH.

"Penthouse? Well, aren't you fancy? You should have told me your lair was this nice. Maybe I wouldn't have been such a pain in the ass about coming here."

Grant lifted a brow. "My lair?"

"I thought it sounded nicer than fuckpad."

He pulled me to his side and kissed the top of my head. "I'm actually glad you refused to come here."

"Oh yeah? So why are we here now?"

"You'll see."

The elevator arrived on the fourteenth floor and opened directly into a huge foyer. A large, round marble table greeted us as we walked in. I looked around. The apartment was enormous. To the right was a sleek, modern stainless-steel kitchen, and straight ahead, a few steps down was a sunken living room with a full wall of floor-to-ceiling windows that overlooked the water. I walked straight to the glass to admire the view.

"Oh my God. This is gorgeous. I don't know why I was picturing some dark and seedy place. Oh wait... maybe I do. It's because of what you *used* this place for."

Grant came up behind me and snaked his arms around my waist. "*Used* is the key word. Past tense."

I turned in his arms and wrapped my arms around his neck. "Are you saying you won't be using this beautiful apartment for any sexual activities anymore? That's sort of a shame."

"Not at all. I plan to use it for lots of fucking. Starting with you bending over and pressing your hands against the glass in just a little while. But the place is now a lot more exclusive."

"Exclusive, huh?" I teased. "Higher end one-night stands?"

Grant rubbed his thumb over my lip and stared at it. "Just you, beautiful."

The tenderness in his voice made my heart flutter. Ever since our talk this morning, my emotions had been all over the place, and I started to feel myself getting a little choked up. Grant saw it in my face and smiled as he brushed his lips with mine.

"Come on. Let me show you around."

We walked down a long hall. Grant opened each door as we passed and pointed from the doorway, but didn't go inside.

"Office."

"Guest bedroom."

"Bathroom."

But when we got to the last door on the left, he opened it and took my hand to lead me inside what was obviously the master bedroom. The room had the same big floor-to-ceiling windows, a beautiful fireplace to one side, and a king-size bed in the center. Like the rest of the apartment, it was pretty stark on decoration, but what was there was beautiful and high quality.

Grant walked to the bed and sat down, pulling me onto his lap. "Mattress is brand new. It was delivered today."

"Was something wrong with the old one?"

He looked into my eyes, and I felt the warmth of his gaze spread through my chest. "It had seven years of things I can't take back on it."

And those bricks just keep falling.

I cupped his cheek. "That was really thoughtful."

"Figured we could pick up some new bedding this afternoon before we christen it."

I smiled. "You better be careful, Mr. Lexington. Buying a new bed, taking me shopping—a girl could get used to all this sweetness."

Grant looked at me in a way he hadn't before. Something was different. And that something made my heart race. I had put off making a decision about the long term, hoping something would organically happen to make it for me. And I suddenly realized it had: I'd fallen for him.

"Get used to it, sweetheart. It's what you deserve."

Falling...falling...falling so deep.

I was basically a pile of mush inside, and my self-protection mechanism had me needing not to fall so far that I lost myself. So I changed gears and smirked. "While we're picking up bedding, maybe we can pick up a few decorative things, too. The apartment is beautiful, but it's kind of...sterile. It needs some warmth."

"Whatever you want."

I kissed him one last time and dragged us from the bedroom. Feeling emotional and sitting on a big bed with this man was dangerous territory on so many fronts. As we walked into the living room, I noticed a tag on the couch.

"Is that a brand new couch, too?"

Grant nodded.

"You needed a new one?"

He shook his head slowly.

Oh. *Oh.* My nose scrunched up at the thought of Grant screwing some woman on the couch. "Did you also get new countertops in the kitchen and a new desk?" I asked dryly.

Grant shook his head. "No, smartass."

• • •

I got the feeling Grant didn't do much shopping. He looked completely awkward in a home goods store. Every time I asked if he liked something, he shrugged and nodded. "Sure, if you like it."

So I picked up the most hideous comforter set I'd ever seen. It looked like someone had taken the ugliest floral pattern in the world and laid it on top of a check print. Not only was it loud and made me a little dizzy, but the material was almost scratchy.

"How about this one?"

Grant barely looked at it. "Sure, if you like it."

I shook my head. "It's the ugliest thing I've ever seen."

His brows furrowed. "So why are you picking it out?"

"I'm not. I just wanted to see your reaction. You aren't really being helpful. I don't know what you like."

He smirked. "You naked. Just pick something you like and will be soft on your back. And your hands and knees."

Mmmm... That sounded good. Desire shot through me. Grant noticed the change in my face and leaned forward to whisper in my ear with a growl. "Hurry. Or I'll be dragging you from this place and fucking you on a bare mattress soon."

Oh my.

I attempted to ignore the growing need between my legs and moved on to a display toward the back of the store. It was simple, a navy blue-and-white striped spread by Nautica. I ran my hand along the fabric—luxurious and soft.

"I feel like this one fits you."

It was the first time Grant gave me an actual answer. "I like it. Simple. Maybe a few of those, too." He pointed to a display of throw pillows I hadn't noticed to my left. They were navy with burlap patches on the front and would go perfectly—continuing a bit of a nautical theme.

"Perfect. Look at you. You're a regular designer when you want to be."

Grant looked over his shoulder and then to the left and right. I thought he was looking for other items to add to what we'd picked out. But I quickly realized he was seeing if the coast was clear. Before I could argue, he lifted me up and tossed me onto the bed. I landed on my back in the middle of the Nautica display. A wicked grin spread across his face as he nodded.

"It looks good together. Let's get it and get the hell out of here."

I was probably as ready to go as he was, but I *so* enjoyed screwing with him. I lifted up on my elbows on the bed. "But you said we could pick up some decorations. I figured we could check out the art store a few blocks away and then head over to that big lighting store on Fairway Blvd. I can spend hours in that place."

Grant's face dropped.

I couldn't contain the smirk taking over my pout. He noticed and squinted. "You're screwing with me."

I smiled. "I figured it was only fair since you plan to *screw* me."

Grant scooped me up off the bed, cradling me in his arms. He shifted my weight to one arm and grabbed the striped comforter set off the shelf. He walked to the throw pillow display and dipped forward.

"Grab a few."

I laughed but grabbed two I liked. He marched down an aisle toward a register on the other side of the store.

"Ummm... You're going to carry me to the line?"

"I am. Keeps you from stopping to look at shit and gets us to trying out the new bedding faster."

I giggled. A few people stared at the handsome man carrying a woman and his purchases, but either Grant didn't notice or didn't give a shit. "You realize you look like a Neanderthal."

"That's the way you make me feel, sweetheart. Don't worry. I'll make up for my ungentlemanlike behavior when we get home."

Home. He'll make it up to me when we get *home.* I liked the sound of that for a lot of reasons.

CHAPTER 30

Ireland

The next week was absolute bliss. Grant and I stayed holed up in his condo for a day and a half—spending Sunday christening every surface we could. Then Monday morning he had to go to a meeting out of town, and a gigantic bouquet of flowers was delivered to the office. They took up half of my desk. Tuesday he met the plumbing contractor at my house so I could work late. Wednesday we ate lunch in his office and locked the door for a quickie. Thursday and Friday, we slept at my place.

On Saturday morning, he went into the office while I waited at my apartment for Mia to come over. She'd come back from her honeymoon earlier in the week and officially moved into Christian's place, but she still had a ton of boxes at our apartment. We were going to take them over to Goodwill today after getting some lunch.

I practically sprinted to her when she walked in. It was probably the longest I'd gone without seeing her since we were kids.

"Honey, I'm home!" she yelled.

We embraced for the longest time, and when I pulled back, I shook my head. "Look at you. You're so tan and relaxed. And you look so...married." I smiled.

"I missed you. Kauai was amazing. But it would have been better if you were there, too. You would've loved the helicopter ride. Christian lost his lunch in a barf bag during the tour."

I laughed. "I'm sure that would have gone over well with your new husband. *I'm taking two pieces of luggage and Ireland with me.*"

"We need to go back—a couples' vacation. Maybe Maui next time."

"That sounds great. Last weekend I asked Grant when the last time he went on vacation was, and he said eight years ago."

"Really? Why?"

I shrugged. "He's a workaholic, and he didn't have anyone in his life to force the issue, I guess."

Mia went into the refrigerator, pulled out the orange juice, and looked at the container. "Pulp? Is this mine from weeks ago and expired? You don't like pulp."

"Grant likes pulp."

She smiled. "So I take it you two have been spending a lot of time together while I was gone, if you're stocking the fridge for him."

I sat down at the kitchen table. "Yeah. We have been. It's been pretty great, actually."

"The last time I saw you two together, at brunch the day after my wedding, I wasn't sure I'd come back to a happy couple, him not wanting kids and all."

Mia took two glasses out of the cabinet and filled them with juice before going to where we kept the liquor and grabbing a bottle of vodka. She poured a shot into each glass and stuck her finger in to stir before sliding one across the table to me. "You can suffer through pulp for me."

I preferred no pulp, but I'd drink it if that was the only choice available. Though that wasn't the issue. I slid the glass back toward her. "You drink both. I'll drive."

"Neither of us is driving. Christian dropped me off on his way to the gym. He's going to come back when he's done and load the boxes into his car." She smiled. "He told me to enjoy my day with you, and he'd take care of the donations and go food shopping."

I shook my head. "I have no idea how you fooled that nice man into marrying you. But you done good, lady."

Since neither of us had to drive, why not indulge? I lifted the glass of orange juice and held it up to clink with my friend. "To good guys for a change."

Mia downed half the glass and wiped her mouth with the back of her hand. "So give me all the dirt. How did things go after brunch? I take it you convinced him having children was not the end of the world?"

I frowned. "Actually, I didn't. He hasn't changed his position. I'm not sure he ever will. And, honestly, he has reasons for not wanting children that I understand... well, mostly."

"So what happens if you two get serious? You just give up your dream of having a family?"

I shook my head. "I don't know. I'm not ready to make the decision to stop seeing him. But I'm also not ready to make the decision to not have a family. So I've decided to put off the decision—hoping something will happen organically."

Mia's lips pressed together in a straight line. "I see only three things that could happen organically." She held up her hand and counted them off, first with her pointer. "One, you split up and there is no decision to make." She added her middle finger. "Two, he changes his mind." She raised her ring finger. "Three, you accept not having children." She shook her head. "You just said you don't think he'll ever change his mind. So that leaves splitting up or you accepting a very different life than you want. I don't think banking on splitting up is a healthy way to be in a relationship, and the last choice is an awfully big concession. Are you sure you would want that life?"

My shoulders slumped. Mia was one hundred percent right, but avoidance was the only way to stay happy, and it had been a long time since I wanted someone in my life so badly.

I sighed. "I know burying my head in the sand is probably only going to make things worse in the future. But...I'm crazy about him, Mia. I don't want to give him up."

Mia stared at me for a long time and then abruptly stood. "January first."

"What about it?"

"That's the day you make the decision. It gives you a few months to enjoy the man and give it thought. But

January first, we'll sit down at this table and not get up until you've made a decision you can live with."

I forced a smile. "That's a good plan." Though, in my heart, I knew it was stupid. Chances were four more months would only make me fall harder for Grant Lexington, especially the side of him he'd been showing me the last few weeks. But my head was pretty damn good at convincing my heart it was in control. So I went with the plan.

"Come on. No more talk about this subject," I told Mia. "Let's go finish sorting your stuff so your hubby can drop the donations off. I want to throw some things in from my closet, too."

"Okay. What do you say we double-date tonight? Have dinner at that new Italian place downtown?"

"I'll text Grant. He's working today, but he planned to come over later. I'm sure he'd be up for it."

I stood to get started, and Mia reached out and squeezed my arm. "One more thing and then no more talking on the subject, I promise."

"Okay..."

"Take it slow. I know you care about him, but go slow. Don't give your heart so fully away that you won't be able to take it back."

I nodded. Except I was pretty sure I already had.

• • •

I hadn't laughed so hard in a long time. Mia kept all of us amused with stories about the odd things that happened at her spa.

"Another woman came in and asked if her husband could watch her Brazilian wax. Aside from the fact that treatment rooms are small, we don't generally allow people to watch while we do procedures with someone's legs wide open on a table when they're naked. So I asked if he wanted to watch because he was interested in getting waxed himself and offered to do a sample strip on his back or leg. The woman, with a complete straight face, said he wanted to watch because he was a masochist, and it gets him aroused to see her in pain. *Uh...no thanks.* I think I'll pass on helping you get your husband's rocks off today."

Grant was definitely the most shocked of the group. Not only was he not used to Mia's dark humor, he had no idea what half the services she offered were for.

"The beauty of owning my own spa is that now I never have to see an ass that looks like a rainforest propped up on a waxing table again." Mia looked at Grant with a straight face and said. "Do you wax your balls or shave?"

He looked like a deer caught in the headlights, which was amusing as hell since he rarely looked rattled. He actually started to answer her, and I had to let him off the hook.

"She's teasing you." Mia and I laughed so hard tears streamed down my face.

The waiter came over to offer more wine, and everyone but Mia declined because the rest of us were driving. Grant had gotten stuck at the office late and met me at the restaurant, so we had two cars. One small glass of wine at the start of a two-hour dinner was my limit.

"So…" Mia picked up her glass and brought it to her lips. She looked across at Grant. "What would you think about going to Maui for the week between Christmas and New Year's? The four of us. I mean, not me and you—I'm a married woman now."

Grant chuckled and looked at me. He reached for my hand under the table and squeezed it. "What do you think? A week in Hawaii?"

My heart raced. Making long-term plans warmed my heart. Lord knew giving most of my exes a dry cleaning ticket to pick up two days later would have freaked them out.

I smiled. "I'd love that."

After we got up from the table, the four of us stood around talking out front for another half hour. I overheard Christian invite Grant to a baseball game, and Mia winked at me with a huge grin. We never got to do things together as couples, and it felt so good to enjoy time with them together.

When it started to mist, it was time to finally go. I hugged Mia and Christian goodbye, and Grant walked me to my car. "It's late. You want to just leave your car here, and we can swing back tomorrow and pick it up?"

"No, I'm fine. I'm actually going to stop back at my apartment and pick up some work I need to do in the morning. I meant to bring it, but I forgot it on the kitchen table. So I'll just meet you at the boat."

"You feel like having wine? I'm out, but I can stop and pick it up on the way."

I pushed up on my toes and planted a soft kiss on his lips. "That sounds great. I'll see you in a little while."

"Be careful driving. It's getting foggy, and the mist will make the road slick."

"My aunt would love you. For all the years I lived with her, not an evening went by that she didn't warn me to drive carefully or tell me about the weather."

Grant opened my car door and held onto the top before shutting it. "Go, smartass. I don't want you to get caught in dense fog. It rolls in fast down by the marina sometimes."

After I stopped home and got back on the road, it actually was getting pretty foggy. I'd teased Grant for warning me to be careful, but it was becoming harder and harder to see. The roads leading down to the marina were winding, and I put on my high beams to get a better look up ahead. But after a few seconds, the headlights of an oncoming car flashed, so I turned my low beams back on. After the car passed, I hit the high beams again, but again an upcoming car approached, so I had to flick them back down. I gripped the steering wheel a little harder during the moments the low beams were on and relaxed when I could switch again. The fourth time an oncoming car passed, I was relieved to be able to return to my brights. But when I did, I was met with two big eyes.

Shit!

A huge deer with giant antlers stood in the middle of the damn road. He'd seemed to come out of nowhere. Suddenly there he was, only a hundred feet in front of me. We stared at each other, frozen in shock, until I thankfully jerked the steering wheel to the right.

Everything after that came in slow motion.

I missed the deer.

But the mist on the road made the blacktop slick, and I started to spin. I pulled the steering wheel in the other direction in an attempt to counter the motion, but it did no good.

My car went off the road and into the dirt.

I pushed all of my weight onto the brakes, and the car slid sideways down the side of the road.

With no lights shining anymore in the direction I was going, I got confused as to whether I was still on the side of the road or had gone back onto the pavement.

I held my breath as the car slowed.

Headlights from the other direction illuminated the street.

Thankfully, I wasn't on the road anymore.

But there was a tree up ahead.

I braced.

And everything became eerily quiet.

Until impact...

CHAPTER 31

Grant

I wasn't a worrier.

Or a nervous person, in general. But I checked my watch for the tenth time in an hour and stood on the back deck of Leilani, watching the dock ramp for any sign of Ireland. Actually, the fog had settled in so thick, I couldn't even see the entrance ramp to get on the dock anymore, or the parking lot. I'd called Ireland's cell fifteen minutes ago and left a message. But I didn't want to distract her by sending a text. When another half hour went by with still no sign of her, I began to pace and called again. Only to get her voicemail a second time.

"Hey. It's me." I looked at my watch and blew out a breath. "I left you at nine, and it's ten thirty now. You didn't mention making any other stops except home. You should have been here almost an hour ago. Give me a call, and let me know you're alright." I swiped *End* and hopped the back transom, deciding to go wait in the parking lot.

The walk up the dock to the ramp was unnervingly quiet. Not a single person was around, and with the fog hanging so low, the anxious feeling in my gut turned into something more ominous.

Where the fuck is she?

She could have fallen asleep. But it hadn't sounded like she planned on spending any time at home. She'd said she was grabbing a pile of work from the table. I suppose she could've stopped at a store—but not too many were open at going on eleven o'clock. Eventually, I gave in and sent a text.

I waited for the *Sent* to change to *Delivered*, but it never did. Restless, I jogged back to the boat, wrote a quick note for her to call me if she got here before I was back, and swiped my keys off the counter.

Getting on the road, I navigated the path she would've taken from her house to mine. I wasn't sure what I was looking for, but I really hoped I didn't find it. The roads were pretty empty for a Saturday night— apparently all the smart people were staying indoors. The more I struggled to see the pavement, the more freaked out I got. But no news was good news. Best-case scenario, she sat down to take off her shoes at home and fell asleep.

Yeah. That's what probably happened.

As I went farther with no sign of her car, I started to feel a little relieved.

Until I rounded a corner and saw a shitload of lights flashing up ahead.

My heart raced. I stepped on the gas, even though I couldn't see more than twenty feet ahead of me.

Something was definitely going on up there. Even through the fog, I could see there were more than a dozen lights flashing at different heights—lights like when both the cops and the fire department respond to an accident.

"It's not her."

"It's definitely not her." I started to talk to myself. *Be reasonable.*

"She's probably stuck behind all of that."

"Some dumbass was speeding in the fog and crossed over the yellow line."

"Damn...there are a lot of rescue vehicles."

Approaching the parade of lights, I slowed when I saw reflectors and what looked to be a safety wand waving up ahead. A cop stood in the road wearing raingear, so I pulled up to speak to him. A firetruck blocked a better view of what was going on.

He leaned over to speak as I rolled down my window. "Accident up ahead. Road's gonna be closed for the next hour or two until we can get things cleaned up and a tow out here."

"My girlfriend was supposed to be at my house an hour ago, and she's not answering her cell. Do you know what kind of cars were involved? Is anyone hurt?"

The officer frowned. "Only one car. Driver was just taken by ambulance to County Hospital. It was a woman. What's your girlfriend's name?"

"Ireland Saint James."

The officer stood and lifted a walkie talkie to his mouth. "This is Connors. You got a name on the woman they just put in the bus?"

My heart thumped, waiting for the answer.

Eventually a burst of static came through and then a voice. "Victim was that lady from the news—Ireland Richardson."

I felt sick. "Is she okay?"

The cop leaned down and shined his light into my car. He was probably looking at a ghost, because I felt all my color drain. His eyes darted over my face, and he frowned again. "Not supposed to give out any information on victims. But I don't want you getting into an accident doing a hundred miles an hour with this fog. She was banged up, but talking." He nodded. "I wouldn't think anything worse than stitches and maybe a broken bone or two."

I blew out a deep breath. "Thank you. Can I turn around here?"

The officer rapped his knuckles on the hood of my car. "Sure thing. Be careful driving. Fog is dangerous."

• • •

"Sir, I told you five minutes ago that I'd let you go back as soon as the doctors are done examining her."

"A guy just walked in and went right back."

The nurse at the registration desk shook her head. "He works here. Please take a seat, and I'll call you as soon as you can go back."

Whatever.

I took a seat and rested my head in my hands with my elbows on my knees. Who did they call for Ireland in an emergency? Her father's in prison, mother was long gone, and her only aunt moved down to Florida. *What if she needs surgery?* Who would make that decision? I should've gotten Mia's cell phone number for emergencies. Maybe she was her designated contact.

I lasted about three minutes sitting before I got up to pace again. I made sure to stay in the nurse's line of view so she wouldn't forget about me. When our eyes caught, she let out an exaggerated sigh and shook her head before looking away. I didn't give a shit if I pissed her off. I only cared that she didn't forget I was here.

About a half hour after I'd walked in, another nurse opened the door. "Family of Ireland Saint James."

I walked to the door, and the woman looked at me. "You're a family member?"

I didn't even have to think about lying. "Yes."

"And you're her..."

I thought they might have asked her marital status when she came in, and I didn't want to contradict her. "Brother. I'm her brother."

The nurse nodded and opened the door wide for me to come into the back. "Right this way. She's in bed four. The doctors just finished examining her."

I followed her to a corner of the large, open room, and the nurse pulled the closed curtain open. "Ms. Saint James, your brother is here to see you."

Ireland's face was confused for a half a second, and then she smiled and nodded. She had a bandage on the side of her head and looked pale. But she was in one piece.

I went to her side, took her hand, and leaned down to kiss her forehead. "Jesus Christ. You scared the shit out of me. What happened? Does anything hurt? Are you okay?"

The nurse shut the curtain behind her.

"Yeah. I'm okay." She pointed to the bandage on her head. "Just butterfly stitches on my head from where I hit something, I guess." She lifted her left arm and winced. "They think I might have broken my ulna. I'm waiting for x-ray to come now."

"What the hell have they been doing all this time if you didn't even get any x-rays yet?"

Ireland smiled. "A nurse came back a little while ago and told me I had a very anxious visitor waiting. I can see you must've been a joy to keep in the waiting room. They did some lab work and examined me. But I'm fine, really."

I dragged a hand through my hair. "Are you sure? County's not the greatest hospital. I can take you over to Memorial."

"I'm fine. They've been really great so far."

"What happened?"

She shook her head. "I was driving, and the fog made it hard to see, so I was switching back and forth between my high and low beams, and the last time I flipped on the brights, I found a deer standing almost right in front of my car. I hit the brakes, but the ground was wet and slippery, and I lost control. Remember in Driver's Ed class when they told you to turn *in* to a spinout instead of away from it?"

"Yeah."

"Well, I didn't do that. I just reacted and didn't even remember that until I got here."

I brushed the hair from her face. "You acted on instinct. It's normal."

Ireland sighed. "I think my car is totaled."

"Who cares about the car?" I began to pat down her body. "Is anything else hurt?"

She laughed. "No, Dr. Lexington. I'm really fine."

A few minutes later, the nurse came back in. She looked at me. "Can I ask you to step back into the waiting room for a few minutes."

"Are you taking her down to x-ray?"

The nurse shook her head. "Not yet. The doctor's going to come back in and do another examination and would like to speak to your sister."

My eyes narrowed. "Why? What's wrong?"

The nurse frowned and looked over at Ireland. "Nothing is wrong. It's just our policy to have visitors wait in the waiting room during an examination."

Ireland smiled. "I'll be fine, Grant." She looked at the nurse. "Can he come back in after the doctor is done?"

The nurse nodded. "Sure."

I leaned down and kissed Ireland's forehead. "I'll be back soon."

Then, begrudgingly, I went back to the waiting room.

Sitting down, I leaned back in the chair and scrubbed my hands over my face. Why didn't I insist that she not drive from the damn restaurant? This was all my fault. I don't know what I would've done if anything had happened to her. My insides twisted at that thought. Ireland didn't know what she meant to me. Hell, I'm not sure I even knew before tonight. But now that she was okay, I was going to make damn sure to show her from now on. I knew all too well that sometimes life changes in the blink of an eye.

CHAPTER 32

Ireland

Dr. Rupert, the emergency room doctor treating me, looked like Penn from the magician duo Penn and Teller. At least I thought it was Penn—I could never remember which was which. In any case, Dr. Rupert bore an uncanny resemblance to the shorter, older one. Since I was pretty sure he was in his late seventies, I figured it wouldn't insult him to mention it.

"Has anyone ever told you that you look like someone famous?"

He smiled, reached into his lab coat sleeve, and pulled out a bouquet of plastic flowers. "Does this answer your question?"

I laughed. "I guess so."

He tucked the flowers headfirst into his lab coat pocket. "No relation, but patients are disappointed when I tell them that. So I find it's at least a consolation prize to perform a trick."

Dr. Rupert picked up the chart hanging from the foot of my bed and flipped through some pages. As he started to speak, the closed curtain opened and another doctor came in, drawing the curtain behind him.

"Good timing. This is Dr. Torres. He's an orthopedic specialist."

"Hello," I said.

"Normally we don't call in ortho for a consultation until after x-rays, but I wanted to have him examine you now, so we can give you all of your options."

"Okay…"

Dr. Rupert pulled up a chair and sat down next to me. He had an old school way about him that doctors didn't have much anymore. Reaching out, he touched my arm.

"The reason we wanted to do an ortho consult before the x-ray is because we found something in your bloodwork."

I sat up in bed. *Oh, God.* The first thing that came to my mind was cancer. Some blood cell count must've been elevated, and now they don't want to radiate me unnecessarily. My heart started to palpitate. "What? What's wrong with my blood work?"

Dr. Rupert squeezed my hand and smiled. "Nothing. You're pregnant, Ms. Saint James."

I blinked a few times. "What?"

He nodded. "I had a feeling the news might come as a shock to you. I noticed on the intake sheet that you said your last period was a month ago, and you answered the *Is there any possibility you might be pregnant* question no.

"I can't be. Are you sure?"

He nodded. "A blood test can pick up hCG as early as six to eight days after ovulation. Urine tests generally can take a bit longer."

Panic set in. "I can't be. It has to be wrong."

Dr. Rupert's smile fell. "Are you saying it's not physically possible for you to be pregnant? There are rare cases of false positives in blood work, such as when you're taking certain medication for seizures." His brows drew together. "Are you on any medications? I didn't see any listed."

I shook my head rapidly.

"So it *is* physically possible you are pregnant? Meaning you've been with a man in the last month or so?"

I lifted my hand to my throat, which suddenly felt tighter. "Yes. But we used protection. And I'm on the pill."

"Did you miss any of your pills?"

"No. Definitely not. And I take them at the same time every day."

"Were you on any antibiotics or sick at any time?"

I shook my head.

Dr. Rupert sighed. "Well, it is only 99.7-percent effective, even under the best of circumstances."

"But we used a condom, too!"

"Well, that obviously makes the odds even smaller that a pregnancy would occur. Sometimes there are just stubborn swimmers." Dr. Rupert patted my arm. "Would you like us to give you a minute before discussing the x-rays?"

I wanted him to rewind time and start over by saying I wasn't pregnant. How could I be? Grant was going to—*oh my God*. I couldn't even begin to imagine what Grant would say. Without realizing it, I must've started to hyperventilate.

"Ms. Saint James? Breathe slowly. Take some long, deep breaths." Dr. Rupert turned to the orthopedist that I had forgotten was even in the room. "Jordan, grab us a paper bag, will you?"

A minute later the nurse came in and asked me to breathe into a paper bag while three people stood around. She held my wrist and took my pulse until she was happy with the results. "You can stop now. Just keep taking big, deep breaths."

I rubbed my forehead. "God, I'm so embarrassed. I've never had to do that before."

The nurse smiled. "I have three kids under four. If my head isn't in a brown paper bag once a week, I'm hiding in the closet to sneak a glass of wine."

After I calmed down a little more, the nurse left, and Dr. Rupert asked if the orthopedist could take a look at my arm. Anytime it moved at all, it hurt. But suddenly I was too numb to even feel the pain.

When he finished assessing, he spoke to both Dr. Rupert and me. "I do recommend having an x-ray. Your ulna is most likely fractured. Bruising is starting to form on your wrist already, so we need to see if the bones are aligned or might need surgical repair or a reduction."

I heard every word he said, but none of them seemed to sink in. They went on to give me the pros and cons of having x-rays while pregnant, and then Dr. Rupert looked at me for a response.

"I'm sorry." I shook my head. "You said it's safe?"

"We'll cover your abdomen with a lead apron and take the minimal amount as a precaution. Your reproductive organs won't be exposed to radiation. In cases like yours, where the risk of harm to your unborn child is very small, and the benefit of the diagnostic x-ray outweighs that risk, yes, I recommend it." He smiled cautiously. "If your ulna needs to be reset and isn't, you could lose mobility in that arm. Which we don't want."

I blew out a giant rush of air and nodded. "Okay."

"I'm going to admit you overnight, just as a precaution for observation. Would you like for the nurse to call someone for you?"

I thought about maybe calling Mia, but it was so late, and I needed to let everything sink in myself before I could actually say the words out loud. "No, that's fine. Thank you."

Dr. Rupert left with the orthopedic doctor, promising to return as soon as the x-ray results came in. I was glad I got a few minutes alone before the nurse came back.

"Would you like me to bring your brother back in? The registration desk said he's asked about you twice and he's pacing." She smiled. "You have a protective big brother."

I closed my eyes. The thought of seeing Grant now made me literally sick. But if he wasn't allowed back here to visit me, he'd undoubtedly make a commotion and suspect something was wrong. There was no way I wanted to have the conversation with him tonight in the ER.

I nodded at the nurse. "Could you bring him back in five minutes? I just need a few more alone."

"Sure. Of course. Let's make it ten."

Not long after, Grant opened the curtain with concern etched in his face. "Is everything alright? That took almost an hour."

I cleared my throat, but had a hard time looking him in the eyes. "Yeah, everything is fine."

"Did you go for x-rays?"

"No, not yet."

He put his hands on his hips. "Let me move you over to Memorial. I have an old friend on staff there."

"No, it's fine. They said it wouldn't be too much longer."

It was impossible to hide my inner freak out. I managed to get through telling Grant about the orthopedic doc's assessment of aligned vs. non-aligned without mentioning the reason he was called in before the x-rays. I also told him I was being admitted for observation. But after that, I was very quiet.

"Are you sure you're okay? Does anything else hurt?"

His concern made me feel even worse about lying. "I'm fine. Just tired."

Ten minutes later, the nurse came in. Before I could say a word, Grant stood. "Can you examine her again? She doesn't seem like herself suddenly. I'd like a doctor to check her out again."

The nurse looked to me, and I suddenly panicked she might say something about my pregnancy. I hadn't specifically told them not to, though obviously there were privacy laws. Seeing me pale and wide eyed, the nurse caught on.

"Umm... I don't think that's necessary. This is perfectly normal. There's an adrenaline surge and then a sudden drop after a trauma. I'd be worried if Ms. Saint James wasn't getting groggy."

Grant nodded, seeming to accept the explanation. Thank God.

"I'm going to take her down to x-ray now. We'll probably be a while. Since she's being admitted, you can go home, and I'll bring your sister a phone after the treatment for her arm is decided."

I turned to Grant. One look at his face, and I knew there was no chance he was leaving. He folded his arms across his chest. "I'm staying right here."

The nurse looked to me, and I nodded. "It's fine if he stays."

She disappeared a moment and came back with a wheelchair. She and Grant stood at my sides to make sure I could get up, even though I'd said I was fine.

"We'll be back in a while," she said to Grant. "Make yourself comfortable."

The nurse stopped at the nursing station and lowered her voice to speak to another nurse. "I'm waiting for x-ray to call down to say they're ready for Ms. Saint James. Can you page me when they do?"

Once the double doors of the emergency room closed behind us, and we were out of Grant's earshot, she spoke while she pushed my chair.

"I sensed that maybe you needed a few minutes without your brother around. I know what you learned was a shock, so I figured you might want to talk about it. Sometimes it's easier to talk to a stranger than a family member. But if you don't, that's fine, too. I'm just going to give you a free ride around the halls until they page me and tell me x-ray can take you."

I sighed. "Thank you."

As promised, she was quiet and left it up to me to decide if I wanted to talk. After a few minutes, I did.

"He's not my brother. He said that because he was worried they wouldn't let him in since he's not a family member. He's my boyfriend."

I looked up and over my shoulder, and the nurse smiled and nodded. "Well, now I'm really glad I didn't ask if your brother was single for my sister. He's very handsome."

I laughed, and my shoulders relaxed for the first time in an hour.

We turned left down a new hallway that was empty. "I take it the pregnancy is going to be a shock for him, too."

"He doesn't want kids."

"Well, if it makes you feel any better, my husband wanted one or two. He wasn't happy when I told him I was pregnant the third time. But I reminded him, I was the one who had to carry a nine-pound bowling ball while it felt like my uterus was going to fall out, and I was the one who was going to get sick for months and get up with the little monster after the delivery. Men sometimes forget that they have a hand in getting pregnant, too. You play, you pay."

I knew that was true. Clearly I didn't get pregnant alone. But...this was different. Grant had emotional scars. His reasoning wasn't exactly the same as a man who didn't want another mouth to feed or diaper to change.

"He has some very good reasons for not wanting a family. He..." I shook my head. It wasn't my place to share the details of Grant's personal life. "He...has reasons."

"Let's forget your boyfriend for a minute. How would you feel right now if the man by your side wanted a family? Would you feel differently?"

I didn't even have to think about that. "Yes. I definitely would. Don't get me wrong, I'd still be in shock. But I want a family someday. I didn't think that would be nine months from now. But if the man I loved wanted children, I'd be okay with it, I think."

We passed another nursing station, and the nurse pushing me said hello to a few people. She waited until we'd passed before resuming our conversation. "So your only real concern here is how your boyfriend is going to take the news."

I thought about it. "Yes. I think so."

"Do you love him?"

I took a deep breath in and exhaled. It probably should have taken me longer to answer that question, but love wasn't something that needed to be analyzed. You either did or you didn't. I nodded. "I do."

"Does he love you?"

I thought back to the worry on his face in the emergency room. He'd seemed truly terrified that I might be hurt. The way he'd looked at me lately had changed, too. I'd find him watching me with a smile when he didn't think I was paying attention, and the other morning I woke to him watching me sleep. "Neither of us have said the words, but I think he does."

"Obviously, under the law you have choices. But it sounds like you want a family and you love the baby's father. I know I'm oversimplifying things, but it seems to me like there's only one choice in this matter, and it's your boyfriend's—whether or not he wants to be with you and your baby more than he wants to be alone."

• • •

I stared out the window from my uncomfortable hospital bed, watching the sun come up. I'd barely slept last night. The x-ray showed I had a clean fracture, which meant no resetting of bones or surgery, and they'd come to cast my arm shortly after midnight. Grant had stayed by my side until I practically pushed him out the door. If he'd had his way, he would have slept in the chair and stayed all night. But with so much to think about, I couldn't quiet my mind enough to fall asleep even after he was gone. I dozed off and on, mostly.

Mia was an early riser, so I thought about calling her. But it didn't feel right to tell her about the pregnancy before I'd told Grant, even though she was my best friend.

Grant knocked on my hospital room door at seven a.m. He had two cups of coffee and was dressed casually.

He set the coffee down on the portable food tray and leaned down to kiss my forehead. "Morning. How's my girl?"

My heart squeezed, and I had to force a smile. "Good. Tired."

"Did you sleep at all?"

"Not much."

"That's understandable. Between the accident and being in this place...then the cast. You'll get some sleep when we get you home."

"The day nurse came by a little while ago and said it would probably be a few hours before my discharge was ready."

Grant took one of the coffees, peeled back the tab to open it, and handed it to me.

Without thinking, I brought it to my lips and almost drank. But *caffeine*. I shouldn't have that. Setting the coffee back on the tray, I said, "I think I'm going to skip coffee this morning. I don't want the caffeine keeping me awake later."

Great. Now I'm a liar and an information withholder.

"Good idea. I picked up some plastic cast shields in the pharmacy downstairs. Doc said you shouldn't get it wet, and I figured you'd want to take a shower when you got home. Maybe a nice hot bath."

"Thank you. That does sound good." Though... oh my God. Could I even take a bath? I honestly knew nothing about pregnancies or babies. And the thought of doing this alone made me feel like I might break out in hives. I scratched my face.

"I spoke to my sister on the ride over and mentioned what happened. She said no problem covering you for however long you need."

I forced a smile. "That's sweet. But I definitely will be back at work tomorrow. It's just a broken bone and a small cut." *And a pregnancy.*

Grant frowned. "You should take it easy. You were banged up pretty good. You're going to be achy, if you're not already. They need to give you muscle relaxers or something for pain."

Yet another thing I can't do. So I simply nodded.

For the next few hours, Grant sat by my side. I was definitely quieter than usual, and he asked me on more than one occasion if I was in any pain and if everything was okay. I explained my mental absence as exhaustion, which at least wasn't fully a lie.

After I was discharged, they made me sit in a wheelchair while Grant pulled the car around out front to pick me up. He got out and helped me into the car, even though I told him I was fine. I got the feeling nothing I could say was going to convince him to stop mollycoddling me.

Well, there was one thing that would probably make him run far the hell away.

We drove to my apartment, and I took a shower and went to lie down. Grant drew the blinds and turned off all the lights so it was practically pitch dark in my bedroom. He stripped down to his underwear and wrapped himself around my body, spooning me from behind.

The room was so quiet, and I thought the intimate moment might be the perfect time to tell him, but I truly was exhausted. It was a conversation I knew I'd need energy for. So I pushed it off, yet again, vowing to tell him when I woke up later.

While I was lost in thought, apparently Grant was, too. He kissed my shoulder and whispered, "I don't know what I would've done if something had happened to you. I realized last night, I can't imagine my life without you anymore."

For some reason, that made me so sad. My eyes welled with tears, and they started to spill over. But I couldn't explain anything to him while I was crying, so I cried in silence, and let him think I'd fallen asleep.

CHAPTER 33

Grant

I was in the kitchen cooking when she woke up.

Ireland had fallen asleep with wet hair, and it had dried with the side she'd slept on pressed flat to her face and the other side all curly and wild. It was a mess, yet to me she'd never looked more beautiful. I was so relieved she was okay.

I turned down the flame on the stove and wiped my hands on a dishtowel. "That was a good nap."

She walked over and peeked at what was cooking on the stove. "What are you making? It smells so good."

I lifted the lid off a pan. "Chicken piccata."

"It looks delicious, too. I didn't even realize I had the ingredients to make that."

I chuckled. "You didn't. I snuck out while you were snoring and picked up chicken, olive oil, and some spices. The only spices I could find in your cabinets were cinnamon and red pepper."

"Yeah. Mia was the cook of the house. They were all hers. She wanted to leave them here, but I snuck them into a box when she wasn't paying attention. Figured they'd go to waste here."

I pulled her into my arms and brought her against my chest. "How do you feel?"

"I'm still tired. But better. How long was I asleep?"

I looked at my watch. "About six hours. It's almost four thirty."

"Oh. Wow."

"Are you hungry?"

"Yeah. Actually, I am."

I smiled. "Good. I'll finish up, and we can eat an early dinner."

Ireland went to wash up and came back out looking around the room. "Did you see my phone? I think it broke during the accident. I tried to fiddle with it in the emergency room and it wouldn't turn on, but I'm hoping maybe it will come back to life when I charge it."

I pointed with a fork to a bag on the counter. "I slipped it out of your bag while you were sleeping and picked you up a new one. It's in the box up there. They said they loaded everything from your old one, but you might want to check that because the sales clerk at Best Buy looked about fifteen, and the whole data transfer only took about five minutes."

"Oh, you didn't have to do that."

"I wanted to."

Ireland was quiet throughout dinner. She still seemed off to me, but I'd never been in a serious accident before and figured it was probably normal to be shaken up a bit. After we ate, she called Mia to tell her what happened, and I could hear her freaking out through the phone.

Later, Ireland was still quiet.

"Are you sure you're feeling okay?" I asked.

She looked away and nodded. "Want to watch a movie?"

I smirked. "Disney? Sure."

Ireland forced a smile. "Not tonight." She sat down on the couch and started to scroll through Netflix, then Hulu, and finally HBO on Demand. Sighing, she extended the remote to me. "You pick something."

Second to porn, I preferred action movies. But I didn't think car chases and shit blowing up was the best thing to put on right now. "Do you like Will Smith?"

"Yeah."

"When in doubt, Will Smith." I pointed the remote to the TV and went back to Netflix. After a search by actor name, I said, "Pick one."

She shrugged. "Any is fine."

I didn't want to keep on bugging her, but she really seemed off—almost depressed. *The Pursuit of Happyness* was the first movie on the list, so I picked that, even though I'd already watched it. I lifted Ireland's feet onto my lap and guided her to lie back so I could give her a foot rub.

The movie was about a down-and-out dad who winds up homeless with his son while he takes a non-paying job in an attempt to make something of himself and better their future. It was a drama, based on a true story, and parts of it were sad. But at one point, I looked over and found tears streaming down Ireland's face. She hadn't even made a sound. I grabbed the remote and put the movie on hold.

"Hey." I scooped her up from the couch and cradled her in my arms. "What's going on? Are you okay?"

She nodded but kept looking down at her lap.

I gave her some time, but she never made eye contact or started to talk, so I put two fingers under her chin and guided her face up to look at me. What I saw caused an ache in my chest. Her eyes were filled with pain, her face completely distraught.

"Talk to me. What's going on? Are you in pain? Are you having flashbacks to the accident?"

She started to cry even harder. "I...I don't want to lose you."

I brushed hair from her face and slid my hands down to cup her cheeks. "Lose me? You're not going to lose me. Why would you think that?"

Ireland reached up and covered my hands at her cheeks with hers. "Grant...I'm..."

"What?"

She shook her head and closed her eyes. "I'm... pregnant, Grant."

• • •

One minute I'm in her apartment, watching her sleep and thinking I should tell her I love her when she wakes up, and then the next I'm out the door like the fucking coward I am.

I didn't yell or argue. Maybe I was in a state of shock...I don't know. But I also couldn't console her or tell her everything was going to be okay. Because it wasn't. It wasn't fucking okay.

I waited until after Ireland calmed down, and then told her I needed to go. She wanted to know where I was going, but I had no idea. The truth was, I just needed to be anywhere but there.

I motioned to the bartender by holding up my empty glass and rattling around the ice that hadn't had time to melt.

"Another one already?"

I took out my billfold and peeled off three hundred-dollar bills. "The hundred should cover all my drinks. Other two are for you if my glass is never empty."

The bartender, who I'd started calling Joe—yet I wasn't sure if he had told me that was his name or I'd made it up in my head—refilled my glass. "You got it."

I sat at the bar and drank three more vodka tonics. I'd never been a big drinker, so four had me starting to see double—which was exactly the state I was going for. The dingy bar I'd wandered into a few blocks from Ireland's place had emptied out, except for an old guy parked at the other end of the bar. The bartender came over and took my glass, which was still about a quarter of the way full. He dumped out the ice and poured me a fresh one. Setting it in front of me, he leaned an elbow on the bar.

"For that kind of a tip, I also provide an ear to listen to the story about whatever went down that brought you here today."

I lifted the newly filled glass and some of it sloshed on the bar. "Maybe I'm just an alcoholic."

Joe smirked. "Nah. Your tolerance is shit."

"Maybe I'm just broke and down on my luck."

"Nah. Broke guys don't carry around a wad of hundreds and look like you do."

"And what exactly do I look like?"

Joe shrugged. "Want the truth?"

"Sure."

He looked over the bar and sized me up. "Clean pants, nice shoes, polo with that fancy whale embroidered on it, and a money clip. You look like a rich asshole who probably grew up with a silver spoon in his hand."

I burst into laughter that wasn't the funny kind. *Silver spoon*. That was exactly what Ireland had said in that very first email that started it all.

I drank more of my drink. "Maybe you're both right."

The bartender's brows drew together. Though he didn't give a shit enough to ask what the hell I was talking about. "So, not broke, not an alcoholic, that leaves the obvious—the reason half the guys come in here to get plastered. Trouble at home. Am I right?"

I grumbled. "Something like that."

"The trouble with trouble is that it starts out disguised as fun."

I'd never heard it put that way, but there was a lot of truth in that statement. "You're a wise man, Joe."

The bartender smiled. "Name's Ben. But for two hundred bucks, you can call me Shirley. I don't give a shit. I'm divorced twice, and my advice probably isn't worth shit. But here it is anyway. If she makes you smile before you have coffee in the morning and you don't have to knock back a few drinks to get in the mood when she's around, she's a keeper. Get some flowers from the twenty-four-hour bodega down the block, and go home and apologize. Doesn't matter who was right or wrong."

If only it were that simple. "You're right, Joe."

The bartender straightened up. "So you're heading home?"

"No. Your advice isn't worth shit."

CHAPTER 34

Grant

W*here the hell am I?*

I lifted my head, and it felt like some of the skin on my cheek stayed on the thick plastic I'd been sleeping on. I rose up to an elbow and looked around. I was in some sort of a waiting room, and it looked industrial. But I had no fucking clue where I was or how the hell I'd gotten here.

"You're at Patton State Hospital," a deep voice said from nearby.

Patton. What the fuck was I doing anywhere near this damn place? I followed the direction of the sound and found a well-dressed man sitting a few chairs away. He closed what looked like a chart he'd been working on and folded his hands on his lap. "I'm Dr. Booth."

The name rang a bell, but it took me a second to figure out why over the pounding in my head. I sat up and realized for the first time that I'd been sprawled out over a few folding chairs with plastic-covered, cushioned bottoms.

My hand reached for the side of my head once I was upright. "Did I get hurt?"

"Not that I'm aware of, other than what I suspect might be a little alcohol poisoning from overconsumption."

Fuck. My head is really killing me. And what the hell was I doing at Patton? "Do you know how I got here?"

"The guard asked you that when you came in. You told him Uber."

I went to nod, but raising my head and lowering it hurt too fucking much. I racked my brain, trying to remember the events of last night. I remembered being at a bar, and I remembered some guy helping me to a car after he locked the door. Joe? Maybe his name was Joe. Yeah, that was it. He was the bartender, and I'd walked out with him at closing time. Damn...that means I was drinking until four in the morning. No wonder I don't remember shit.

"Did we meet earlier?" I asked Dr. Booth.

He smiled. "No. This is the first time we've met. You came in about five thirty this morning and asked to see one of my patients. All visits require the inmate's psychiatrist's approval. The guards knew you were drunk and turned you away. But they called me to let me know what had happened, and I asked them to let you sleep it off in the waiting room, at least until visiting hours start at noon. The hospital allows visitors twenty-four hours a day, but the correctional facility ward follows state prison protocol when it comes to letting people in."

"What time is it?"

He looked at his watch. "Ten fifteen."

I raked a hand through my hair. Even touching the strands hurt. "I take it you're Lily's doctor?"

He nodded. "I am. Lily tried to get you to come see her for the first four years of her admission here. You never would respond to any of my messages or her letters. So I was curious what made you come by today. But by the time I got here, you were out cold."

"You've been sitting there for four hours waiting for me to wake up?"

He smiled. "No. When I saw your condition, I made my morning rounds and told the guard to page me if you woke up. I came back after I finished to work on some of my charts." He pointed his eyes down to a stack of thick manila folders on the chair next to him.

"Why?"

"Why what? Why did I ask the guards to let you sleep it off, or why am I here working on my charts?"

I shook my head. "All of it."

"Well, like I said, I was curious about you. And Lily is still my patient. She's made great progress over the years, but I often learn things from family members that help me in treatment. When she was first admitted, she signed a release that all of her medical information could be discussed with you. Every year we go over her permissions on file. It's been seven years, and she still hasn't withdrawn permission for me to discuss her health with you. So I'm legally free to discuss her case. I thought it also might be helpful for me to understand why it was you were here to see her today."

"When she was first *admitted*? She wasn't *admitted* to the hospital, Doc. She was *sentenced*—to twenty-five damn years. And you people keep her here to do easy time. She deserves to be locked in a cell, just like all the other murderers."

"I see. Did you come today to speak to her?"

I cleared my throat. My mouth was so damn dry. "No. I have no desire to see her. Or help her. I don't know what the hell I was thinking last night, or this morning—whenever I showed up. But it was a mistake."

Dr. Booth examined my face and nodded. "I understand. But perhaps you and I could still talk." He stood. "How do you take your coffee? Let me at least give you some caffeine and Tylenol. It looks like you could use both."

The thought of standing made me feel nauseous, much less jumping in a cab and taking the hour-and-a-half ride back home. I rubbed the back of my neck. "Yeah. Alright. I could use some coffee before I get out of here. Black, please."

The doc disappeared and came back a few minutes later with two Styrofoam cups and a small packet of Tylenol.

"Thank you."

He took a seat across from me and stayed quiet, watching me.

"I don't normally do this. Haven't tied one on like that since college."

Dr. Booth nodded. "Did something happen that set you off? Drinking and showing up here, I mean?"

"Nothing that has to do with Lily." *Or everything that has to do with my ex-wife.*

"We can talk about whatever you like. It doesn't have to be about Lily."

I scoffed. "No, but I'm sure you'd psychoanalyze anything I say to relate it back to her. Isn't that what shrinks do? Find a cause for everything that happens so there's someone or something to blame other than their patient? A man murders another man while robbing him—his father molested him, so it's his father's fault. Not the crack he smoked an hour before because he's an addict. A woman kills her own child—she shouldn't be blamed because she's depressed. We're all fucking depressed at some point in our lives, Doc."

The doc sipped his coffee. "I wasn't planning on psychoanalyzing you. I figured if you were here, you could use someone to talk to. I'm not your doctor, but I'm a man, and you're a fellow man who seems in need. That's all."

Well, now I felt like shit. I raked a hand through my hair. "Sorry."

"It's fine. Trust me, I don't get offended easily. Hazard of the career. Most people who show up at my door aren't there because they want to be. Either the court or their family forced their hand. It's not uncommon for me to be told to fuck off because I'm an asshole in the first fifteen minutes of a session."

I smiled. "I'm usually good at holding my tongue for the first half hour of a meeting."

Dr. Booth smiled back. "May I ask you a personal question?"

I shrugged. "Go for it. It doesn't mean I have to answer."

He shook his head. "No, it doesn't. Are you married?"

"No."

"In a relationship?"

I thought of Ireland. *I was. Or am I? I don't fucking know.* "I've been seeing someone, yes."

"Are you happy?"

Another loaded question I couldn't answer easily. "It's hard to be happy when you've lost a child. But, yeah...Ireland makes me happy." I shook my head. "For the first time in seven damn years."

Doc was quiet for a long time again. "Is it possible you came today because you want forgiveness so you can move on?"

I felt the veins in my neck pulse with anger. "Lily doesn't deserve forgiveness."

Dr. Booth caught my eyes. "I wasn't referring to Lily. Forgiveness is something you have to find within yourself. No one can give that to you. Yes, I believe your ex-wife suffers from bipolar disorder that caused her behavior to be manic, and that, coupled with severe postpartum depression, made her do something unthinkable, but you don't need to agree with me in order to find forgiveness. Forgiveness doesn't excuse Lily's behavior. Forgiveness allows that behavior to not destroy your heart anymore."

I tasted salt in the back of my mouth. I'd cried enough in the last seven years; I wasn't about to sit in the same building my ex-wife breathed in and shed any more tears. I cleared my throat, hoping to swallow my emotions.

"I know you mean well, Doc. And I appreciate it. I really do... But Lily doesn't deserve forgiveness." I shook my head. "I should really get going. Thanks for the coffee and Tylenol."

I stood and extended my hand to Dr. Booth. When he clasped mine, he again looked into my eyes. "I don't think you want to forgive Lily. I think you want to forgive yourself. You did nothing wrong, Grant. Give yourself that forgiveness and move on. Sometimes people don't allow themselves to forgive because they're afraid they'll forget—forgive and forget. But you'll never forget Leilani. You just need to realize there's room in your heart for more than one person again."

"Tell her to stop writing the letters, Doc."

CHAPTER 35

Ireland

Almost two weeks had passed, and yet it felt like a year.

Between my construction and work, I had enough to keep me busy. But every time I passed the exit that led to the marina where Grant lived, it felt like ripping a Band-Aid off of a fresh wound.

It was Saturday afternoon, and Mia and I were meeting for lunch at our favorite Greek restaurant. I'd gotten caught in traffic, so I arrived a few minutes late, and she'd already gotten a table.

"Hey." I slid into the booth across from her.

Her face wrinkled up when she looked at me. "Did you come from the gym?"

"No. Why?"

Mia frowned. "No offense, but you sort of look like shit."

I sighed. "I didn't feel like doing my hair. I thought the messy bun was still in?"

"It is. But yours looks more like a rat's nest. And your shirt has a giant stain on it, and either you have black eyes coming in or you didn't get all of yesterday's makeup off."

I looked down at my sweatshirt. Sure enough, there was a giant, round spot. I rubbed at it. "I had a container of Ben & Jerry's for dinner last night. I missed my mouth a few times."

Mia raised a brow. "So you slept in that shirt?"

"Shut up. I've seen you wear the same outfit for days when you're sick."

"That's because I'm sick. Are you?"

"No."

She made yet another disapproving face. "I take it you still haven't heard from Grant?"

My shoulders slumped. "No."

Mia shook her head. "I can't believe he turned out to be such a piece of shit."

"He's not a piece of shit. He just...really didn't want children."

"Yes. And five years ago, I didn't ever want to get married. I really didn't want my mom to die at fifty-nine last year either. This is life. We do our best to live it, but we can't be in control of everything."

"I know. But having children is something we can control."

"Did you take all of your pills?"

"Yes."

"Did Grant wear a condom every time you had sex?"

"Yes."

"Then obviously there are times we can't control it. Nothing in life is foolproof."

"I know. But he has a good reason for being upset." A few days after Grant walked out, I'd unloaded everything on Mia—from my pregnancy to the reason I'd found out he didn't want children.

"Of course he does. He's experienced an unthinkable trauma. I understand that. So he deserved a little time to be shocked and upset, but it's been almost two weeks now. What is he going to do? Pretend he doesn't have a child and this entire thing doesn't exist?"

I'd been wondering the same thing lately. The first few days he didn't call or come by, I understood why he was upset. But at what point did he plan on dealing with the reality of our situation? I'd been so certain he'd come around...even if he didn't want to be with me or want to be involved with this baby's life. I thought he would at least own up to it and we'd talk. But the past few days, I'd started to lose the last shred of confidence in him. Hence the ice cream dinners.

"Can we just...not talk about it today? I need a day off from dealing with everything. Let's stuff our faces and go to the movies like we planned and eat buttered popcorn with Snowcaps until we feel nauseous."

Mia nodded. "Of course. Sure. But can I say one more thing? And it's not really about Grant."

I smiled. *So Mia.* "Sure."

Her face lit up as her lips curved. "I went off the pill."

My eyes widened. "Really? I thought you and Christian wanted to wait a year or two before having kids."

"We did. But things change. I've been thinking about it since the day you told me you were pregnant. Then, a few days ago Christian came into the bathroom while I was brushing my teeth. You know my routine in the morning—teeth then pill. He looked at them in my hand and said, 'I can't wait until you're pregnant. The thought of you with a big belly just turns me on like you wouldn't believe.'

"So I turned around and said, 'I could stop taking them now.' I guess I expected him to backtrack. It's one thing to say you're looking forward to seeing your wife pregnant and another to want that to be next month. But he took the pills out of my hand and tossed them in the garbage. Then we had a quickie on the bathroom sink."

I laughed. "Well, it would be awesome to have kids around the same age. But are you ready for that?"

She picked up an olive from the dish in the middle of the table and popped it into her mouth. "I don't think anyone's ever ready for kids. But yeah...I don't really want to wait."

I took Mia's hands. "I love you, my crazy friend."

"I know you want to stop talking about this. So I promise this is the last thing I'll say today..." She squeezed my hand. "I will be here for you every step of the way. Holding your hair back through morning sickness if you have it, getting fat with you, even if I'm not pregnant, and by your side in the delivery room, if you'll have me. There is nothing you'll be alone for."

I felt my eyes watering and fanned my face with my hand. "Thank you. And now let's move on. I refuse to cry anymore."

"You got it." She picked up her menu and pointed to the waiter heading our way. "Do you think that's a banana he's carrying?"

I turned to see what the waiter had in his hands just as he arrived at the table, though I had no idea what the hell she was talking about. The only thing he had was a small pad and pencil. I ordered first and waited for Mia to order. But picking up my menu to hand it to him, I came face to face with his crotch and realized she hadn't been talking about anything in his hands. It was in his pants.

My eyes widened, and I had to lift the menu back up to my face to hide my smile. Seriously, the man either had an erection or had to be stuffing. I cracked up and had to force it into a cough so I didn't laugh in the waiter's face while I handed him back the menu.

"Are you okay?" he asked.

I grabbed the water off the table and brought it to my lips. "Fine. Just swallowed down the wrong pipe."

After he left, the two of us laughed for a solid five minutes. It was the first time in almost two weeks that I'd really laughed, and it made me feel like maybe, just maybe, I could get through this on my own, if I had to.

• • •

The tile in my bathroom came out beautifully. I'd just finished sweeping up after the contractor left and stood admiring it. The tumbled marble that the guy in Home Depot had recommended gave off a rustic look that really went with the lake house feel I was going for.

Unfortunately, thinking of that contractor reminded me of Grant—he'd been jealous of the construction guy who was just being nice at that store. How did one go from being jealous to disappearing from someone's life in the span of a few weeks? And don't even get me started with the fooling around that had gone on in this room when he'd spent the day helping me.

Everything reminded me of Grant—my apartment, work, even the construction of my home. Unconsciously, I reached down and covered my belly. Realizing what I'd done, I sighed. He was everywhere, even inside me. How the hell was I supposed to escape it?

My head hurt from so much thinking, and my heart ached in my chest. I'd decided if I didn't hear from Grant by tomorrow morning, which would be two full weeks, I was going to go see him in his office. If we weren't going to be a couple, that was one thing, but I needed to know if he planned to be in his child's life.

I looked around the bathroom one last time and switched off the light. I emptied the dustpan into the garbage bag in the kitchen and set the broom against the door. The last of the day's sun streaked in through the adjoining living room windows, and I thought I might walk down to the lake to watch it set—yet another thing that reminded me of Grant, though I refused to let him take the beauty out of a sunset for me.

My land was about three blocks from the lake, but it was a straight walk down a paved road. One of the nearby lakefront parcels hadn't been sold yet, so I sat down on the grass at the lake's edge on that property and watched as the sky turned shades of orange.

I shut my eyes, took a few deep breaths, and wrapped my arms around my knees. I heard a jingle behind me, but was so lost in my head that I didn't register the sound until I was nearly knocked over by a dog. The most adorable golden retriever puppy started to lick my face. It made me smile and laugh.

"Aren't you cute. Where did you come from?"

A few seconds later, the answer came. "Down, boy!"

I froze, hearing Grant's deep voice behind me.

I couldn't bring myself to turn around until I felt the vibration of footsteps next to me on the ground.

"Grant?"

Just seeing his face made my heart beat wildly. I reached up to cover it and felt the thumping underneath.

"Sorry," he said. "I didn't mean to startle you."

"What are you doing here?"

"I came to talk to you. I saw your car at the house, but needed a minute to clear my head." He thumbed behind him. "So I parked here. I didn't mean to interrupt you. When I opened my car door, he jumped over me and took off like a bandit running this way."

"He? Meaning the dog came with you?"

He nodded. "Yeah. He's mine."

The dog spotted some birds a few yards away and took off chasing them.

"I better get him on his leash."

Grant followed, managing to hook the dog's collar as he jumped up on him. I watched, feeling so confused. *He has a puppy? When did that happen?*

He walked back with the dog on a long leash, and for the first time, I took in how he looked. My reaction was probably similar to Mia's when she got a load of me the other day. Grant looked terrible—or as terrible as he possibly could, which at the moment really pissed me off because his terrible was still a shitload better than most men's best. He had dark circles under his eyes, his hair was disheveled, clothes were a wrinkled mess, and his skin had a sallow tone to it.

My first instinct was to ask if he was okay, but then I remembered how okay I hadn't been the last couple of weeks and how much he'd cared. So I turned back around and faced the lake.

"What do you want?" I said.

He was quiet, but I felt him standing behind me.

"Do you...mind if I sit?"

I picked a blade of grass from in front of me and threw it. "Whatever."

Grant sat down next to me. His dog started to dig a hole a few feet away, and we both stared. I refused to look at him, even though I felt the pull I always experienced when I was near him, since right from the start.

"How are you feeling?" he asked softly.

My lips pursed together. "Alone. Scared. Disappointed. Let down."

I felt his eyes on my face, but still didn't turn my head.

"Ireland," he whispered. "Look at me. Please."

I turned with my best icy glare, but one look in his eyes and I softened. *God, I'm an idiot.*

"I'm so sorry." The pain in his voice was palpable. "I'm so fucking sorry for running away."

My eyes filled with tears. But I still refused to shed any for him. So I blinked and looked down until I could force them back.

"There's no excuse for what I did. But I'd like to tell you about Leilani, if that's okay. It doesn't justify the way I treated you, but it might help you understand why I did what I did."

He had my attention now. I looked over at him with a sad smile and nodded.

Grant took a few minutes to collect his thoughts and then spoke softly. "Leilani May was born on August fourth. She was eight pounds, four ounces." He smiled. "Eight four on eight four. She had big blue eyes that were so dark they were almost purple. Pops nicknamed her Indigo because of it. She had a mop of dark hair that looked like a wig."

He paused, and I suddenly forgot all of my anger. Reaching over, I took his hand and squeezed. "She sounds beautiful."

Grant cleared his throat and nodded. "The only time she really cried was when she needed to be changed. And she loved to be swaddled so tightly she couldn't move her arms." He paused. "And she loved it when I would sniff her feet and tell her she smelled. They say most babies aren't really smiling until they're a few months old, that it's just a reflex. But Leilani, she smiled at me."

Grant got quiet again. This time it was him who looked away. He stared out to the lake and setting sun. I watched his face go from warm to somber, so I knew I needed to brace for the next part of his story.

His voice was barely a whisper when he started talking again. "I've told you that Lily was a foster care placement with my family. Over the years, she bounced around back and forth from her mother's house to ours. Her mom suffered from mental illness, and the state would intervene and remove her at least once a year when her mom went off her meds. Lily was always different. But I didn't recognize it for what it was until we were older. And by then, it was too late. I was all-in with her."

A pang of jealousy chimed inside of me, even though it was ridiculous.

Grant hung his head. "Doctors say she's bipolar like her mom. And that, mixed with postpartum depression, made her..." He shook his head, and his voice cracked. "She..."

Oh my God. No!

Grant had said there was an accident, but no...not this. Please God, no. Don't make him have endured something so inconceivable. I crawled from my spot to kneel between his knees and cupped his cheeks in my hands. His eyes were closed, but tears streamed down his face.

He swallowed, and the look of pain he wore sliced right through me. It felt like someone had stabbed a knife into my chest.

Grant shook his head. "We were arguing. I fell asleep. I should've known better. When I woke up, Lily was sitting on the deck crying, and Leilani was gone. She...threw..." He started to sob.

I pulled him into my arms. "Shhh. It's okay. It's okay. You don't need to say any more. I'm so sorry, Grant. I'm so, so sorry."

We stayed that way for a long time, both of us crying and holding each other as if our lives depended on it. In the moment, I thought maybe his did. Maybe he needed to get this out in order for his life to move forward.

Eventually, he pulled back and looked into my eyes. "I'm sorry I walked out on you. You didn't deserve that. And I'll never do it again. I promise."

I was such an emotional wreck, I was afraid to believe he was telling me any more than he'd said— afraid to get my hopes up that his apology was a promise of a future and not just an explanation of the past.

He looked into my eyes. "I'm so sorry, Ireland. I've felt buried these last seven years, buried in darkness in the ground—until I met you. You made me feel like maybe I hadn't been buried after all, but planted in the ground, waiting to grow again."

I gulped in a breath of air to stop the last of my crying. "Please don't apologize anymore. I understand. I'm sorry this happened to us and stirred up all these difficult memories."

Grant shook his head. "No. Don't say that. Don't be sorry you're pregnant. I'm not."

"You're not?"

He shook his head again. "I'm scared shitless. I don't feel like I deserve another child. I'm worried something will happen again. But I'm not sorry you're having my baby."

Hope bloomed inside of me. "Are you sure?"

Grant pulled my face to his until our noses were touching. "I love you, Ireland. I think I did from the very first time you gave me an attitude in that coffee shop. And I've tried to fight it every step of the way, but it's physically impossible for me not to love you. Trust me, I tried as hard as I could. I'm done fighting it. I want to love you."

All of my tears came flooding back. Only this time, some happy ones were mixed in. "I love you, too."

Grant's dog finished digging his hole and started to try to lick my face again. I sniffled and laughed. "Your dog is as pushy as you."

"He's not my dog."

I pulled back. "What? But you have his leash and said he was?"

"Spuds is your dog, if you'll have him."

Spuds. Oh my God. He remembered what I'd said I wanted. *"Two or three little ones close in age, maybe a golden retriever named Spuds—a real full house."*

We sat on the grass, kissing and saying I love you to each other over and over. Eventually, the sun was gone and the stars came out. I could barely see the lake anymore.

Grant stroked my hair. "I went to visit Leilani every day over the last week. Some days I'd sit leaning against her headstone from dusk until dawn. It wasn't pretty. I definitely scared away a few people visiting nearby graves. But I hadn't been there since her funeral. I just couldn't bring myself to go. Instead, I stayed on that damn boat so every day I was reminded of the worst day of my life. It was impossible to move on living where it happened. I was keeping the memory of my daughter alive, but none of the good ones I should've been focusing on."

He paused and took a deep breath. "One morning I ended up at the prison psychiatric hospital where Lily lives, and I talked to her doctor. I've been so lost for so long, and I guess I thought I needed something from them to move on. But it turned out I don't. I need something from you."

I looked into Grant's eyes. "Anything. What can I do?"

He smiled, a crooked, adorable, half smile that told me he'd expected my response. "Give me another chance."

• • •

A beam of sun streaking through a window directly onto my face woke me on the floor. Naked and confused, I squinted and shielded my eyes while reaching down for the blanket at my waist. Memories of the night before came flooding back, and a goofy smile spread across my face. Grant and I had spent half the night talking and half the night making up for the last two weeks of not being able to touch each other.

For as long as I lived, I'd never forget the look in his eyes when he told me he loved me as he pushed inside of me. The words *making love* had been just that—words—before last night. But we'd connected in such a way that it truly felt like we became one. Which made me wonder...why wasn't my other half lying next to me anymore?

I wrapped the blanket around my body and went in search of Grant.

I found him and Spuds on the front porch.

He turned as I creaked the door open. "Morning."

I smiled. "Good morning. What time is it?"

"About ten."

"Yikes. You must've been up for hours already."

"Nope. Slept until nine." He lifted a Styrofoam cup from next to him, one that matched the one in his hands. "Went to the store up the road and got us coffees. Yours is decaf. Though it might be a little cold by now."

"Oh. Thanks. I'll drink it cold. I don't care." I sat down next to him on the top step of my porch, and he leaned over and kissed my forehead while I peeled back the top of the container. "Does that mean you missed the sunrise?" I asked.

"I did. Slept right through it." He smiled.

"You'll have to catch the sunset then."

Grant shook his head. "As much as I like you in that blanket, drink a little of your coffee and go put some clothes on. I want to show you something."

I swallowed a few mouthfuls and went in search of my clothes. I found them scattered from the kitchen to the living room and smiled as I went to the bathroom to change. Spuds followed and waited outside the bathroom door.

"Where are we going?"

"Just for a walk."

"Alright. But it better not be too far, or you might have to carry me. I have no energy after last night."

Grant looked over and grinned. "I plan to keep you that way: thoroughly fucked and smiling."

We walked hand in hand down to the open lot at the lake where we'd sat last night. When we got to the edge of the water, Grant looked around. "This would be a nice spot for a house."

"It would be. I actually looked at this plot before buying mine. But it's ridiculously expensive."

He nodded. "I know. I just bought it."

I blinked a few times. "You what?"

"I called an hour ago and made an offer. They called back five minutes before you woke up and accepted."

"I don't understand..."

Grant took both my hands. "You wanted this property. I want to give it to you, if you'll let me. I'd like to build a house on it. One with a big fenced yard and a bunch of bedrooms we can spend the next few years filling."

"Are you serious?"

"I am." Grant's smile fell. "I've been living on that boat for seven years. Every day it ripped my heart out to step onto the back deck and remember... I need to move. Leilani will always be a part of my life, but there's room in my heart for more than one."

"Oh my God, Grant." I wrapped my arms around his neck. "But what about my house?"

"Sell it. Or rent it. Or maybe just keep it, and we can use it to sneak away when the kids are driving us nuts someday. You are kind of loud, and I don't want that to have to change."

I laughed. "Keep a whole house just so we don't need to have sex quietly? You're insane."

"We'll figure it out. We have plenty of time. It'll take us a while to build something anyway."

"Oh my God. I just envisioned your house being done before my house."

Grant leaned in and brushed his lips with mine. "That's not possible."

"Why not?"

"Because there is no *my* house. There's only *our* house."

I smiled. "I love you."

"Love you, too." He pulled back and bent to kiss my belly. "And I love you, too."

After we kissed, I had to come back to reality. "I have a lot of work to do this afternoon. Would you want to come hang out at my apartment for the day while I get it done? We can get takeout, maybe?"

"Can you bring your work to my condo?"

I shrugged. "I guess. I just need my laptop and some files. Did you want to watch the sunset from there or something?"

Grant looked into my eyes. "Nope. Just figured I'd make my girl and our baby a good meal. Then rather than watching the sunset, I'm planning on watching the face you make while I lick your entire body."

I liked the sound of that. But... "You missed the sunrise this morning. I thought you watched either a sunset or a sunrise every day as a reminder that good things in life can be simple?"

Grant cupped my cheeks. "That was the past. I realize now that not all the good things in life are simple. Some of the best things are complicated, but beautiful and worth all the risk. I don't need to watch every sunrise or sunset for a reminder that good exists anymore. I have you."

CHAPTER 36

Grant

Ireland took my hand. The doctor had just done an exam and said everything seemed fine. But since it was our two-month checkup, he wanted to do a sonogram to see if he could hear the baby's heartbeat.

I watched as Dr. Warren squeezed a dollop of gel onto Ireland's flat stomach and started to move a wand around. Shadows flashed on the screen across from me, and all three of us stared at the monitor. The doctor zoned in, pushing down a little more firmly on the wand, and suddenly a sound began to echo throughout the room.

A heartbeat.

My baby has a heartbeat.

Ireland had been reading to me from her *What to Expect While You're Expecting* book, which said the early months of pregnancy produced a surge of hormones that made many women more emotional than usual. But the damn book failed to mention that the father-to-be would get all choked up.

My eyes welled, and it was impossible to hold back the tears, no matter how hard I tried. Ireland squeezed my hand and smiled.

Fuck it. Who cares if I'm a total pussy? I didn't want to fight it anymore. I let the tears flow as I leaned down and kissed my girl's forehead. Seven years ago, my own heartbeat stopped, and today mine found its purpose again. I wanted to take Ireland in my arms and dance with her to the rhythm of our baby's magical beat.

The doctor pressed a button and a few inches of the heartbeat printed out from the machine. "Heartbeat sounds good. Strong. I'm just going to do a few quick measurements and I'll have you out of here." He turned a knob on the machine, and the heartbeat disappeared. I felt a stab of panic.

"Could you...leave it on until you finish the exam?" I asked.

Dr. Warren smiled. "Sure thing."

He clicked around and printed out a few more sheets over the next five minutes. When he finished, he gave Ireland a paper towel to wipe off her stomach. Nodding, he said, "Measurements look really good. We can see you back here in a month, and hopefully you'll continue to have a morning-sickness-free pregnancy." He extended one of the little slips of paper with the baby's heartbeat he'd printed from the sonogram machine. "Thought you might like to keep this, Dad."

"I would. Thanks. Sorry about getting emotional."

He waved me off. "No need to apologize. This is a big time in your life with a lot of change. Give in and go with the moment. Enjoy the happy times, even if they come with a few tears."

"I will. Thanks, Doc."

Dr. Warren closed the door behind him, and Ireland started to get dressed. I'd been doing a lot of thinking lately and decided the doc's advice was spot on. I needed to go with the moment, and this moment had never felt so right. The fact that I had the box in my pocket made it seem like destiny, if you asked me.

Ireland buttoned her pants and wadded up the paper gown she'd been wearing. She turned to toss it in the garbage, and when she turned back around, I was...

...down on one knee.

Her eyes grew wide and her hands flew up to cover her mouth. "What are you doing?"

I dug into my pocket and pulled out a dingy, old white box. "I'd planned to give this to you in a few weeks, not today. But you heard what the doctor said—'give in and go with the moment'."

"Grant...oh my God."

I took her hand and held up the box. "This was my grandmother's ring. I was going to get the stone reset for you and put it in a nice, new box. But..." I shook my head. "But I didn't want to wait. The moment feels right." I opened the old box and showed Ireland the contents. It wasn't the biggest ring or the shiniest, but it was filled with so much history and hope. "Last week, after we went to tell Pops about the baby, my grandmother called the next day and asked me to come by alone. The two of them sat me down and told me they wanted me to give this to you when the time was right. It was my great grandmother's, then my grandmother's, and then my mother's."

"It's beautiful, Grant."

"The funny thing is, I never knew my mother, grandmother, and great grandmother had all shared the same ring. My mom had passed away before I married Lily, and they hadn't given me the ring then. I was curious why now, so I asked. You know what the response was?"

"What?"

I held up the tiny paper the doc had given me. "Pops said you had given me a heartbeat again. And he knew you were my forever."

Ireland started to cry. "That's beautiful."

I took the ring out of the box. "Ireland Saint James, I know we've known each other for less than a year, but I never thought I'd find someone to love the way I love you. I didn't just fall in love with you, I fell in love with life with you by my side. So will you marry me? We can get a different ring, or set a date a year from now if you're not ready. None of it's important. All I want to know is that you'll spend the rest of your life with me."

Ireland practically knocked me over wrapping her arms and body around me. "Yes! Yes! I will. And the ring is beautiful. I don't need anything else. And I don't need a year. All I need is you."

CHAPTER 37

Grant

I sat on the back deck of Leilani by myself. The bay was eerily quiet this afternoon, which seemed fitting right about now. I felt the same strange calm as the water, even though I'd expected to feel just the opposite on this day. Saying goodbye to this boat was so much more than leaving a place I'd lived for years. Though she wasn't going anywhere—not as long as Pops still wanted to visit her. But it was time for me to move on. Time to stop starting and ending my day with the memories that would forever haunt me, and time to start making new ones—ones filled with happiness. There was just one more thing I needed to do.

I took a deep breath and picked up the pen and paper I'd left out when I packed the last of my things. A sealed envelope sat on the bench seat next to me, one of thousands I'd received and thrown out over the years. But today when my daily letter arrived, I tucked it into my pocket rather than tossing it into the trash. I didn't intend to read it, but I needed the return address today.

More than three thousand of these envelopes had to have come and gone since I first met Lily at fourteen. I'd had the power to stop them at any time—yet I never did—and now I wasn't sure why. Maybe I wanted the daily reminder as part of my punishment. Maybe I wanted Lily to have the same daily reminder of what she'd done every time she picked up a pen. Maybe I was just so fucked in the head, I was afraid I wouldn't think about my daughter without that daily letter. I don't know. But whatever the reason, today was the day it came to an end.

I looked around one last time, imagining Lily standing on the deck that night. I had seen that image in my mind a thousand times before. Squeezing my eyes tight, I swallowed back the taste of salt in my throat before finally lifting the pen to the paper.

Lily,

I don't know how to forgive you.

Maybe by now I should have found God or something—found some way to accept what you've done and make peace with the idea that it wasn't your fault. But I haven't. That's not what this letter is about.

I need to tell you I'm sorry.

I'm sorry I fell asleep that night.

I'm sorry I didn't see the depth of what you were going through and take Leilani far away.

I'm sorry I put what you needed above what our little girl needed.

I'm sorry I didn't see it coming.

I'm sorry I didn't protect our little girl.

I fucked up. I fucked up, Lily.

I've spent the last seven years avoiding anyone I might love. Because I thought when you fall in love, you become blind to that person's flaws and only see what you want to. I was afraid of not seeing who someone is again. I thought I could control who I loved.

Until Ireland.

Ireland made me realize we don't have a choice who we fall in love with. We fall in love by chance. But staying in love and making it work isn't something that happens by chance—that's a choice. And I've chosen to love Ireland.

Because of that, I'm writing today to tell you I've fallen in love with someone else and to ask you to stop writing. Who knows, maybe it will help you move on, too.

I wish I could tell you I found a way to forgive you. But I haven't yet. Maybe someday that will happen. It's not something I can force. I have a long way to go and a lot of healing to do, but I've decided that forgiving myself might be the best place to start. So while I'm not able to fully open my heart and grant you forgiveness, I'm asking you to forgive me. I need to move on. I want to stop hating myself and work toward finding peace. That starts with us.

Please forgive me. Someday I hope to return the gift of forgiveness.

No more letters.

Goodbye, Lily.

Grant

EPILOGUE

Ireland – 15 months later

"I still can't believe you did all this." I looked out the window and watched a team of people stringing lights from palm trees and laying a wooden dance floor over the sand. Grant came up behind me and wrapped his arms around my waist. He kissed my bare shoulder.

"You don't make it easy to surprise you."

Grant and I had gotten married when I was five months pregnant. A big party wasn't important to either of us, and I didn't want to walk down the aisle with a giant bump. So we'd gone down to City Hall and quietly made it official. But he'd always felt guilty that we didn't have a big celebration, so for our one-year wedding anniversary, Grant surprised me with a trip to the Caribbean to renew our vows. I had no idea when I walked into the hotel that he'd flown all of our friends and family down, too.

And now a staff of twenty was busy preparing for a sunset vow renewal in a setting I'd once described to him as my ideal wedding: palm trees lit with tea lights on the beach at sunset. He'd even arranged for Mia and me to go to a wedding shop on the island and pick out dresses when we'd arrived two days ago. Which wasn't easy, considering Mia was six months pregnant herself now.

I turned in my husband's arms and wrapped my hands around his neck. "This is amazing. Thank you for doing all this. I still can't get over how you pulled it off without my knowing."

He rubbed my bottom lip with his thumb. "Anything for this smile. Plus, I had an ulterior motive. Since Mia is right next door, she's going to keep Logan for us tonight. I haven't had you all to myself in a long time."

"It always comes back to sex with you, doesn't it?" I teased.

"I'm still making up for lost time, sweetheart."

When I was seven months pregnant with Logan, I went into premature labor. The doctors were able to stop it, but they put me on bed rest and restricted all sexual activity. That meant we had gone the two months before delivery and six weeks after delivery without sex. Grant wasn't kidding when he said he was still trying to make up for the lost time—we'd been like horny teenagers the last few months. Which was why I had a surprise for him today, too.

"I have something to show you," I said.

Grant flashed a wicked grin and squeezed my ass. "I have something to show you, too."

I chuckled. "I'm being serious."

My husband took my hand and slid it from around his neck down over a steely erection, guiding my fingers to grip. "I'm serious, too."

I'd picked up a pregnancy test while Mia and I were out shopping on the island yesterday and saved the stick to surprise Grant. He was an amazing father to our son, Logan, but I was still a little nervous to tell him because of the reaction he'd had the first time I'd gotten pregnant. It was silly, I knew that, especially since we'd agreed to not use birth control and spent a lot of time *practicing* making a baby. But nonetheless, I wanted to get it off my chest.

"Sit for a minute. I'll be right back."

Grant pouted, but released me so I could go to the bathroom. I'd hidden the test in my makeup case under the sink in the plastic bag it had come in. Tucking it into my shorts pocket, I walked back to the bedroom and found Grant taking off his T-shirt. My heart squeezed seeing the tattoo he'd gotten inked onto his chest a few days before our wedding last year.

I brushed my finger across it. Grant had gotten the printout of Logan's first heartbeat, the one the doctor had handed him during our very first sonogram, tattooed onto his chest, along with the words from the sign that hung above my bed: *No rain. No flowers.*

I kissed the tattoo. "I love this today as much as the day you got it. But something is off. I think you're going to need to go back and add a little ink to fix it."

Grant's brows drew together as he looked down at his chest. He pulled at the skin to get a better look. "What's wrong with it?"

I took the stick from my pocket. "It only has one baby's heartbeat."

Grant's forehead wrinkled and his eyes quickly went wide. "You're..."

I nodded. "Pregnant again."

Grant shut his eyes, and for a few long seconds, I held my breath. When he opened them, it only took one look to see the joy in his eyes.

He smiled. "You're pregnant. My wife is pregnant again."

I smiled. "Yeah. I guess that's what happens when your husband is insatiable."

Grant lifted me off my feet and swung me around. "I love you pregnant. I love your big belly. And your big tits. I even love shaving your legs for you when you can't bend down anymore. You gave me life again, Ireland, and you being pregnant is proof of that."

"That's the sweetest thing anyone has ever said to me. Well, minus the tits comment."

Grant smiled. "Good. Because it's the truth. Now get your pregnant ass on the bed so I can give you my gift."

• • •

We renewed our vows barefoot in front of all of our friends and family at sunset. Pops stood by Grant's side as his best man, and Mia stood next to me with one hand holding her growing belly. Leo, who now lived with us, held our son in his arms in the first row. He'd moved in four months ago when his aunt had suffered a stroke that left her unable to care for him. The court granted us temporary custody, but if we had anything to do with it, he'd be with us forever.

Toward the end of the ceremony, the pastor officiating said, "At this time, the groom would like to give his wife a new ring, as a sign of his love and commitment."

I leaned to Grant. "I thought we weren't exchanging new rings."

He winked. "*We* aren't. I don't need two. But I wanted you to have something to remember today."

Grant turned to Pops and whispered. "*Psst.* Pops... in your pocket."

Pops's face wrinkled up. He seemed to be having a moment. That had happened more and more frequently over the last few months.

Grant whispered again. "You have the box in your pocket."

Still confused, Pops scanned his surroundings. Our friends and family in the audience were all watching and waiting. Turning back, he looked at me holding hands with Grant and smiled. "Hey, Charlize."

I smiled back. "Hi, Pops. How you doing?"

Grant chuckled. "Always distracted by the pretty girls. The box is in the left side of your suit jacket, Pops. Can I have it?"

"Box?"

"Yeah, in your suit jacket."

"Oh, you want the..." Pops snapped his fingers. "Damn it...what is it called again..." *Snap. Snap.* "You want the..." *Snap. Snap.* "You want your *balls*!"

Everyone started to laugh, including both of us. Grant walked over and slipped his hand into his grandfather's suit pocket, pulling out a black box.

"Nah. She can keep my balls, Pops. She's had them since the first day we met. I just want the ring."

The End

ACKNOWLEDGEMENTS

To you—the *readers*. Thank you for allowing me to be a part of your hearts and homes. Life seems to move so fast these days, and I am so grateful to be with you at those moments when you relax and pick up a book to escape. I hope you've enjoyed Grant and Ireland's tangled story and you'll come back in the summer to see who you might meet next!

To Penelope – 2019 was full of twists and turns. I'm glad you're the Thelma to my Louise for this crazy ride.

To Cheri –This year was one to remind us both how precious time is, and it means that much more to me that you step away from your family to join me on our crazy trips! Books brought us together, but friendship made us forever.

To Julie – Thank you for your friendship and wisdom.

To Luna – No rain. No flowers. 2020 is your year to blossom and I can't wait to watch it.

To my spectacular Facebook reader group, Vi's Violets – Every morning I wake up and have my coffee with you. You start my day, encourage me when things get tough, and celebrate my successes. I've said it before, but as each year passes, it only holds truer: This group is a gift. Thank you for being part of it.

To Sommer – I don't know how you do it every time. Thank you for yet another amazing cover.

To my agent and friend, Kimberly Brower – Thank you for never accepting *good enough*. You always go above and beyond what is expected. I can't wait to see what unique things you find each and every year!

To Jessica, Elaine, and Eda – Thank you for being the dream team of editing! You smooth out the all the rough edges and make me shine!

To all of the bloggers – Thank you for inspiring others to take a chance on me. Without you, there would be no them.

Much love

Vi

ABOUT VI KEELAND

Vi Keeland is a #1 *New York Times*, #1 *Wall Street Journal*, and *USA Today* Bestselling author. With millions of books sold, her titles have appeared in over a hundred Bestseller lists and are currently translated in twenty-five languages. She resides in New York with her husband and their three children where she is living out her own happily ever after with the boy she met at age six.

OTHER BOOKS BY VI KEELAND

Standalone novels

All Grown Up

We Shouldn't

The Naked Truth

Sex, Not Love

Beautiful Mistake

EgoManiac

Bossman

The Baller

Dirty Letters (Co-written with Penelope Ward)

Hate Notes (Co-written with Penelope Ward)

Park Avenue Player (Co-written with Penelope Ward)

British Bedmate (Co-written with Penelope Ward)

Mister Moneybags (Co-written with Penelope Ward)

Playboy Pilot (Co-written with Penelope Ward)

Stuck-Up Suit (Co-written with Penelope Ward)

Cocky Bastard (Co-written with Penelope Ward)

Left Behind (A Young Adult Novel)

First Thing I See